ON MISSING LINK ROAD

ON MISSING LINK ROAD

Bruce Dale

Copyright © 1994 by Bruce Dale.

Library of Congress Number: 99-90824
ISBN#:   Hardback   0-7388-0528-9
              Softback   0-7388-0529-7

All rights reserved. No part of this book may be reproduced or transmitted in any form or by any means, electronic or mechanical, including photocopying, recording, or by any information storage and retrieval system, without permission in writing from the copyright owner.

This is a work of fiction. Names, characters, places and incidents either are the product of the author's imagination or are used fictitiously, and any resemblance to any actual persons, living or dead, events, or locales is entirely coincidental.

This book was printed in the United States of America.

To order additional copies of this book, contact:
Xlibris Corporation   1-888-7-XLIBRIS
123 Chestnut St. Suite 402   1-215-923-4686
Philadelphia, PA 19106   www.Xlibris.com
USA   Orders@Xlibris.com

CONTENTS

PROLOGUE 9

CHAPTER 1 15
CHAPTER 2 22
CHAPTER 3 30
CHAPTER 4 40
CHAPTER 5 46
CHAPTER 6 56
CHAPTER 7 67
CHAPTER 8 75
CHAPTER 9 80
CHAPTER 10 91
CHAPTER 11 100
CHAPTER 12 110
CHAPTER 13 119
CHAPTER 14 131
CHAPTER 15 140
CHAPTER 16 148
CHAPTER 17 161
CHAPTER 18 172
CHAPTER 19 181
CHAPTER 20 191
CHAPTER 21 203
CHAPTER 22 212
CHAPTER 23 220
CHAPTER 24 225
CHAPTER 25 232

CHAPTER 26	241
CHAPTER 27	253
CHAPTER 28	262
EPILOGUE	267

*To Chuck, for giving me a spiritual home,
and to my own family, the greatest in the world.
Also my closest friends: I am astonished
at the blessings I've received.*

PROLOGUE

Dorian took his bike off Main Street and down the steadily sloping road to the river. It made him mad. All the elm trees destroyed. All right, Dutch elm disease was spreading, but every damn tree? It wasn't necessary. They just didn't want to take the time to save some of the trees. Quicker and cheaper to cut them all down. Dorian hated what they were doing to his town. They hadn't quite ruined the river yet. Lots of filth spewed into it so not a good idea to swim, but it still looked beautiful. North—all misty and spooky with Mt. Ascutney looming. South—the direction of his dreams—where does the river end after passing all those strange towns he was taken as a kid? What he called subconscious erotic. Deep mysterious feelings exuding from a particular landscape, smell, sound. Oh, to be driving south in an open convertible, the music drowning out all human talk, the scenery rushing by like a movie, only better because the movie surrounds you, the main character, and you keep moving through one lovely scene after another.

He stopped, left the bike on its side, and climbed a small hill so he could look at the river through a web of trees. Already he was getting an idea for a new painting. He sketched it out on a small pad he carried everywhere. Unfortunately he'd have to go home to turn it into a painting. A crow's cry overhead seemed to call him back to that woeful place. Or was that his mother howling for him? He was only a half-mile from the house, and she had a huge lung capacity that years of smoking Chesterfields had barely diminished.

The home of Eddie and Esther Osborne was a hundred-and-fifty-year-old dilapidated tripledecker saltbox near the train tracks and the center of town. Esther was calling from inside and actually could be heard from well down the road.

"Dorian! Where are you? Dorian? You upstairs? I need you! Come down here!"

At the foot of the stairs, her bony hand resting on the rotting bannister, Esther had no desire to make the two-story climb to Dorian's bedroom, his hideaway. He should come when she called, whether he was painting or not. If she kept it up long enough, loud enough, she knew he would. Unless he'd managed to slip out, but she was getting better at catching him in the act. Not that she couldn't understand why he'd want to get out every chance he could. His bedroom was the only place in the whole house that had escaped her own 'brush strokes': a moodswinging stab at housework that did more to destroy the place than clean it. Junk and so-called memorabilia formed a foot high obstacle course wherever one turned. Even neighbors who understood the country habit of hording were overwhelmed at the doorway of the Osborne place.

"Dorian! Please——I can't climb all these stairs! Come see the black eye your dad gave me."

Dorian had left the river, quickly crossed Main Street and its vanished elms, and immersed himself in the kind of death he preferred: the cold stone quiet of the Hillside Cemetery. From midway up, it gave the best view of Charlestown, its finest houses framed by magnificent tall pines. Dorian hopped off his bike and started sketching immediately. He was barely conscious of crossing over from the domain of the living to the land of the dead, except for a slight shiver, an inner thrill that here, finally, people behaved as they should.

"Death is the last great adventure," said Dorian aloud. If only his mother understood that. If only Karin could see that it's no tragedy. He felt bad for her, but she'd see her family soon enough. He wondered if that was literally true: do we join our loved ones in the after life or is it a much stranger, grander kind of unity? Dad and his war stories—he didn't actually see people die. Maybe because he was stationed in Greenland during the Korean War. Only dead things he saw were deer, and dead animals tell us nothing. They just have a group soul, no matter how close we may get to one pet or another. That's what Mrs. Bingham had told him; for someone who ran a Christian pet store, she was fairly smart.

He remembered being dragged into Mrs. Bingham's store the day after Blondie died. He was still crying and Esther wanted him to help her pick out a new dog. So determined, as she usually was after her midmorning beer. "We have to get one today! You're off to school half the time. I don't know what I'll do in that house all alone with Eddie. Oh, look, isn't he cute? How much, Sally?"

The new puppy, Jute, was a great pal, but he should have known better than to get attached. Esther had him put to sleep just six months later when she couldn't afford the vet bills. Jute returned to the group soul of dogs, and Dorian had nothing so friendly left to come home to.

He put it all out of his mind, exercising the will power of which he was so proud, and got back to sketching, enamored of everything he saw in the Hillside graveyard. New Hampshire's unstable weather played right into his hands, casting light at odd angles, throwing the whole hill into shadow, now sending a beam onto a group of tombstones. Dorian was working so fast he got to the end of his pad before he knew it.

"Why spoil a perfect day by going home? Lie down amidst the grass and monuments, and stuff the glorious sky into my eyes."

The best fantasy was to fly up into that sky, soar over Charlestown, then take off to mysterious Southern climes. Sure, everyone wished they could fly, but it would be wasted on them if the wish were granted. Most people treated everything like a new toy, playing with it constantly till it's broken or boring, then back to their silly routine. Not Dorian. He would never tire of victory over gravity. When he couldn't paint he would fly, when he couldn't fly, he would die. Come straight here, set up a plot of earth with a great view of his town, and enjoy death as much as he enjoyed life.

"Oh that sky. The edges of the clouds are starting to turn maroon, ever so slightly. What color would you call that, just beyond the hilltops? It's going away, have to hold on to it, mix up something similar at home... at home... oh, not now, not yet. No one can see me between these stones. The dead will protect me."

"Dorian!"

"He's not up there, Esther. Can't you figure that out?" The tip came from Karin, Eddie's live-in nurse. Hired by Esther almost two years ago and now as much a part of the family as Dorian, and certainly in the house far more often.

"Aw, he's up there, with his head in a can of paint."

"Oils come in tubes. If he heard you, he'd answer."

"Ha! That's a good one. He played deaf and dumb till he was five years old. When he finally admitted he could talk all he said was two words. I was Daddy and Eddie was Unh-unh. "

"Oh, that must've been cute." Teasing Esther brought a smile to Karin's face that showed her potential beauty through the exhaustion. But then Eddie wrapped his arms around her and she remembered how burnt-out she felt at twenty-four.

"You shaw what she did, Karin, h-honey." It was hard to say whether Eddie looked older than Esther. He claimed to be six years younger, only fifty eight, but seemed far more battered by the long years of loving and clobbering.

"I know, Eddie, but you mustn't hit her."

Nursing her shiner, Esther came back from the hall. "Now that's good advice.

That what two years of nursing school taught?"

"I'll never be half the nurse you were, Esther."

"Go up and get Dorian. I'll see to Eddie."

"I don't think so."

"Don't leave me alone with her, hon-hon-hon, d-don't!"

"Aw, like he's so defenseless."

Eddie started to cry when he saw what he'd done to Esther's eye. His stroke made him lose control. Sometimes his hands just flew out for no reason. He pulled her close and blubbered into her dress. Karin knew it was make-up time and all right to leave them on their own.

"I'll go see what's up with Dorian," she said, making her getaway to the hall.

"He's not up there, Karin. Don't you know that? He slipped out. Got some ladder trick he uses." Esther's mood-based conclusions seemed to change faster every day. But Karin still wanted to check out Dorian's room, the only oasis of order and beauty in the deteriorating hulk at the corner of Southwest and Dell. At times like this she especially wanted to lose herself in Dorian's paintings: surrealistic pastorals and strange haunted chambers. Light from the southern window put "The Four Evangelists" in a lovely glow that made the apocalyptic animals leap out of the picture. Karin turned to the window and hoped what she'd see outside could match the colors within. She got there just in time to see the sun go behind some clouds. She looked up into essentially the same sky as Dorian gazed at from the cemetery. But flying was the furthest thing from her mind. From her corner perspective, she could see far down both roads and neither one seemed to go anywhere.

She had forgotten to close the door, so Esther and Eddie's renewed shouting invaded the otherwise serene gallery.

"It does too hurt more than your heart!"

"You-you can't die from a black-black eye!"

Karin sighed and fell back onto Dorian's neatly made bed. On the headboard was a copy of "The Time Machine." Yes, yes, what a wonderful notion. Escape to the Age of Chivalry. Or the heights of the Renaissance. She reached for the book, but it slipped from her lazy grasp and fell to the floor. It was a two-sided book from the fifties and landed with its opposite cover face-up. "The War of the Worlds" shot back at her as the screaming from below grew louder and the sun once again vanished, maybe this time for good.

CHAPTER 1

Ethan loved the looks he got as he drove down Charles Street in his green Jaguar, Bessie Smith blaring. It was fun to bust up the genteel world of those Beacon Hill Brahmins and the nouveau riche who felt so serene strolling along the brick sidewalks, gazing into pricey antique shop windows. Somehow he'd been born here, but it had to be a mistake, some mixup at birth. He would never be content to sit by the fireplace perusing Proust.

Ethan doubleparked and ran into a flower shop. Moments later he emerged with a beautiful bouquet. It was a hasty purchase, but decision-making was not one of Ethan's hangups. Back in the Jag, he turned up the hill and maneuvered into a parking space with amazing efficiency. There were hardly any spaces on Beacon Hill, and especially not on Louisberg Square if you didn't own property there, but Ethan's family had that one licked. He took the flowers in one hand and a fat art book in the other, locked his car with a thrust of his hip, and hurried into the nineteenth century mansion he called home.

His parents, Dr. and Mrs. Leblanc, were in formal attire, looking all the more odd as doctor and patient, the husband checking the wife's blood pressure, pumping up the gauge. Ethan nonchalantly waved the bouquet in his mother's face.

"I hope these brighten your day."

"Oh, how exquisite! And you went overboard for Mother's Day so recently. I'm overwhelmed!"

Systolic and diastolic went haywire making Dr. Leblanc moan, "Oh Jeez, now I'll have to start all over." He rewrapped the instrument's black padding around his faint wife's upper arm and started to pump again.

"Nonsense, Andrew—our handsome son has brought my blood pressure back to normal." Rachel closed her eyes and gripped Ethan's wrist, seeking in vain a bit of his strength. He tried to control his enthusiasm, remaining silent just long enough for his father to get a reading.

"Aren't you guys late for your thing?"

"Your mother's threatening to dance the night away, and she always collapses the next day. She forgets herself, she's having so much fun with me."

"And I do have fun," said Rachel, moving her hand from Ethan to Andrew's lowered shoulder. "I was feeling terribly weak, then I got a spurt of energy and insisted your father take me to the naval club. Or should it be the air force monthly danceoff?"

Ethan recalled with a flash of pride that his father had been an officer in all three branches of the armed services, a singular accomplishment during the Second World War. He didn't understand friends who disdained their parents and failed to appreciate what they'd been through, how much they'd achieved. Of course that was why the world's such a mess. Hardly anyone sees clearly, gets past their own ego. Ethan knew when he was being a cocky son of a bitch, but he could also step back and give others their little moments of glory.

"You'll be O.K., Mom. Just keep up those yoga exercises I showed you. Oh, Dad, I got you something too. Happy Father's Day!"

He held up the huge book entitled, "Life vs. Art—Save me, Doctor!" Leblanc put away the blood pressure device and Ethan plopped the book into his lap, forcing him down into an armchair under its weight.

"Whoa, that's a book. Maybe your mother can exercise with this."

"Mom will think there's too many pictures of bloody things. It's paintings of all the great moments in medicine. What's this guy doing? Oh, fourteenth century."

"We really haven't improved on that method, you know," Dr.

Leblanc said with an absolutely straight face.

"Oh, Andrew, he'll believe you. No progress since the fourteenth century? Let me see that."

"Wait, Mom, don't—"

She couldn't get the book away, but she did get an eyeful of some leeches draining the blood from an emaciated maiden. "Oh, I think I'm having a relapse, honey!"

"I told you not to look. It's a gross book."

Mrs. Leblanc squeezed her eyes shut, folded her hands and lay perfectly still on the couch. Ethan looked pained, but his father motioned reassurance. "She'll be fine. These pictures are really something. I saw scenes like this in the South Pacific. It wasn't paradise, not when malaria and dysentery were in full swing. I want to tell you—"

"It's amazing you made it through in one piece, Dad. It's so weird when you think of how many ways you could've been killed."

"Thanks, Ethan. And thanks for the book. A few days early, isn't it?"

"Yeah, well it had to be this way cause I won't be around too much the rest of June."

"Taking some time off from work?" Rachel didn't miss a thing, even if she was still as a mummy over on the sofa.

"Alot, actually. I kind of fixed it so they had to fire me. It wasn't enough to say I needed a few extra days to pick up Jeff."

"That wasn't necessary, Ethan. Oh, God, your job." Dr. Leblanc closed the bloody book with a thump.

"You didn't tell them about Jeff. How he is, or where—" Mrs. Leblanc sat straight up and even opened her eyes.

"No, Mom, the family secrets are safe with me. And that job was no big deal."

Ethan stepped into the middle of the room so he could angle his persuasion at both folks at once. "See, actually, once I get him, I thought we might spend a few days in the country, just the two of us. I know you want him back here right away, Dad, but I really think he needs a break. Not from you! But he's told me how he feels like you're always watching him, waiting for him to crack up or something. Fine, he'd be free from the hospital, but living with a doctor is not exactly not a hospital."

"Andrew, tell him you don't understand what he's saying, dear."

"I understand, Rachel. Lie back down and let me handle this." She immediately returned to her mummified state, eyes shut too tight, but Ethan could see her trembling as his father went on, "We really thought the whole business could be done in a weekend. It's only a four hour trip each way. Let's talk about this after dinner, Ethan. It doesn't look like we're going to any naval club."

"Now I've spoiled your night out?" Ethan felt genuine remorse. "It shouldn't be such a big thing. If it doesn't work out, I'll bring him right back, but at least some time in the mountains, or at the beach, just him and me—"

"Oh, darling, I'm so queasy, I should go to bed."

Ten minutes later Ethan's mother was under the covers and he was hanging up her party dress. He started a tape of Erik Satie piano music and she smiled appreciatively. "I'm trying to learn this piece, but it's slow, slow, slow with all this discomfort."

"I'd feel lousy if I wrecked your night."

"You didn't wreck anything, dear. Poor judgement to quit your job. As for Jeff, we can leave him up there. Your father has his hands full with me. What can he be thinking, telling you to go get Jeff—"

"Don't you want him home? He'll make you feel better."

"He'll put me in an early grave."

"Quit exaggerating, Mom. Listen, just let me work my magic. I think part of your thing is psychosomatic and once you see Jeff getting better you'll wonder why you spent so much time in bed. Hey? Mom?"

"I'm listening, dear. Even though my eyes are shut and the music is glorious. I'm listening, but I won't respond because I'm much too weak. It does me good to hear you speak. Everything you say is so well-thought out and reasonable even though I completely disagree."

Ethan gave her a gentle kiss, fixed her blankets and went up to his room to pack. When he came back down it was evening and his father was slowly turning the pages of the medical art book by the light of a Tiffany lamp. He seemed so absorbed in the intimate portraits of sick people, strange healing methods through the ages, compassionate physicians doing more than was humanly possible, that Ethan did not want to disturb him with more talk of Jeff. But as he passed through the room, his shadow fell across Hippocrates lecturing on the location of the soul in the body, and Dr. Leblanc was jarred back to 1972.

"Ethan, are you sure you want to do this thing with Jeff?"

"Yeah, why not? Dad, let's face it. he's not responding to the therapy or the medication, it's time for a radical approach. Radically simple. You keep telling him there's no pressure on him so he should relax. But the nothingness of relaxation itself is too much stress for him. I'll keep him totally preoccupied. I make him laugh. He appreciates that I pay attention to all the strange things he comes up with."

"I suppose there's nothing to lose. You know what an awful handful he can be. Do you need extra money?"

Ethan didn't refuse, but chattered on. "I'll get a new job when I come back. The ethics of marketing strategy just drove me up a wall. I'm thinking more seriously about med school."

That did the trick. His father handed him a thick wad of bills. Nervous about easily accepting so much, Ethan kept it up. "Or finishing that MBA. Maybe international diplomacy. The world can use my well-thought-out reasoning, don't you think?"

His son's self-mocking confidence made Andrew Leblanc smile. "Do what you think is right and come back when you need to. I'm making your mother some very thin spaghetti. Do you want any?"

A huge helping of vermicelli and a night full of strange dreams took Ethan to a pre-dawn departure. Brisk for early June, gas lamps still illuminating the gated garden of Louisberg Square. Ethan felt incredibly healthy, wondered why his mother and younger brother were so unwell, then shrugged off his fears, closed the trunk on his possessions, and assumed his favorite position, the driver's seat. He adroitly maneuvered out of the tight space, let his car roll to the bottom of Beacon Hill, took a left on Charles Street and was on his way before the sun came up.

Zipping along unfamiliar roads in his Jaguar was the best way Ethan could find to deal with feelings of strangeness that he'd only recently begun to notice. He didn't have to go over the speed limit. Just the sensation of movement brought him a spell of happiness.

Just yesterday winter was driving everyone nuts. Now it's practically summer again. That's New England, god, I love it here. Where's this exit go? Man, beautiful stuff. Don't get too lost. About an hour I should be there. If I don't become a doctor I could be. . . . an architect. Throw up a city. That falls apart, I fix cars in my spare time and read all the timeless philosophers. Grab an MBA and manage some firm, make a bundle and lose it all playing the stocks. Teach kindergarten, open a shop on Charles Street, join the FBI and go undercover for good. Oh, I know it could evaporate just like it did for Dad's dad in the dismal Depression. He still came out on top. And now I'm stressed cause I'm his heir apparent. Medicine's in my blood, yeah right. Got to give myself a solid month or two before making any crucial decisions. I'm Dr. Faustus, fuck , that's all—finding fault with every field. No need to sell my soul—you can be a nice guy in a meaningless world. I'll prove that if I accomplish nothing else. Never can tell what lies ahead. Well, dead skunk obviously, so swerve to the left! Wow, those pink blossoms make me want to just. . . . fuck. Money, money, money. It can buy happiness but not sanity. Look at Jeff. Yeah, look him through and through and you'll never figure him out. It'd be nice to do something for him, crack through the wall. These are weird times. Hard enough when you're completely with it. Damn it, he's my brother. Only three years apart. Some of his blood's in me. So something in Jeff might tell me why things are suddenly not working out. But that's just it—there's nothing I can point to that's not working out. Six months I worry, worry, no way out of getting sent to that shitty war. Even Dad, one of the best soldiers there ever was, says this one's immoral. We shouldn't be over there, and nei-

ther should I. And now it's two weeks since I found out I'm definitely not going. Lucked out in the lottery. So what the fuck was the half-year of nerves for? Am I a stupid hypocrite or what? I'm safe, I'm not going to die in a putrid jungle, my guts in the mud. So now I get antsy over doing nothing. Why can't I wallow in relief? I don't have to do a fucking thing. All choices are fine. Even choosing to be a nervous wreck. But that's never been my style. So why now? Can anyone tell me? Can Jeff? I'll find out soon enough.

CHAPTER 2

It was the time of day at Walpole Manor when there was no scheduled activity for Jeff which was fine by him. He most enjoyed just sitting absolutely still on his bed and staring deeply into the wall.

 Aha! I knew there was a path behind that huge compost heap. You're not supposed to go back there because the woods are full of wild animals or something. That doesn't worry me. I'll run along this path. So far I don't hear a sound. Do the animals only come out at night? But it already is nighttime and now it's day again and once again pitch dark and still nothing. They made up the animals just to scare us. I've been in the woods for at least three weeks and haven't seen so much as a squirrel, not even a worm. That's what they didn't want me to find out—that the woods really are nothing but a bunch of trees and they go on forever. So why leave my bed when I already know that? Why go anywhere if I can predict exactly what's going to happen when I get there? Or won't happen, which is more often the case. Everyone makes such a big deal—"I'm off to see the world!" They end up sweaty and tired and disappointed cause things were less than they'd imagined. All that running around for nothing. I don't miss the world. And it turns out all the places I've been were right in this wall all along. Stroke of luck when I got sent here. But even the hospital routine is ridiculous. All the programs, schedules, special activities—all for nothing. A lot of running here and there, aw you fell, get up and try again, who are they kidding? I know better. So do they. But they like fooling themselves. And I just can't do it anymore. "But you're so young!" say all the people, with increasing emphasis till they hit ninety and then they mostly don't give a shit either. Yeah, how did I use up life before turning twenty? Now I'm here and I can go anywhere without budging from my bed.

 Outside the window through which Jeff didn't need to look,

heavy fog still clung to the wooded hills of southwest New Hampshire. Only a mile down the road, patches of cool dampness nestled against the sides of the old colonial clapboards, resurrected barns and tin sheds. The rolling mist made the townfolk appear more bucolic than they actually were. And it seemed to increase their distance from the asylum, Walpole Manor so mercifully lost amidst birch and maple and fog.

Upon its broad verandah sat a lonely woman babysitting a babbling boy with her anxious eyes, intent on weeding out all intrusion. The child scrambled about, cheerfully oblivious to his paranoid chaperone. His laughter was the only sound in mid-morning stillness.

Shrouds of mist and solitude lifted over the prow of the electric green Jaguar. The invading car brought shocking light and sound to that place of damaged souls, already unable to accept the slightest of life's offending sensations. The woman covered her face and the child fell backward onto a bush. The music flowed from within the sleek car-thing: the Who were "goin' mobile," and inspired the driver to go roaring up the drive. He stopped one space from Handicapped, but let the band finish their raucous anthem before killing the engine. A glance in the mirror, a comb slipping through a great head of hair, the magnanimous smile—Ethan stepped out of his car.

Cool. Old lady and kid. Big porch, fancy grounds. Cool. In and out, like five minutes. Mental hospital, my ass.

Ethan helped the kid out of the bush, tousled his hair and took the steps in three bounds, setting him down next to the woman he presumed was its mother. He watched his shadow approach as he advanced on the great oak door. Confidently took the iron handle, swung the door wide and strode in.

The immediate urge to put back on his sunglasses struck Ethan as stupid at first, but his eyes only reluctantly adjusted, verifying the gut impression. The charming New England mansion was inside cold and starkly bright. Ethan thought of the kinds of places to hide from the world—outside in wooded splendor or in here, a pastel green refrigerated purgatory. All the old opulence of the estate had been sucked out by some Freudian vampire's stab at appropriate asylum decor. But shallow disdain quickly slid out of Ethan's mind as he glimpsed a few of the clinic's inhabitants through half-open doors.

A contorted woman, writhing naked and tangled in her bedsheets. Gliding toward him in a distorted silhouette an old man in wheelchair, eyes glazed, all-seeing except for all that was in front of him. And at the end of the hall a careening hermaphrodite, hissing and mumbling, trying to draw Ethan into his manic fantasy.

No place for Jeff, this is no place for Jeff. There are people so far gone you can't call them people anymore. I know that's wrong, that's mean to even think, but Jeff is, never was, can't possibly have become— like that.

Stepping into the office, he saw that here, at least, some of the rich veneers had been spared the therapeutic brush-off. The front room was empty; it boasted a large fireplace for New Hampshire's long deepfreeze. Even at the start of summer, it had obviously been used in the past week. Ethan smiled at the thought of the patients frozen in Currier and Ives Christmas scenes. Knitted sweaters, ski caps, hot cider, and a drooling psychopath foraging through an oversized gift fruit basket from relatives who had not forgotten him.

The sound of medical jargon and case histories read into a dictaphone brought Ethan into the main office where he observed the director collapsed in her squeaky leather chair. As she wriggled her bare feet under the desk, Dr. Farber breathed out patient protocol into a handheld microphone which did not seem up to the immense task. It took in words like schizoid personality, hebephrenic mania, and bipolar dementia while being fondled by the doctor's puffy white hands. She was just beginning another case and uttered the name which brought Ethan fully into the room: "Jeffrey Leblanc."

She stopped the tape to think this one out, and Ethan imagined for a moment that perhaps it wasn't her chair that squeaked, but her odd-shaped head. As if feeling his smirk, Dr. Farber locked on his eyes and turned the recorder back on. "Jeffrey Leblanc, age twenty-one, acute cyclical schizophrenia, one thousand milligrams Elavil daily, two thousand milligrams Dilantin daily, fifteen hundred milligrams Valium twice daily, prognosis poor." She turned off the microphone. "So you're the brother."

She led the way out to the back of the asylum, through a struggling flower garden and a grove of sumac.

"We have to drag him kicking and screaming from his room, then once we get him outside he's just as hard to coax back inside." She hoisted a hefty arm in a grand gesture of "he's out there somewhere," and turned away, leaving Ethan to scout the outer perimeter of the grounds. An overgrown imposition of ivy and dried out trees. He followed an old stone fence to a sparse glade. And there was Jeff, propped in the fork of an immense tree. With his own personal attendant, no less. At least that was something for the big bucks. But moving closer Ethan could judge from the tired and disinterested face that this was no well-schooled psychiatric aide. Part time grease-monkey was more like it, licking his lips in a comic book, dressed in drab overalls, a medical Gomer Pyle. Looking up from "Spiderman's Greatest Battle Ever!" he acknowledged Ethan and glanced at his treebound ward.

"Physical therapy," he spoke to the air between them, hoping to avoid more clinical questions. Ethan squinted up with a genuine smile of love for a lost-and-found brother. "Don't say hello or anything." He let the words drift up to Jeffrey, knowing that a response would be slow in descending.

The eventual reply floated down from Jeff's haunted image, Spidey gone mad. Disheveled and enervated, his good looks, in fairer shades than his older sibling, seemed the lesser of the two. Ethan wondered if he was scouting for Sandman or Dr. Octopus when Jeff said, "They never let me stay out here at night. It's so beautiful then."

Ethan was determined to goose up the exchange: "Oh yeah,

man, this whole area's just fantastic! Hills, lakes, woods, God, look at that sky!" But his avian brother wanted more. "Come up here, Ethan."

"No way, I don't want to get mussed up, you know?" Ethan was feeling dirty just standing there. "You'll want your feet on the ground for the news I've brought."

His brother was dangling now, a frantic spider monkey. "Nobody just comes, they have to bring news." Jeff hovered and dropped a couple of notches. "The best thing about this place is being spared the news. News and views and blues, it never changes, but you on the outside have to be entertained. Ho-hi-de-ho!" It wasn't easy to see if he was happy or not, especially twelve feet in the air, hanging upside-down by his knees, head swaying to a peculiar inner beat.

"It sure does change, buddy. I'm taking you home. Eventually. After a little—well, I'll tell you when you come down." But Jeff continued to dangle, a cyclical schizoid's way to dilly-dally. "So? What do you say? Excited or what? It's a new start. A different kind of day. We on the outside are very entertained. And we want to spread it around. So please spare me one of your moods and get the fuck out of that tree!" Ethan had also wanted to wake up the watcher, but the rube was far too engrossed in Peter Parker's super-transformations.

"Hey, Ethan," from above, "I have lots more than one to spare. For starters, how about six!"

"Six what?"

"Here—have elation. No, make that ecstasy! Brain-curdling astonishment!"

Jeffrey hurled moods out to his earthbound brother, first with no more sincerity than a whore's makeup, but finally the very profusion of false feeling stuck to his face with an anguish unbearable to behold .

"Despair . . . crushing despair. Rage! Mild, casual contentment. Mmmm—desire, craving, drooly hunger. And you watching me watching myself—all with the most perfect imperfect indifference."

He punctuated his patter by relaxing his leghold on the branch and slipping to the ground, arching feet first to the dirt. The amazing Jeff then paused a beat and fell flat on his ass. It made Ethan laugh, but as he tried to smooth his brother's unkempt hair, the barely audible sobs caused him to choke back even a smile.

Jeff hugged his knees to himself and was rocking and weeping. Ethan wasn't sure how to handle it, his nineteen-year-old brother bawling worse than that little boy on the front porch. And over what? They'd just gotten started. Fear of leaving the asylum or the futility of going home? "Come on, Jeff, ease up, huh?" A glance at the guardian under the tree brought no assistance. "I don't imagine packing being much easier. But with or without your stuff we are hitting the road and soon."

While Jeff wiped his nose on his sleeve, Ethan took him back toward his home of the past two years. The grounds were good, but definitely not as healthy as some he'd seen in Brookline where his latest ex-girlfriend lived. He had visions of acid rain browning the grass and maiming the trees. All the green gone. The flagstone walk was an obstacle course, each slab tilting to its own desire. It led past the ruins of a flower arbor and on into the long since faded patients' sunroom where the ping-pong table had been sorely maltreated. The last hurdle was Dr. Farber. Ethan had to confront her one more time to ensure freedom for Jeff. His brother lurked by the fireplace, breathing and moaning, but only Ethan and the doctor brought the office to life.

The glasses had before hung around Dr. Farber's thick throat; now they perched on her nose. A precarious placement at best, they pronounced her arcane wisdom.

"Your brother's quite the handful. Knows how to keep the staff working overtime." She chatted on while rifling through one of many overburdened file cabinets. Within moments she had produced a rainbow of papers in her paw. "You'll need this pink one for the clearance of medications, the robin's egg blue for the county officials, the warm orange—sign twice please—for those nosy state inspectors, the page with the big logo for damn Washington bureaucrats, and of course the boring beige—initial here and here—so your parents won't sue our pants off!"

Ethan grimaced at the pile of responsibility in front of him, sad to see his brother reduced to a stack of ragtag documents.

"Your parents tell me you may take a side trip?" She cast a glance to the dim shape at the far end of the room. "With your brother, I mean."

"Yeah, I thought maybe rent a room for a week or something, away from the folks." He was still staring at the puddle of colors on his lap.

"Well, " she stiffened, "I don't think a session of handholding is going to be all that therapeutic for the boy, and you must consider the pharmaceuticals needed for his comfort and your peace of mind." Though she was receiving a tidy sum to close this account, Dr. Farber rather enjoyed needling the preppie punk.

"Oh, yeah, what about his supplies? Do you do prescriptions?"

"See the girl at the front as you leave. Jeffrey has some leftovers that he can take along." The brothers were beginning to blur together for her now. Two losers in the psychogenetic sweepstakes. "Well, you'll have better luck at McLean or wherever. My, the advances they've made these past few years with incurables." She smiled and drove in the last nail.

Ethan proceeded to sign. *She's only being phenomenally rude cause she's stuck around this shit all the time. I get to leave, even Jeff gets to go, but Dr. Squeaker has a life sentence to serve.*

"Yes, they have. You'd be surprised what they can cure." He sighed and held back, "Pathetic bitch."

Through the voices passing back and forth, Jeffrey's world remained unpolluted. Neither combatant noticed his fixation with Dr. Farber's wall. Not quite so vast a world as the one in his room, but it had its own beckoning roads, enticing precipices. His eyes saw such perfection in dust motes and sunlight that tears welled under the lids. Prickles of sensation poured down his body. His joy was only outside, damn it, none within. Still no escape from the dancing images of shadows, rearing up out of infinite plains of white sand. Maybe if he could draw his tears back in, some joy might follow. Jeff's ears responded to the tinkling sound of a hallucinated Calder mobile, one nobody could touch because its edges were razor sharp. He hoped that Dr. Farber would look up, enraptured, as the multi-colored blades fell right on her face and . . .

Both Ethan and the doctor looked back at him as he sat in bemused silence, a subtle grin focussed on Farber's sourball puss. "As I said, you won't have much time for sightseeing, and I suppose that smart green number out front has only one seat restraint for him. Too bad."

Ethan's face only registered concern as he stepped over to Jeff, holding out a hand to offer continuance outside the sick place. But would it be received as honest or some inconsequential gesture? Jeffrey's uncertain smile and wet eyes looked up to him with a hope that even the blind physician might see.

CHAPTER 3

Carrying Jeff out to the car, Ethan laughed at his earlier notion that "we'll take turns driving." Jeff's meager things all fit in one small suitcase and went in the back seat while Jeff was strapped in next to Ethan. The Jaguar's startup got the little kid on the steps screaming up and down, his "mother" holding her head like it would explode, and Gomer Pyle waving his arms, trying to corral them back inside. Ethan exhaled as much pain as he could. "I got you out of that place just in time."

"Just in time for what?" came from Jeff, and then he imitated Ethan's exhalation, making it bigger, longer. He pressed his face against the window and watched the roadside go by, a hypnotic blur of greens and browns, since he never looked up high enough to see the shades of blue in the lightening sky.

"I mean it's lucky I came today. It was that place making you batty."

"There wasn't anybody really like me."

"That's what I'm saying. I've been such a jerk leaving things up to Dad."

"Is Mom still sick?"

"Comes and goes. Not so great yesterday. I'm not blaming them, Jeff—they can't help how they are either. Dad takes care of her, sometimes he seems so helpless but he covers it up. I just woke up to the fact that it's ultimately up to me."

"I miss them sometimes, Ethan. They don't think I hate them, do they?"

"Sometimes you have a right to. They're not perfect. Anyway, it's not like you're dying to get home right away, are you?"

Jeff had to think about that. Ethan turned on the left hand

turn signal and forgot to turn it off. The clicking sound built into something not unlike bombs exploding in Jeff's head. Although he'd never really heard bombs exploding, not like his father in the war. Thousands of explosions, shooting and screaming everywhere, yet somehow controlled by a consciousness that could simply process any horror and move along. If this disease that made a car's turn signals into bomb blasts was genetic, it was a gene that lay dormant in dad, and had missed Ethan entirely.

Jeff wanted to say that he felt persecuted by Ethan's high spirits. How could it be that great numbers of people like his brother could simply go about living their lives, intrinsically feeling good, moving from one activity to the next as easily as slipping out of clothes into a warm bath? While for Jeff and his type, the clothes would become tangled, an impossible chore to take off or put back on, and the tub would be boiling hot or freezing cold, an abrupt shock that would ruin the rest of the day. These were the two classes of people, as Jeff saw it, even as he criticized himself for dividing the world into types of people, the way so many ignorant people do. There were people for whom life comes naturally and those for whom every thought, word and deed seems like an overwhelming task. Not that the former were totally without problems; of course the weight of practical life challenged them, but at least they had the benefit of a healthy attitude of hope, a sense that even if life were frequently frustrating, disappointing, and maddening, at least it was that way for everyone else. One could accept the nature of existence and get on with improving things in the immediate surroundings with confidence. For Jeff's breed, it was a matter of every opportunity becoming a mistake, a constant inner reminder that all we are doing is dying, and feeling choice eradicated by a cloud over the entire brain. People like Ethan were unaware of the abuse they caused by virtue of their ordinary behavior. Jeff knew Ethan was far from evil, even that he loved him and would like to help, but a disease that was every bit as crippling as the most violently physical of pains had invaded and conquered his mind, snuffing out notions like closeness and caring.

These thoughts erupted in words that came out of Jeff so incoherently that Ethan had no idea what he was talking about.

Jeff is going off about something. Why's he have to be this way? That's a dumb question. Everyone's the way they are and you have to deal. How I see it—our family's been lucky. There's a couple billion less fortunate in the world. That's what keeps me going. But what was it in him that tipped the balance? What's doled out to people isn't fair, isn't fair, isn't—oh what the fuck. It's so beautiful out here. The mountains, that view is better than any movie. And Jeff just wants to drag me down, don't look at anything but me, no that's not it, he can't help the way he is, but, but—if anything's possible, and I'm sure great philosophers have proved it, if anything's possible, then I can figure Jeff out and cure him. Well, cure's not the word, but I can help him, get him to a point of—self-sufficiency? Nah, probably not anytime soon. Do I devote my life? Nobody'd blame me if I didn't. Mom says, 'how can brothers be so different?' Dad knows the answer to that. He knows the answer to almost everything. But even he can't get to the bottom of Jeff.

"Look in that tape box and pick out something you like. Jeff? The box by your feet. I feel like music. Pick out something good to drive by."

Jeff passed his hand over the titles, sucking the tunes into his fingertips. Ethan had eclectic taste, but Jeff turned it all into noise with that hasty caress. If the noises had meaning, then Jeff's choice would define his own taste to Ethan, and then Ethan would know, "So, Jeff, you like that one, huh? Boy oh boy, you really go for that particular singer, he really touches something inside you, well, well, doesn't that say it all about you."

No, no, no, Ethan is not going to be able to look down on me for liking one song over another.

Jeff had the window down and was tossing tapes out in an instant.

"Hey! What the fuck are you doing? Stop throwing my music away! Hey, Jeff!"

Ethan slammed on the brakes, got riled by a honking car that came out of nowhere, figured the tapes were ruined and were all replaceable for a little money, so he kept going. He grabbed the box so Jeff would stop his destructive inventory.

"I can't believe you'd do that!"

Jeff looked despondently at the floor, feeling as lousy as he would have anyway if he hadn't gotten rid of all that noise. His father's voice in a silly self-mocking tone saying, "Damned if you do, damned if you don't" came back at Jeff. Dad loved the triteness of life as though it gave him pleasure to rub in how predictable everything was. And now the stupid "nugget of wisdom" gnawed at his heart, repulsively true.

Ethan shrugged off his loss with annoying equanimity. "Well . . . guess you don't feel like music right now."

And then a silence that made Jeff long for any kind of music, whether it defined his soul or not. Let people think of him what they would, *but please, please me and play a song for me, Mr. Tambourine Man, Mr. Piano Man, you heavily sedated singer in a rock and roll band!*

"Ethan, I don't mean to be horrible. But it hurts. In my stomach. And all over my face. And then it runs down into the rest of my body. There and there and there and—god, Ethan, it feels so terrible. The pills used to help. Makes me mad. They make some people completely better. But not me. I'm in the thirty percent it does no good. So they try new things. And combinations. So I might have a good hour or two, before I sink back down. All those others being cured, able to function. Why not me?" .

"I found this cool antique shop on the way up, Jeff. You know Mom's thing for tiny animals? Look at this cute little pig. Here, let's tie it by its tail to the rearview mirror, make it jiggle. There— fat little dancing pig! Couldn't find anything for Dad yet, but he hadn't gotten halfway through the book I gave him before leaving. You should've seen it. Paintings of doctors from all over the world. He ate it up. Vesalius pulls the skin back and has this big cheesy grin over how perfectly the organs are mushed together. Eureka! I could just dissect the whole thing and put it together again my own way. Yuk, all that blood pouring around those Greeks' feet!

And still they sit there, lost in amazement. There's a whole section about great men and their stomachs. Pepys was dyspeptic. And Samuel Johnson never had an unconstipated moment. If these guys did it, Jeff, then so can we. Right? Right?"

Great men and their stomachs. What about not so great men and their bladders?

"Better pull over quick, Ethan."

"Let's make some headway before a rest stop."

"O.K. I'll go in my pants, no problem."

Ethan screeched off the road next to an especially wooded area. He left the motor running, assuming Jeff would jump out and go behind the nearest tree. But Jeff didn't move.

"I thought you had to go real bad. Jeff?"

Was he waiting for the seat restraints to be removed? "The shoulder thing comes off as soon as you open the door," said Ethan, unbuckling the part across Jeff's lap. Jeff still didn't budge. Ethan reached over and opened the door. As soon as the safety strap pulled away, Jeff climbed into the back seat. He opened his suitcase and rummaged through it, quickly making a mess. Before Ethan could deal with his brother's unexpected imitation of a manic bellhop, a stranger appeared by the side of the car. It was a hitchhiker who'd mistakenly assumed that Ethan had stopped for him.

"Thanks! I've been standing out there all day. Can't believe the attitude of drivers in this state."

"Uh—I wasn't stopping for you."

"Aw, come on," pleaded the hitcher.

"Look, there's no room. My brother has to sit next to me." Ethan was normally well-disposed toward hitchhikers, but this was not the time.

"I'm short, can stretch out in the back, whatever." Seeing logistics was not the obstacle, the hitcher tried a different tack. "I have some great dope."

"Yeah?" Ethan was briefly moved. Then, glancing at his brother who was frantically seeking nothing, he thought better of it. "Nah, I can't."

"Come on, you'll love it."

"Yeah, I probably would but—"

The guy was starting to get in. Ethan couldn't allow it. "Sure, sure, slide on in. I just picked up my brother from a mental hospital. I could use a hand when he throws another fit."

The hitchhiker looked confused, then laughed it off. That offended Jeff no end.

"Ethan! Turn back! I'm off schedule! I'm going to die!" and Jeff was all arms and legs, raging in the back seat, clawing at the "wall" that kept him from returning to the front.

The hitcher darted away from the car and ran back down the road. "Next time I'll take the bus! Fuck all this!"

Ethan patted Jeff on the head. "Good job." He felt they were actually starting to communicate. Then Jeff returned to the business of digging and sniffing in his flung-apart suitcase. He was grunting like a badger in heat until he found a particular bottle. He put a pill on his tongue and gulped it down, then collapsed in the back amidst the strewn clothes.

"I thought you said those things don't make that big a difference," said Ethan.

"Mmmhmm," muttered Jeff, praying they would. "They pulverize the pain in my brain. Squeeze the mulch into a fine dust." He mimed such an action, making his whole body go limp, frighteningly lifeless.

"I still think you should go off them. The side effects probably make you worse and you don't even know it."

"If I wasn't here, you'd have picked up that guy."

"So?"

"You wanted the dope. You like how it makes you feel. There's no difference."

"There sure is. I only do dope when I want to and it doesn't run my life. I definitely wouldn't take any while I'm driving," he said, overstating the case.

"I'm sick of people making like I'm an addict just because I need these pills to get normal."

"I haven't seen you normal yet, Jeff. And I don't think you're an addict. After I've had you with me for a month or two, just the two of us having fun and working things out, I bet you'll come around."

"Or you will," snapped Jeff, less a threat than a sad prediction.

Ethan pulled the door shut and started to drive. Jeff might as well stay in the back for the time being.

"Hey, I forgot to go!" he yelled, and Ethan burst out laughing. He would have pulled back over if Jeff had insisted, but the catatonic routine resumed. Jeff lay rigid, watching life up through the back window, now blue, now crossed with power lines, until twenty minutes later when Ethan pulled into a gas station.

He walked his brother to the men's room, aimed him at the toilet, then ducked to avoid the erratic spray. At first he thought, "I don't envy the next user," then realized that was himself, and he laughingly escorted Jeff back to the car so he could have a bit of privacy. A young blonde woman was having her tank filled by a shirtless attendant. Ethan fantasized momentarily on the blonde's exposed shoulders as he tucked Jeff away. Through the windshield, Jeff was equally riveted by the movements of the sweaty attendant. Ethan winked at Jeff, shaking his finger in a gesture of no-no, as much to himself as his brother, then hurried back to the dirty little men's room.

Jeff remained quietly in the safety harness this time, staring out at a swampy area behind the gas station. He regretted faking that tantrum because it probably indicated to Ethan he could act out his fits and that meant much of his illness could be brought under control by a sheer act of will. *Probably saved our lives—who knows if that hitchhiker had a gun or what—but Ethan was mad because he wanted some normal company, someone who'd respond and shoot the shit and play along. How dare he even consider offering that guy a ride when he waved coke, dope and smoke in his face? Why is my need for prescribed drugs a crutch while Ethan can say he's just out for a little fun? Nobody ever tries to see the world the way others do. Except for schizophrenics who can't help seeing the world the way everybody does. And all at once.*

Jeff emerged from his reveries to notice that Ethan had left an open can of coke on the dashboard. What was taking Ethan so long? It felt like hours. Jeff knew not to trust his own sense of time, but he was helpless to affect his feelings about being abandoned for however long it had been. *Ethan is probably proud of leaving me on my own. "I'm proving he doesn't need constant supervision," or some such bullshit. It's not independence I'm after—it's freedom from this constant agony. People like Ethan like to say perceptive crap like: "crazy people are the sane ones in this insane world." I only wish. So when Ethan does some minor socially inappropriate action, like throwing a milk carton across a crowded lunch room, he gets real pleased with himself. I'm not hampered by arbitrary rules, or so he likes to think. As if a psychotic person has the goal to be liberated from social conventionality. It's that simple, and not some oozing bloodsucking marauder lurching maniacally throughout my body, bringing limitless torment to every particle of my being.*

"People have to understand!" suddenly said Jeff out loud. *Ethan thinking he gets it—that's worse than all the idiots who just are scared of the insane and move to the other side of the street. Ethan wants to be inside my head and have his own thoughts too. Like someone who wants to be filthy rich but doesn't want to have to do the filthy things to get the money and keep it., but Ethan thinks he can have a great fulfilling life—out there in the men's room, then off on the open road, climbing every mountain—and simultaneously hallucinate the impossible. He can't! Fantasy has a price! I'll show him. I'll fix him. If he wants to see things the way I do, he's going to have to pay the price.*

While his mind speeded along, Jeff involuntarily poured out a half-dozen of his anti-psychotics into his hand. He made a fist around the pills and waved it around, pretending to be the conductor of his seething brain orchestration. The fist opened over Ethan's coke and the pills bounced off the rim. Thin tinny sounds, but they reverberated like kettle drums to Jeff. This minimal activity exhausted him and his head fell heavily against the back of the seat. Several pills still stuck to his palm. His arm jerked out of control. The can of soda was huge, all that red and white and red smacking him across the face. *The can, the sky, the swampy bog, the hot sun, the dancing pig on the rearview mirror, the gas tanks with their shuttling numbers, Ethan, how dare you, how dare you presume to, how dare you presume to know to know to know!*

Jeff put the open pill bottle on the dashboard and retrieved the capsules that had dropped, blowing them off and inserting them on his tongue. He picked up the coke to wash them all down at once. But just as the soda was entering his mouth, he saw the rim was dirty. *Ugh, look at all that shit. Isn't there a law against putting them in the machines all covered with crud? And Ethan's been drinking from this putrid can?*

Jeff spat what he'd been drinking straight back into the can, shooting three of his capsules right along with it. He wiped the top all over his sleeve, determined to make that can shine. Once again a wave of exhaustion overwhelmed him. *All I've done is clean up a can . . . and I'm wiped out! People fly all over the world, hustling and bustling their important things, catch an hour of sleep and are back at it again. But I fade away trying to cross a room . . .*

Jeff didn't seem to notice that he'd done something at least a little gross in spitting into Ethan's soda, and probably worse than gross considering that several of his anti-psychotic meds were now dissolving in the carbonation. For the moment, all he could fathom of the whole event was that he'd attempted to stay on his medication schedule and had been confronted with that disgusting coke can. *Have I taken any pills at all today? They went all over the floor. There's one. What happened to all the others? The bottle is half empty. Gimme!*

He grabbed for the bottle, wondering if the pills had spilled out and he was instantly granted an image of small particles leaping from the bottle and heading out the car window. *So that's where they went!*

He undid the seat belt, wriggled from the shoulder harness, and was out the door, feeling his way around and under the car when Ethan came out of the bathroom. He shrugged and grinned at the attendant who was watching Jeff crawl around the car like a dog orbiting a hydrant. "My brother's always losing his contact lens."

"I don't think he's having a good day," returned the teenager, brushing grease and bugs off his naked stomach. "Did you need gas or anything?"

"Nope, just dropped by for a coke and a whiz. Hey, Jeff, buddy, whatcha lose now?" Ethan got Jeff off the ground and back in the car, not wanting to really hear an answer. An older man, maybe the teenager's dad, had come out of the station office and motioned for an explanation of what the guys in the Jaguar were up to.

Ethan called over, "It's O.K." The older man might not pass off weird behavior like a spacey teen. He shut his door crisply, restrapped Jeff and hit the gas.

Jeff had closed his eyes so he only felt the jolt of motion. He was safe for the moment in the dark, letting the rapids of his mind rush by. It was not impossible that he had done something inappropriate, but if he kept his eyes shut tight it would pass and be forgotten.

He opened his eyes to see Ethan eagerly swigging down the soda. Jeff saw a pill lying in a crease of his trousers and noticed that another was stuck to his hand. What had become of the others he honestly could not say. Ethan's smile made the entire gas station stop dissolve into memory and the car engine drowned out, for the moment, even Jeff's noisy clatter of thoughts.

CHAPTER 4

Jeff was cognizant they were back on the highway, putting the gas station and the asylum (where had he been longer?) into the past, and whatever was in the past took on a comforting haze, became a falsely serene memory. It was only the fact of things moving inexorably into the past that kept Jeff from killing himself. Somehow he realized that the hell of each moment would soon be gone, which in turn made continued existence just acceptable enough.

Ethan was singing. The price Jeff had to pay for tossing tapes out the window. Ethan was singing, sipping his soda, awfully perky considering what a burden Jeff had been all day. Ethan was singing, nothing seemed to bother him, he actually enjoyed the passing of time, looked forward to the future, regretted nothing in the past, and especially got off on the here and now. That singing, that not quite on-key singing . . . Ethan was acting pretty ebullient, even for Ethan. And his eyes were so big. But that was lucky because he should keep them on the winding road while Jeff kept his shut whenever he felt like it. Big eyes, loud singing, pat-pat-patting the steering wheel. And the speedometer steadily rising.

Ethan glanced at himself in the rearview mirror. He sensed Jeff watching him and wondered if he looked funny. Nope, same good-looking, ready-for-anything kind of guy. Singing and driving and helping his brother, doing his family a favor, lots of money in his pocket and no boring job to go home to. *The future's wide open, billions of people less fortunate, life too short to complain about the obvious. It's all just a party and even that dancing, jiggling little pig on the rearview mirror knows it. Forget all the bad, feel good, project it to other people, they'll give you what you want. A conspiracy of happiness. We're all in this together and we all know what sucks about it, so let's laugh and help each other and we'll turn it all into a plus. Whooppee! How does that song go? Lookit, Jeff's starting to smile. I'm right, this is contagious.*

But Jeff wasn't looking at Ethan anymore. He was smiling at something else in the mirror. A brilliant blue—going around and around. Ethan did not seem to notice until a whining siren started to blare. That made Jeff's smile fade, but only because the abstract pleasure of a favorite color elicited profanity from his brother.

"What the fuck! Where'd those assholes come from?"

He looked at the speedometer. Over ninety?!

Jeff put color and sound together and came to a scary conclusion.

"They've come to take me back!"

"What? Oh, shit, yeah, I really pissed off that doctor. Did she have them tail us, I wonder? What a bitch! I signed all her fucking papers! I am doing ninety, but what the fuck—there was nobody around."

"Ethan, what are you doing? Slow down!"

"Huh? Nobody's going to touch you, Jeff! If they blamed you for this, I'd never forgive myself. Hang on, we can lose these creeps!"

He accelerated into another lane. The police were momentarily left behind. But seconds later they were breathing down Ethan's neck.

"Stop, Ethan, stop! They'll hate us worse!"

"Oh yeah? It's you they want, not me, pal. I've never done anything wrong in my life!"

Ethan weaved in and out of other cars. He swerved off at the next exit, followed closely by the police. The driving got more hazardous on treacherous back country roads. Jeff's heart practically burst out of his chest as Ethan gunned the Jaguar, taking it around curves like it was an extension of his supple body.

"You can't keep this up forever!"

"Sure I can! If they make me!"

Woods and fields rushed by so fast Jeff imagined he was travelling in time. The hordes of Attila, the bubonic rats from Brussels,

Vesuvius raining down on everyone, China sleeping for a thousand years, Tyrannosaurus waking up to the smell of meat in motion. Were they at the center of the Earth yet? Or was Jeff actually still back in his tiny room at the hospital and all of this was happening in the wall? That was not impossible. Many were the times he'd left the hospital on perilous, joyous journeys across the globe, even to other parts of the universe, only to find he hadn't budged from his bed. The wall had so much to offer. "I don't really need to go anywhere," Jeff surmised. "Every place is right here inside my wall. Look! There's a road that winds off toward infinity!" But, wait, there was that image of Ethan carrying him out of the hospital and strapping him into the car. His trips through the wall had never required such specifics as mode of travel. This hurtling piece of steel was quite possibly real—and real things often came to bad ends. In which case, Ethan was doing something real crazy.

Jeff grabbed at Ethan, flapping his hands in front of his face. "You have to slow down!"

"Get out of here, Jeff! " Ethan had to use his right hand to fend off Jeff while keeping up the daredevil maneuvers with only his left. The wheels skidded on the edge of the dirt embankment and he nearly lost control of the car. It jerked from side to side before he mastered the wheel once more. A glance in the mirror—that stupid little pig is driving me nuts!—and he saw the patrol car was matching his every move. "Stay over there, Jeff! Don't know how long I can keep this up—."

Ethan swooped around a deceptively wide smooth curve. The road abruptly whipped back the other way. Ethan's fierce concentration helped him pull it off, but the cop car wasn't so lucky. Just after Ethan passed, a small animal darted out into the road, daring to run the split-second avenue between one flying object and the next. It didn't make it, and as its furry corpse got sucked into a wheel, the patrol car leapt off the road, flipping over several times before coming down on its roof. The momentum kept it going, scraping along the embankment upside-down until it slammed into a tree and blew up.

Ethan caught barely a glimpse of the stunning flash before another curve in the road blocked his rear view. But the horrific sound poured over the Jaguar. Even Jeff knew something terrible had become of their pursuers.

"That didn't happen! It didn't happen, couldn't have—." With that declaration, Ethan had suddenly become a master at what Jeff had awkwardly practiced for almost twenty years: being a slave to illusion. And since Jeff tended to trust Ethan (who had always had a firm grip on what most people seemed to agree was actually going on), then perhaps that explosion and flash of light actually did not happen. Maybe the cops gave up the chase, conceding that Ethan was the superior driver. A sonic boom just coincidentally came from overhead, and the flash of light had to do with the angle of the sun or a mischievous UFO, a ubiquitous event in these parts of New Hampshire. Because otherwise, the chasing car had blown up and its inhabitants were obliterated. And if that was the case, Ethan would surely not still be coaxing his snazzy sports car into the stratosphere, a wondrous look of triumph on his face.

I saved Jeff. I got him out of that fucking sty and I got him away from those storm troopers who just wanted to beat the shit out of an escaped lunatic. Now they're off our tail, they're gone, that's all I know, and we just keep going, going, putting all that behind us. I'm going to amaze everyone and cure him! It's the gravity of the world that makes my brother crazy and we left that behind long ago. Mach Two Mach Three Mach Four, this Jag has never let me down, best car I ever owned. Damn, did I wet my pants?

Ethan looked between his legs. He had put the coke can there before the chase began and it had behaved itself until just now, tipping over and foaming up his crotch. Jeff also looked at the spilled soda and had vague memories associated with that red and white can—but of what? That specifically escaped him.

And then he felt awash in guilt. It was a feeling he got many times in a single day, so there was no cause to relate it to the current situation. *Of course it's for my sake Ethan is going so fast.*

Those cops would like nothing better than to beat me into the ground. What a good guy Ethan is! Ooops, we're off the road . . .

The Jaguar had once again slipped onto the rocky embankment, only this time Ethan hit the brakes instead of trying to steer it back on track. That caused a snake-like skid, the car spun a hundred eighty degrees, swung backwards , around again, flying off the road and down the gully, propelled all the way across a field and into a patch of tangled trees where it finally slammed to a stop.

Protected by the seat belts, the brothers suffered minor injuries, cuts from shattering glass and bruises from being bounced around. But the force of the landing briefly knocked Ethan out. A fire started in the engine. Jeff surprised himself by instantly undoing his seat belt and roughly shaking Ethan awake. "Ethan! We're on fire!"

Ethan sprang up. "Out of here! Quick!" His door was smashed stuck. He crawled over Jeff and got the other door open. Spilling onto the dirt, he pulled Jeff out on top of him, then clawed away from the car with Jeff on his back. He held Jeff by the arm until he felt they must be far enough and he couldn't handle his weight for another instant. In the panic, Ethan had gone into the woods instead of finding the clearing. Now, as smoke continued to pour from the engine, filling the air with a stinging mist, Ethan kept pushing forward no matter where that might take him. He prayed Jeff would follow.

"Hey! Where are we going? Ethan!" Jeff chased dependable Ethan further and further into dense woodland. Ethan's haywire driving had given way to frenzied running, a mad dash toward everywhere and nowhere. Even when Jeff caught up, Ethan initially pushed him away and kept running.

Their pace didn't slow until they were deep in the woods. Ethan tripped, Jeff ran into him, both went tumbling down. They looked at each other directly for the first time since the crash. Ethan's eyes reflected his shifting awareness of what was going on. For once, Jeff's were clearer and so full of need for his brother that

Ethan was touched and stopped thrashing about on the ground. He hugged Jeff tightly and burst out laughing.

"Hey, Jeffrey, whatcha doing? We're all right, kid, we made it!"

"I—I had to get you to stop. I'm sorry, Ethan, sorry . . . "

"Look at all the trees! My God, they're all over the place!" Ethan was flat on the ground, his face to the sky. The treetops did indeed seem to be all there was. Jeff stood up, but could not dispel Ethan's amazement. "Let me—let me catch my breath. Let me—"

Jeff let him and after a few moments noticed he was breathing in perfect sync with Ethan. The woods were so quiet and they could just lay there, inhaling, exhaling together, sharing finally, finally a moment of relief. The sedating effect was irresistible. Coupled with a delayed reaction of exhaustion, both brothers lost consciousness in less than a minute.

CHAPTER 5

By the time they woke, most of the day had passed. Jeff raised his head first. It took him a solid minute to realize the comforting arms of an American soldier rescuing him from a Siberian prison camp had been a dream, and these quiet green woods were his lamentable reality.

"Come on, get up! They blew up! They're probably dead!"

"Huh? Who?" Ethan was shocked out of a dreamless sleep and calmed down only when he remembered he was with Jeff who frequently spoke nonsense, such as screaming about death in the middle of a burgeoning forest.

"I'm going back. With or without you." And Jeff made good on his threat, heading off arbitrarily in one direction. Ethan rolled around in the dirt, stretching out like he could easily revert to unconsciousness. "All by yourself? I'm impressed. Mom and Dad will be pleased. Taking things into your own hands. We're making progress already."

But Jeff returned within seconds. "Which way was it? Our car? The road?"

Ethan stood up and brushed himself off. His wounds and cuts had dried while they slept so he saw no evidence for alarm. Looking up and circling around the tall canopy of trees, he lost his balance and Jeff had to help him up again.

"I remember that road. Don't go down there! It goes nowhere that road, we'll never find our way back to the main highway . . . I have to remember the name, the name of that road. Missing. . . . something. Missing Link! What kind of name is that for a road?"

"What are you talking about missing links for? You Darwin all of a sudden? Very original, Jeff. Most of your type goes for Napoleon or some fucked up conqueror. A man of peace, a man of science, that's more like it."

Jeff shook Ethan to make him stop this weird talk. He was serious, as serious as it was ever possible for him to be when the world was such a sick joke, but Ethan still had that ludicrous grin on his face and was fighting off the giggles.

"You O.K.? You look O.K. Couple bruises." Ethan resembled his old man as he gave Jeff a surgical once-over.

"I'm fine. Now let's try this way." Jeff yanked Ethan down a promising path that only yielded more bushes and vines and not the way out that Jeff so desperately wanted. For the life of him, Ethan could not figure what the urgency was about. They were safe, alive—whatever had happened, now it was over and they were in this paradise of trees and wild flowers. It was the latter part of a nearly perfect day, the only cloud being the one that had mysteriously descended over his own mind.

At the same time, the dark shroud that normally enveloped Jeff's mind had effortlessly lifted. Being thrown around in the car, strapped in tight while the machine flipped and rolled, skid and slammed, like some kid's idea of the world's greatest amusement park ride—that could well have shook the shroud. But since Ethan was acting like none of that had happened, Jeff had no way of confirming his theory. And besides, now that this brilliant clarity was his after what seemed like years spent in muffled darkness, what did it matter what had caused it? Maybe something terrible had occurred, maybe not. Abruptly, there came a startling sense of freedom. Now what to do with it? First, explore the woods.

Two trees growing out of the same stump. Faces in the bark, definitely faces, full of expression. A squirrel nestled in the crux of a branch. "You know Mom's thing for tiny animals." I'm like those trees, stuck with my roots. Although, unlike them I can move around—and here I am doing it. Moving away from Ethan who doesn't seem to want to go anywhere all of a sudden. Now I can't even see him. He was near the trees with the faces. But there are so many trees, so many faces—"Ethan!

"Jeff! Where'd you go?"
"Ethan!"
"I'm over here!"

Jeff found Ethan back by the trees with a common stump. He looked so dizzy Jeff could virtually feel Ethan's wobbly sense of balance. *I wonder if Ethan can do that? See me seeing him from inside my head. Or if that's a power I alone was born with?.*

And just as he thought of his troubles, a conflicting image came to mind. He was twelve years old and speeding around a rink on ice skates. His parents were skating side-by-side, smiling and moving through the steps of a waltz. His father making sure their feet moved together, his mother trying hard not to look at her feet, looking straight ahead with a strained expression of pleasure. And Jeff sped past them, again and again, going as fast as he could. At that moment he was free, the movement made him feel utterly free, and all the burdens of complex thought, ponderous feeling and his resulting lack of will vanished. He was moving faster and faster in an endless circle. His parents were happy and so was he.

Jeff's looking at me that way again. Pleading eyes. Frisky as a dog in winter. His yearbook quote. Everyone else is like National Honor Society, World Affairs Club, Varsity Soccer, Student Council, Morse Code Club—and my brother's "frisky as a dog in winter." He's counting on me. I should help him find what he's looking for. A way out of these woods. But it's so nice right here. What's the hurry? That's his whole problem. He thinks there's something else to do besides enjoy the moment. Who ever gave him that idea? Dad, probably. And Mom, telling him he could only go to summer camp if it was a Math Camp. "You have to do something with your life." How fucked up. Do something with your life if you want to. Like I'm going to. Eventually. Until then you don't worry about it. Course it is getting dark. Are we camping out in the woods? Where are our things?

"Ethan! Aren't you worried? You have a huge bump on your forehead!"

"Huh? Oh. Must've banged it against a tree."

"It wasn't a tree! I'll show you what it was."

Jeff now pulled Ethan along, trying this path and that, through the woods. Black smoke rising over the trees—the car must be over there! Jeff hurried down a trail and came out into a clearing. But it wasn't the scene of the crash. Ethan emerged a few moments later and saw that Jeff had found his way out to a hilltop overlooking the edge of a town.

"I see lights!"

"Jeff, try and control your—oh, God, there's a town down there."

"We should try and find a place to call."

"Call who? About what?" *Jeff sure knows how to spoil a walk in the woods.*

Jeff ran down the hill and found himself in someone's back yard. The smoke he'd seen was coming from a fire on the other side of the house. He turned the corner where an old woman in overalls was putting out a fire in her barbecue grill. She saw Jeff and interpreted his desperate expression as a sign of concern for her accident.

"Hello there! It's under control now. Just turned my back for a few seconds and the sparks got out of hand." She sprayed out the remains of the fire, causing more thick smoke to billow up. "There goes my cookout. Sorry I can't offer you anything."

Ethan came down the hill to get Jeff before he did anything weird in front of some unsuspecting person. Too late. Jeff had already entered into animated discussion.

"We used to have cookouts every Sunday afternoon. Right after coming home from ice-skating."

"Cookouts? Ice skating? What country are you from?"

"Jeff, this is private property. I'm sorry, Ma'am."

"No, no, that's all right. He just wanted to help. You boys out for a hike?"

"No, we're looking for a green Jaguar on fire." Jeff was on a roll.

The woman gave a great guffaw. "Goodness, me! My treasure

hunts used to be for rabbits and squirrels. Say, you got scraped up pretty bad in them woods."

For the first time, hearing it from someone besides Jeff, Ethan took stock of the condition of his face and arms. Blood from a reopened cut smeared his hands and clothes.

"Ought to get home and see to that," advised the woman. "You live close by?"

"No," muttered Ethan. "No, we're from . . . far away."

"Head on over to the hotel. They'll have first aid stuff there."

Jeff immediately pulled Ethan in the direction she pointed. He didn't want Ethan striking up a conversation with such an accident-prone woman.

"I'd offer you a burger, but I've burnt them to a crisp." She was laughing heartily at herself as Ethan waved thank you and gave in to Jeff's manic grip.

"Where did we park?" he said once they were out of the woman's earshot.

"Park?" Jeff practically screeched it.

"How'd I get so bloody?"

Jeff felt like he'd been trying to tell him all afternoon. He wasn't going to stop now to inform Ethan of the obvious. Especially when the town they were entering was so strangely intriguing. He didn't want to say, "I've been here before," because he had an obsession with not saying things that others said too lightly. But the small farm and mill town whose center they were rapidly approaching stirred something inside Jeff, vivid feelings that were so alluring he longed to be everywhere in the town simultaneously. Jeff was crying, but walking ever faster as if getting to the hotel would somehow solve everything. Ethan grabbed him.

"Where are you going? We were in some kind of crash . . . we hit a tree, right?

And that—that cop car—oh my God! They blew up!"

"I told you that before. Let's go."

"Go where? We're in a fucking mess!"

"I tried to get you to slow down."

Ethan was stupefied at Jeff's newfound objectivity. He muttered to himself, trying to piece things together. They had reached the center of town. A freight train was moving a seemingly endless number of boxcars along a track just behind the hotel. It blared its deafening horn twice. Jeff jumped and Ethan worked hard to organize his thoughts. The train went clacking along, prodding a similar rhythm in his brain; things suddenly came together.

"The car was stolen! Yeah, that's it! We weren't driving. Hitchhikers robbed us, made us get out and took off!" Ethan's masterstroke did nothing to un-confuse Jeff who wondered, "And then what happened?"

"The punks who robbed us caused, you know, whatever happened."

They couldn't cross over to the hotel till the train went by; Jeff had long moments to mull Ethan's strange rationale.

"So . . . we're going to lie?"

"Oh, come on, Jeff. As if you could ever tell the difference between what's real and what's not."

Ethan's strongest point yet. At times like this, Jeff envied his brother's commanding way with the world. Jeff began to wonder whether anything at all had happened the way he'd perceived. "Maybe I'm still back in the hospital," he concluded. "This is all happening in my wall."

Ethan put his arm around Jeff. "Yeah, I wish. Now, not a word out of you when we go in here." The last boxcar went by and they crossed the tracks, heading around to the front of the hotel. A turn-of-the-century, less-than-grand affair even in its day, now very much on its last legs. A large black dog was tied to a dying tree on the back lawn. If it had been in front, few would have dared attempt to register for a night's stay. The dog barked ferociously whenever it wasn't drooling and gnawing at the rope. It strained to pull up the tree and maul Ethan who steered Jeff in a wide arc as they went around to the front. Nobody was in the stale lobby, so they went through a swinging door into the hotel bar. Jeff was overwhelmed by the sense of maroon—seats, walls, carpet. Ethan felt instantly superior to anything shabby. He went right up to the bartender as she refilled the glasses of two old drunks. The three spoke in low voices, at length about nothing; Ethan's bloodiness barely caught their attention.

"Excuse me, I don't see a phone. Miss? A phone?"

"There's no phone here, Mister. We had it taken out. People would come in and use it for the wrong things. Know what I mean, wrong things?"

Ethan had no idea, but he joined in the laughter of the drunks to get them on his side. "Yeah, yeah, but listen—we're kind of in a jam. Our car was stolen."

"Yeah? What kind of car? Nice one?" The lively interest came from the drunks, whom Ethan could see were much younger than he'd thought.

"It's my car. Sentimental value, you know?" It was important not to come across like some hot shot. The bartender felt a twinge of sympathy.

"Well, you can go on down the road and tell Tom. He's the sheriff," and then with a nudge to her only customers, "Might be beyond him though."

"Right! Tell Tom! Tom's on the case! You can go home and forget about it!" The drunks were ready for another refill.

Despite their roaring non-recommendation, Ethan figured Tom was the inevitable next step. "Thanks. Do you have anything we could use to—?" He felt silly having to point out his bloodstains, but it was that kind of day. The bartender handed him her last two tiny drink napkins and knelt down to find another package. When it seemed apparent she wouldn't be standing back up for awhile, Ethan turned to apply one of the pathetic little napkins to Jeff. Where'd he go?

Jeff had drifted away to wander among the bar's sparse furnishings. He was far too sensitive a schizo to watch his older brother so offhandedly mistreated. *A lot of sad, lonely people drank themselves to death in this place.* He actually could see them coming through that creaky door and sitting down to drink till they dropped. A cast of rejects from "Our Town." The petering out of a long line of American dreams. Oh sure, they laughed in their beers and threw up in private, but nobody fooled anyone else.

That over-madeup woman has such a sweet face . . . we should give her money. Even though she'll only use it for booze. She dragged her kid along. He's not having the greatest time. But he keeps her friends amused. He's tasting her drink while she's not looking. Ugh, spit it out all over everyone. More laughs. "They all drank themselves to death, to death, drank their way to bottomless graves."

"Thanks for the pep talk, Jeff. I don't see a lot of progress in here myself. Let's go find this Sheriff Tom person."

He was gently nudging Jeff toward the exit when a lovely woman roughly his age came into the bar. Before uttering a word, she swept so much energy into the place that Ethan couldn't take his eyes off her. She returned his stare, conveying lively flamboyance and dark brooding, somehow both at once.

"Evening, Harriet. Eddie says he lost something in here last night." Karin's voice carried authority and Ethan could not have guessed how tired and worn down she felt.

"Howdy, Karin. He say what it was?"

"His wallet or his keys or maybe some memento from his air force days."

Jeff blurted out, "How could he not know what he lost?"

"You're no one to talk, Jeffrey." But Ethan was glad he had spoken up and commanded the wide-eyed brunette's attention.

"If-if-if you don't know what you lost, it could be anything! You could lose something you never had!"

"Don't mind him." Ethan smiled an apology to the woman he'd heard called Karin. He never forgot names or faces. Or telephone numbers. His reputation for trustworthiness was about to get a good workout.

"Oh, but he's got a point. When you work for the Osbornes, you have to keep on your toes for all the bullshit." Jeff enjoyed being proven right and he also instantly liked Karin, if somewhat more platonically. She went on, "Eddie and Esther, you know? Well, Harriet, I don't think these boys are from around here."

"They haven't head of the Fighting Osbornes, that's a sure sign."

For the first time, Ethan realized that Harriet was as loaded as her customers. Time for some sober assistance. "Our car was stolen. Can we come use your phone?"

Karin purposely didn't look at him. "What do you think, Harriet? Can I trust these strange guys?"

"Sure, but can they trust Esther and Eddie?" blurted out the two town drunks, each eager to take credit for the day's best crack.

The barrage of inside jokes was lost on Ethan who at the moment could not imagine anyone being worse off than himself. "I just want to use the phone." He and Karin met eyes again, affirming a great first impression. Jeff felt obliged to chime in.

"That's really all he wants!" and his tone broke any remaining ice. Karin gave a short laugh and motioned them outside. "So give a call if anything of Eddie's turns up."

"Will do, Karin. Can't have Eddie running around without his air force mementoes."

"Charlestown's war hero!" proclaimed one of the guys spinning on his stool. That brought down the house as the brothers fled into twilight with the seemingly no-nonsense lady.

Jeff kept chattering away as introductions were exchanged. "It's no big deal, but it's kind of life and death." The Osborne house was only about two hundred feet once they re-crossed the railroad tracks, but Ethan knew it would be a job to keep a lid on Jeff all the way.

"Nothing's life and death, fella. Jeff, I mean. Not here." Karin took it in the most innocent spirit. "Not too many tourists bother with Charlestown."

"I'll bet it has its attractions," said Ethan, determined to flatter her attention away from Jeff. But that boy was definitely frisky, even in summer.

"We lost our car. We're not tourists. Boy, you have to repeat everything around here."

Ethan poked him in the ribs. "We're making small talk."

"Huge incredible universe and everyone makes small talk," Jeff complained. "No wonder some of us have to be locked up."

"Why would they lock you up for having your car stolen?"

"My brother has a couple loose screws, that's all."

"Does it run in the family?" Karin shot back and Ethan instantly laughed. Luckily they were already heading up the walkway to the Osborne's front door. The yelling from inside the house quashed anymore threats from Jeff's twisted insight.

CHAPTER 6

"What do you want now, you old pig?"

"Eshter, pleash, jus-jus one more beer."

"No way! I don't want to get beat up before dinner."

"Bashtard, woman, bashtard! Who beats who around here?"

Esther and Eddie's conversation spiced up another dull country evening. Ethan, who had not been terribly bored lately, wondered if he was ready for whatever was inside. If not for Karin holding open the door, he was certain this would be the last house on the block he'd stop for help. His first glimpse of the "Fighting Osbornes" and their battlefield made even his lowest expectations seem rosy. In an instant Ethan had passed from a low-lit scene of small-town tranquility to a Fourth of July riot. No one was safe in this free-for-all. The condition of the living room, its appearance and odor, would have sent a veteran sanitation engineer screaming for cover. The kitchen, just visible through a lazy butler wall space, promised a deeper descent into filth. Ethan's eyes darted about for the phone. Hopefully, he'd only have to go a few feet more to accomplish his task and get the hell out. But picking a phone out from this century-old explosion of trash Americana would have required a surgical skill beyond that of his own doctor dad. No, he was clearly in Karin's hands, and she presumably knew the way around the crazed pair that employed her.

But Karin gave a laconic, "These guys need to use the phone," which surely couldn't be heard above the din of that rampaging couple. Astonishingly, Esther stopped her verbal pounding, whirled around physically and emotionally, and met the brothers with an ingratiating grin. "Who's that? Company? Come on in! Welcome, boys! Nice to see you!"

Eddie fell back in his chair, knocked over by the wind of Esther's turn.

He made a loud moan which could have been the sound of the whole house settling while Esther determinedly hurled out the welcome mat. "Door's always open at our place! Ain't that right, Eddie?"

"God damn plase ish turning into Grand Shen-shen-tral." Eddie was exhausted but damned if anyone was going to barge into his house. He got up and waved his cane at Jeff. Moving objects always left strobe-like tracks in front of Jeff's eyes, so the cane made a wondrous show that drew him further in.

"Don't mind Eddie. I'm just teaching him a little self-discipline." Esther lit a cigarette and cracked open a fresh beer for herself.

"Grrr, gimme dat!" Eddie shoved past Jeff and went roaring across the room at his mocking spouse. Esther ducked behind Ethan.

"Help! Karin! You guys! Stop him!"

Baffled, but pulled into the fray by Karin, Ethan tried to restrain Eddie. Jeff laughed. There were more fast moves and blocking than in a Celtics game.

Esther made for the telephone. "Hold him tight! I'll call Tom!" She managed to dial half the number before Eddie got loose, ripped the phone out of the wall and smashed it to the floor. Finally, Karin got upset.

"Eddie, sit! You sit down this instant or I'm hiding your pills again!"

"God damn crazy woman!" Eddie was in tears.

Esther was not. "Idiot! Psychopath!" Then with her homespun smile, "Excuse my language, boys, but he did the same thing to the TV just last week."

Ethan was beginning to see the big picture. "Uh, I think we'll try next door."

"Next door, ha-ha, fat chance!" Another of her Larry Bird blocks separated Ethan from freedom. "That's Clara Muff's house. She's my friend but I've got enough courtesy to warn folks away from that dump. Do you know the only time she moves her fat butt is when she sees UFO's peeping in her trailer park?"

"UFOs?" Jeff heard something he could relate to.

"Yeah, we got lots of them around here. The trick is stay in your car, lock your doors. They can only suck you up into their ships if you're out in the open. Stupid Clara, though, she opens her windows and starts waving—come on down! Like they're in-laws that got lost. I'm trying to tell you boys my old friend's gone nuts! Everybody knows UFOs can be explained. It's a bunch of no-good husbands in souped-up airforce junk trying to pull a fast one."

"O.K., so next door's out, but even so—" Ethan was going to get by Esther even if it meant agreeing with her.

Karin put her hand on Ethan's shoulder. "Wait a second. Things are calming down."

"But he smashed the phone—"

Esther was unfazed by that logic. "American Legion across the street's got a lock on theirs. Instead of trying to find a decent phone in Charlestown, you might as well just open the window and holler."

"She's got a point."

"You're very nice, but we've got a problem and—"

"You think I got it easy? Come in here." Ethan ducked, so it was Jeff that Esther got hold of and dragged into the kitchen. Eddie's cane kept Ethan at bay long enough for the manic woman to hold up a big pot of beef stew for Jeff to smell.

"Don't make me throw all this out. Dorian doesn't appreciate it either. 'I just want to paint. I'll eat later.' " she mimicked. "Boy oh boy. With them baggy clothes off, I'll bet you're as skinny as him."

Ethan was at the point of begging Karin. "I'm sorry, but we don't have the time for all this. Get him off me!"

Karin separated Eddie from Ethan. "Don't worry. I'll get Dorian to run upstreet and report your car." She went to the foot of the stairs and called up two flights. "Dorian! Come on down! It's important!"

"I'm painting! I'll do it later!" came the flat response.

"You have to get Tom, Dorian!"

"Why? Who's beating up who?" and that was the last word from Dorian.

Ethan whirled in frustration. He made for the door and was almost out when he remembered it wasn't a good idea to leave Jeff behind.

Esther tried to spoon-feed the stew to Jeff. He was real hungry and he opened wide. But the first taste was so dreadful, he was dead set on avoiding seconds. Esther was aiming another heaping tablespoon. Jeff shoved it away with such force the pot tipped over. Beef stew splashed down his clothes.

"What a waste!" She was suddenly more concerned about Jeff's appearance than a floorful of stew. "Come on, out of your things. I'll have to run a machine." Anyone so compulsively concerned with clean clothes could not possibly be responsible for the hopeless condition of this house, could she? Jeff pondered the question and remained compliant while Esther stripped him down to his underpants.

Ethan whipped into the kitchen and the sight of his near naked brother would have unhinged him if not for Karin's warm hand on the back of his neck. Somehow that made up for everything. And then there was her voice, full of honest concern. "Say, you're cut up pretty bad."

As Esther drew Jeff back into the living room, Ethan was gently set down in a remarkably empty kitchen chair by Karin. He helplessly became her charge, watching her delectable hands pick out a first aid kit from the horrendous mess on the overflowing table. Those hands gave the illusion of a sanitary procedure as she began to treat his wounds.

"You're like a live-in nurse? That's what you do here?"

"That's what I do. I'm aiming for medical school, but who has money or time for that?"

"My dad did. Ouch.... oooo... "

"Really? A doctor's son. Quite a find in the hotel bar of Charlestown. Eddie's my fifth, no sixth, patient since I got my LPN. God, but they seem to drop like flies."

Ethan shifted uneasily in his chair. Maybe not such sanitary hands. But he let her go to work on him while trying to eavesdrop on Jeff's ongoing troubles with Esther in the living room.

"How about that now, Eddie? Your old thing fits him real good!" Esther had put a musty oversized blue bathrobe on Jeff and was spinning him around in front of her husband like some frazzled fashion model. "I usually have to cart whole bag-loads over to the church rummage sale," she confided to Jeff. "Nice to be able to help someone in person."

I'm in a big blue sack. Bad food, no clothes, marched around—I haven't left the hospital! But it's way past time for my afternoon dosage. "Ethan! I lost all my pills in the car!"

"Oh, you take pills too? So does Eddie. What kind are you on?"

Eddie had no idea why he was being subjected to this wild-eyed stranger. "Blah, blah, blah, motormouth never quitsh. Pleash, Eshter, lemme shleep!"

"Ain't twenty-five years of married life sleep enough?" spat Esther, and then to Jeff, "That shuts him up every time. Now you go upstairs and get in the tub." Already halfway into the foyer, she hollered as loud as she could, "Dorian! I'm sending this boy up to get washed. You leave him alone!"

Dorian, who was never too busy when a boy was being sent up, instantly responded, "I'll be right there."

"Just go on with your painting!" Esther started Jeff up the steep, junk-laden steps on his own, figuring she could talk him through the mess. "It's the last door down the hall. Toilet stopped overflowing last time I looked. Go on, go on, I can't have you wandering around my house all dirty." Jeff made his way step by step, like a zombie wading through mud. His footing seemed so uncertain Esther considered climbing after him, even with her aching legs, but then she saw Eddie sneaking out of his chair to get a beer. He didn't get five feet along when something fell over and the sound brought back a blast from a distant battle.

"They're dropping—things! Look out!" He crouched by the chair, holding his hands over his head.

"Shell-shocked old shithead. Karin! Watch Eddie!"

"I can only handle one case at a time, Esther!" huffed Karin who had no intention of letting Ethan out of her sight.

"I have to see to the wash. Get Eddie out of his pants and bring 'em to me!"

Esther did what she always did when household events were slipping out of her grasp. Fill the machines and get those clothes clean. Let these fools knock the house down around their ears. At least they'd all be in fresh underwear when the wreckers arrived.

She slipped into the laundry room, more a nook separated from the kitchen by a thin wall, and had the washer going almost before there was anything in it.

Hearing it start up, Karin breathed easier. Esther out of the way for the duration of the cycle. "How did you do this?" as she bandaged Ethan's worst wound.

"Oh, ah—those guys—hitchhikers—roughed us up before taking off with the car."

"Picking up hitchhikers these days? God. You never know what kind of lunatic you're letting in."

"Yeah, I feel like a jerk."

"Who am I to talk? I've done dumber things. A lot dumber." But picking up Ethan and his strange brother at the hotel was not one of them, she was quite sure. "So how many were there?"

"How many what?"

"Hitchers."

"Three," somehow leapt out.

"Three! My God, go looking for trouble. Picking up three guys."

"It was one of those things where only one guy is out in the open and he was kind of small, looked like a high school student."

Ethan was pleased with his acting so far. *The story is taking shape. First the people in the hotel, now this nurse. Hell, even I'm already starting to believe it.* But then the feeling of the car heading across the field, completely out of his control, swept back over him and he knew he still had a lot of work to wipe that from his memory. He shut his eyes and let himself be comforted by her touch. And her voice.

"Awful how you can't trust people anymore. You're driving along and you see this worn out young guy, down on his luck, everyone passing him by, what the hell, give the poor jerk a lift. Who'd have thought he and his pals are wanted in seventeen states for robbery, treason, and a million worse things? What happens to the basic trust when we were little kids? Where does it go? I tell you I'm a nurse, I'm going to fix you up, and you have every right to believe me. And I believe you're a nice decent guy from—from—"

"Boston. I just dropped out of Harvard med school."

"See, I know so much about you just from that. Why can't everybody be like us? Blowing great opportunities and still able to say, what the fuck, I'm gonna ruin my life as I see fit."

"I don't think I've ruined any of my chances just by dropping—"

"Listen, you know as well as me, you'll never get anywhere if you can't trust people for two seconds." She was applying iodine too heavily and it stung like crazy.

"Ooowoooh, it's a good philosophy. Hang on to it."

"I intend to. You're not the first person to try and talk me out of it."

"No, no—I believe you, I said. And—and I believe in you." *God, that's going overboard.*

"This has got to be the best conversation I've had in months."

Ethan couldn't hold back a proud smile. Then he thought of the woman in overalls and the people in the bar, even of the other inhabitants of this house. Maybe "best conversation" wasn't a terribly high achievement. And there was one member of the household he hadn't met.

"Did that guy go for the sheriff yet?"

"Dorian? I assume so. There, I think we stopped the major bleeding in time. So, what did your car look like?"

"Green Jaguar," said Ethan.

"That would show up for miles in Charlestown. Once they find it—and they might find it, don't give up—where are you off to once you get it back?"

The structure of opportunity Ethan had been piecing together suddenly fell apart. He was so busy remaking the past he didn't know what to say about the future. He decided to be honest for once. "I don't know."

Even that lame comeback pleased his private nurse. "Yeah, kind of open-ended. Kind of wild and free. That's the way to live."

"It is?"

"Oh, yeah." She sighed as she replaced the unused bandages on the table. Her work was done and she fidgeted pointlessly, unnerved at having run out of things to say. Ethan looked away to ease her discomfort.

What a bitch life is for most people. She actually envies me having been beat up and getting my car stolen. Hey, I'd envy myself at the moment if that's what had really happened. Wild and free, the only way to live. We'll see. Gonna find out all about it. Wild and free, wild and free . . .

It had taken all this time for Jeff to get to the second story landing and pass about halfway down the hall. The decor echoed the lower floor, the piles perhaps two feet higher, but to Jeff it was a return to the woods, and from the woods back into his wall, and within his wall was a world whose strangeness he could embrace. Each stack of junk became a gnarled little tree and the narrow space through which he moved was that road whose name he'd lost, even after swearing never to forget.

Dorian came up from behind and grabbed him. "Gotcha!"

Jeff shrieked and turned to see a charmingly good-looking blondish guy in his late teens. His face, hands and clothes were covered with paint, but that actually increased the appeal. The boy's eyes swam with such naive bemusement he could not possibly be a threat. "What are you doing in Dad's robe?" That reminded Jeff he didn't even look like himself anymore. It was the startling sense of his own identity heading further into oblivion that really scared him, not this strangely assertive guy.

"Esther put it on me."

"Liar. You did in my Dad and robbed him. Took it right off his back."

"No, no, he's O.K." *He looked like he'd keel over any second, but that wasn't my doing, I don't think.*

"Oh hell, I was going to thank you." Dorian chuckled so good-naturedly Jeff forgot even to be afraid of himself.

"Your Mom wants you."

"I know that. And she gets me too. Breakfast, lunch and dinner. She should be full by now, but there's always room for dessert."

"Is she always so . . . lively?" That wasn't the right word, but it was this guy's mother after all. Dorian put his arm around Jeff's shoulder and confided two inches from his face. "I probably shouldn't tell you, but Mom's a complete manic-depressive. I always know when she's gone manic by listening for—yep, there—it's going."

He put his hand over Jeff's mouth so they could listen together to the steady rumbling of the washing machine. Dorian nodded as if that strengthened his case. Washing machine. Manic mother. Listen to it go. Jeff wanted to start making sense of things. "I got dirty."

"Well, I'm sure glad you came along. Otherwise she'd have Dad and me strip down to make her laundry quota."

"I could barely understand what he says."

"He's getting over a stroke. But nobody could understand him before," Dorian concluded with an uncontrolled laugh. The strangely desperate sound that Eddie made preceding every utterance, a kind of melancholy sheep's bray, was something probably only a family member could see as funny. Jeff thought he'd best move along before Dorian found something amusing in his condition.

"I'm supposed to take a shower now."

But there was no easy way to get rid of Dorian. "It's kind of a weird faucet. Here, I'll show you," and he coaxed Jeff into the bathroom. It was a long narrow space; from the tub you could lean over into the rusty sink and maybe even take a leak if your aim was good. Buckets, paint cans and tools were abundant enough to insure you'd be dirty again by the time you finished washing up. Dorian helped Jeff out of the baggy robe and hung it on a mop handle. Jeff blushed, seeing his bare skin in the cracked, spotted mirror. He caught Dorian taking a longing look at his underpants before glancing away to monkey with the tub faucets. A trickle came out. Dorian banged on the pipes, turned the sink handles on and off, and jiggled the toilet flusher as if priming the pump. Jeff held himself, exaggerating his sense of cold, but not thinking to wrap himself back in the robe. "It usually doesn't take this long," muttered Dorian. He knew it always took this long when Esther was running the machine. He smiled to himself that Jeff did not move no matter how close Dorian passed in his plumbing maneuvers. Everything was just a matter of time. The tub, this guy . . .

Down in the kitchen Ethan was mostly patched up. Once Karin's hands were no longer all over him he remembered that his purpose in coming to this house was rapidly losing focus. He stared up at the ceiling wishing for X-ray vision to keep an eye on Jeff. *I'd better get him and get us the hell out of here.*

"Ceiling's kind of sturdy. Not going to fall in quite yet, " said Karin, thinking reassurance was needed. Ethan felt it was Karin that needed some kind of assurance.

"I can help you become a doctor. I mean, my Dad can."

"You can? Really? I didn't exactly save your life here."

"He's got the clout to get you into a great school."

"God, you make me feel like I've already cut open my first cadaver."

"Well, but I kind of need your help too."

"I—I'll do whatever I can, Ethan."

They were caught in a silence, each daring the other to be bolder. Esther, emerging from the laundry room, could always be counted on to break any silence.

"Karin! You should be through with him! I need your help with Eddie's pants. They're still on him."

"Oh. Right away, Esther." She gave Ethan a quick kiss that doubled as a healing balm and a tease and hurried to join Esther in the living room. Ethan shivered and looked back up at the ceiling, now fully expecting it to come crashing down.

CHAPTER 7

The washing machine shifted cycles and the tub sprayed to life. Jeff gave a cry of astonishment, something fell over, and Ethan knew he'd better get up there fast. He sneaked past Karin and Esther struggling to yank off Eddie's trousers and made his way up the stairs. He banged his leg and felt something crunch underfoot. A ski fell over and nearly decapitated him. He knocked everything out of his way, got to the end of the hall, and barged into the bathroom.

The door opened to reveal Jeff sitting in the rapidly filling tub. Dorian was thickly lathering his back with suds.

"Hey! What is this?"

Delighted by an unexpected third, Dorian did his best to appear innocent.

"He didn't know how to use the tub."

"Yeah, well, I think you've shown him enough. Aren't you the one who's supposed to go tell the sheriff about my car?"

"What about it?"

"It's stolen!"

"Already? You just got here."

"I know we just got here. So how come you're giving my brother a rubdown?"

"He seemed confused."

Ethan had no time to untangle the fact that Jeff was definitely confused, but that the teenager all covered with paint had an odd way of dealing with confusion and probably hadn't the faintest idea that the confusion was psychosis. "Just hurry up now. Go up the street or down the street, wherever the hell you go and tell them it's a green convertible 1971 Jaguar, license plate IKSYO64—"

"Whoa, slow down, I can't remember all that." In fact, Dorian was terrible with numbers, and not so great with facts, especially those that had no place in his self-created world.

"This is insane! You should have been there by now," insisted Ethan.

Dorian had him there. "How would I have known what to tell him when you just now told me the kind of car it was?"

"That's a point," piped in Jeff.

Ethan was not going to stand for two against one. He brought Dorian to his feet and shoved him out the door. "Go! Go tell him! Come on! Jesus!"

Having heard the word 'brother', but not certain what kind of relationship he was intruding upon, Dorian thought it best to let himself be tossed out of his own bathroom by a complete stranger. His mother had taken in so many boarders to make ends meet ever since he could remember—drifters, oddballs, fragments of families. These guys were cute, but dirty, so they were probably the next of a long line. Trying to remember the kind of car that had followed "green" and imagining what shade and tone of green, Dorian headed downstairs. He heard his father screaming, "Inspection! Inspection!" and didn't even want to look at what Esther and Karin were doing. Eddie's pants came off with a ripping sound as Dorian bolted out the side screen door. All he wanted was to put distance between himself and that damn house.

Jeff splashed water all over Ethan to get back at him.

"Why are you so mad at Dorian? You just met."

"So did you! What was this cozy scene in the tub?"

Jeff shrugged. "He's friendly, I guess."

"You guess? Christ, Jeff, if I hadn't come in when I did, there's no telling—I just don't trust how this whole family's being so fucking friendly. Don't you find it kind of weird?"

"Compared to where I've been?" Jeff flung that with another handful of soapy water and Ethan got a vivid picture of Jeff's life over the past few years. Nothing, not this creepy town, not this house that could be the town dump, probably not even those

UFO's snooping around in the trailer park next door, none of it was going to faze his brother who'd been confined with a bunch of "incurables." Ethan clutched the edge of the tub, wanting to feel something solid before drifting too far with Jeff's question.

"I'm still so fucked up," he conceded. Fighting wooziness, he stood up and looked at himself in the steamy mirror. He wiped it off so he could study the redness of his eyes and the startling dilation of his pupils.

"It was you who wanted to come here." Jeff seized the upper hand. Ethan saw tears coming out of his eyes. He was suddenly overwhelmed with sadness. The crash, the chase, the cops, and worst of all his own face seemed to jump out at him from the mirror. "What the fuck was I thinking about?" Jeff felt like his accusation had brought on Ethan's abrupt collapse.

"It's all my fault," he consoled.

"You tried to get me to stop. I remember that much."

"That's not what I meant. I was so mad at you. It's OK to do dope but not my pills. That's what everyone thinks. You were supposed to be different."

Jeff's unclear demand drove Ethan back into the mirror. Better to look at his own bruised and swollen puss than his brother's—so blank, so unknowable. The mirror became a different mirror. In the world of that mirror, Ethan saw the image of the men's room at the gas station where they'd stopped. *I'm in some strange bathroom, filthy pipes dripping from above, shit coming up from below. Jeff's depending on me and I'm falling apart. Can't let him down. I made a promise. I'm going to amaze everyone and cure him. Long way to go—look at him sloshing around in the water like he's barely able to keep from drowning. No, he's not here. He's out in the car. Waiting for me. Counting on me. And I'm going to amaze everyone and cure him!*

While Ethan continued to roam in the labyrinth of the mirror, Jeff lowered his eyes to the scum-caked ledge of the tub. A razor, a plastic bottle of shampoo, tube of conditioner, everything he would need if he decided to stay in this tub forever. Which would be nice. To sink below the anguish of the open air where things were constantly being thrown at him. Under water, under waves, deep down, muffled in silence, immersed in watery stillness. But he couldn't hold his breath for more than fifteen seconds. He sprang up from the dark and the wet. His eyes cleared and saw the items on the ledge. Razor, bottle of shampoo, coke can, conditioner—*coke can? I'm out of my wall, out of the tub, back in the car. It's not the ledge of the bath, it's the dashboard. Ethan left his Coke here while he went to the men's room. Soon he'll be back here, sipping and driving, driving and guzzling, bragging about his exploits, his affairs, his perfect life, swigging down that coke like he's the star of his own commercial. I'll show him, I'll fix him.*

Jeff couldn't take his eyes off the non-existent soda can next to the shampoo. He looked at his palm, cupped with grimy, bloody water, and saw a handful of pills, brightly colored antidotes for the anguish of the open air. He reached over to the mouth of the can of coke and poured in the pills. What he was really doing was scooping up water and splashing it over the side of the tub. And like the water, the imaginary pills were going all over the place, not inside the can. *I didn't do it. It crossed my mind, but I wasn't able to follow through. Normally it's a curse not being able to follow through, always thinking but never doing, but not that time. Thank God I didn't follow through!*

It was a liberating notion that became an emphatically liberating gesture—swooshing the water out of the tub, carrying his mind away with his body, until he was no longer in the Jaguar, no longer in his wall at the asylum, no longer in a bathtub in the house of friendly strangers, but in a sinking boat that needed bailing out. He created a wave with both arms and sent it swirling up over Ethan. Hot slimy wetness brought Ethan out of the mirror, out of his inner self and back to the matter at hand.

"Stop that, Jeff! You're making a mess!"

"I'm trying to drown myself. Wouldn't that help? You'd have a much better time without me. You could have a great summer, Ethan."

"Great summer! Those cops might be dead! What the fuck

came over me? Sure, they were tailing my ass, but I could've pulled over. I kept going for some crazy, stupid reason. Help me remember. Did I say anything? What the hell was I doing?"

"I told you it was my fault."

"Don't be ridiculous. Me driving too fast was your fault?"

"When you went to the men's room? And left your soda on the dashboard? And I was pouring pills out to figure which ones to take?"

"Yeah? So?"

"It was awfully tempting."

"What was?"

"That open can. Your cocky attitude. I wanted you to see things the way I do."

"Oh, no—you didn't."

"Right. I didn't. But I thought about it."

"Well, did you or didn't you?"

"I think I tried and missed. Even so, you've been acting like you—well, like I do when I, oh God, it's awful the things I almost do.

'What a dumb thing to—you asshole! How could you? It's so fucking crazy—right. Shit. Oh, Jeff, we were almost killed!"

"I'm sorry, Ethan."

"Haven't I always looked out for you? Christ, I would have pulled over if I was feeling halfway like myself. God, it's still a big blur. If there's one thing, one thing, I learned in med school it's that a normal person can get pretty fucked up on anti-psychotics. Jeff, I know you're sick and all, but what a fucking fucked up thing to do!"

Jeff sunk back down below the water. Now it was definitely time to drown himself. But Ethan, stupid inconsistent Ethan, yanked him up. Jeff gasped pathetically, wondering why his brother didn't just leave him down there. As the water drained from his eyes and he saw Ethan's frantic expression, Jeff realized perhaps he wasn't acting out of sympathy. Ethan needed him alive for someone to talk to.

"Pay attention, Jeff! You can't imagine what they'll do to you if we're caught."

"I remember that road! Missing Link! Missing Link!"

"That's fine. Now I want you to forget it."

"But I worked so hard to—"

"Forget it! Forget the fucking Missing Link, forget all of it! We were never there. How could we know where the car crashed when we weren't in it anymore?"

"I'm . . . I'm really working at not being a mess, Ethan, but you're—you're confusing me worse all the time."

Ethan's head was reeling, but he was going to clarify things for Jeff and in doing so, nail them down for himself. "It's very simple. That hitchhiker we almost picked up?

What if he'd gotten in and I drove off? And what if he had a gun, yeah, pulled out a gun on us, forced us both to get out and then he took off in my car? It could have happened that way. And I'm saying it did. That is all you have to remember. Hell, don't even remember that. You've been in a delusional haze ever since we left the hospital.

You're staring at a million roads coming out of the walls, dodging huge trucks and tractor trailers, zooming and zipping! Here comes a motorcycle gang! Barrrrrooooom!"

Jeff bought it completely. "They're going to hit us! Aaaaaaggggh!"

"Stop it, Jeff!" Ethan tried to hold him in his arms, but his brother was too slippery.

"This house is in my wall! I never left that place! You're not my brother! The end of the world happened ten years ago, during the Cuban Missile crisis, and now everyone's rotted away and the bugs rule the world and—and—and—that's a lousy plan."

He emphasized just how lousy by standing up in the tub, his nude young body proclaiming his innocence louder than his hysterical words. Ethan grabbed the opportunity to start wiping him off with a ratty red towel.

"The car will be reported stolen. Karin thinks we were roughed up by hitchhikers. We're stuck in this house. We can beat this thing!" He vigorously dried his brother.

"So. We just do nothing."

"You have lots of practice at that."

A banging at the door. "Hey! What the hell's going on in there! Chrissakes, you'll wake poor Eddie."

"It's O.K., Esther," Ethan called out the door. "Jeff slipped getting out of the tub and I fell trying to catch him."

The door wasn't locked, merely jammed, and Esther was able to come crashing in on them. "Slipping and sliding, huh? You know, if it's dancing you're up for, we can all go to Meatland. Are you decent?" Not that it mattered.

Jeff could have whipped the towel around his middle if he'd felt the slightest embarrassment. But something more urgent had seized his attention; it was vital to immediately wrap it tightly around his right hand.

"Did I hurt you?" Ethan asked, thinking he'd gripped Jeff's hand so hard it restarted some bleeding.

"Good, good, you're all clean," Esther scanned Jeff up and down. "I haven't been to Meatland in months. It used to be a slaughterhouse, but that folded and they turned it into a disco."

"Sounds nice, but I really don't think we're up for a night on the town." Ethan played it as cool as possible, sandwiched between two unpredictable personalities.

Esther was demonstrating how she could keep up with the latest dance steps while Jeff grew concerned about the shadowy tentacles he saw spreading out across the bathroom window. Some disgusting creature that had spontaneously generated from the chemical aggregation of homegrown filth. *How big is it? Is it covering the whole house? Nobody sees it yet but me. I'll make up for what I did to Ethan. I'll save the day!* Jeff pushed past Ethan and smashed his towel-protected hand through the window, socking the slimy monster in its tenders, making it hurtle off into oblivion. "Got it!"

"Stop, you nut! Moron!" Ethan grabbed Jeff too late.

"My window!" Esther stopped dancing.

"I scared it away!" Jeff was fairly bursting with pride.

"There's nothing there!"

"Not anymore."

"That's two hundred bucks, at least," spat Esther.

"We'll pay you for it," promised Ethan.

"Hell, I don't want your money."

"You don't?"

"No, sir. You'll work it off."

"Work?"

"Bet your ass. I need a million things done round here before the Fourth of July."

Jeff looked more terrified than he had before striking out at the house-sucking monster. But Ethan thought this might not be such a bad thing. "Are you offering to put us up for a couple of days?"

"Offering? I'm telling you what you're going to do to stop me from calling the sheriff."

"No, you should still report about my car being stolen, but in the meantime—"

"I don't even think you had a car. I know drifters when I see them. You wrecked my kitchen, tore apart the guest bathroom, made eyes at the live-in help. I can lodge a lot of grievances."

She didn't miss too much, thought Ethan. She's playing right into my hands. Yeah, this could work out. "O.K., O.K., you got us."

Jeff had experienced first hand the uselessness of resisting Esther. But he also knew his brother was no slouch in the juggernaut department. Ethan had caved in far too readily. *I'm out of my wall. I'm in his hands. We're on some UFO and Ethan thinks he's at the controls. Where in the universe is he taking us now?*

CHAPTER 8

Karin was sitting on Dorian's bed. She'd satisfied Esther's craving for a second washload of Eddie's things and gotten her employer sufficiently hypnotized watching the spin-dry cycle. Or so she thought. Evidently right after she left, Esther broke the spell and went to collar Ethan and his brother. She could hear 'those poor guys' receiving the brunt of Esther's second wind. "At least it keeps her out of my hair. Eddie will sleep till dinner. Now if only Dorian had stuck around."

Missing Dorian, Karin took comfort in studying his paintings. An abundance of green leapt out at her. One magnificent landscape depicted the four evangelists as animals—eagle, bull, lion and man—in harmonious meditation on a hilltop that she recognized as a place where Charlestown's woods met the Connecticut River. Nearby stood the portrait of a wide-eyed teenager, projecting self-conscious pride about the bulge in his pants. An angel hovered in the cradle formed by two trees curving toward one another. A lusciously bare-bottomed youth waded in a hidden pool. Karin marveled at Dorian's easy transition from the sensual to the sublime. Unlike most boys in their late teens, Dorian did not think of them as the same thing. He had developed so much talent barricading himself in this room. The harshness of the world down below was absent from even his most realistic pictures. Indeed, he'd begun a portrait of his mother that most visitors to the house would have viewed as supreme idealization. But Karin also had observed Esther in her withdrawn moments of silence. Dorian had captured the pervasive sadness of the woman. Karin realized there was no helping her at such times and did not intrude when Esther chose to hide away in the shadows of the second floor.

What Dorian called his Self-Portrait was a featureless robed figure whose impassive gray and white face loomed ominously over Dorian's desk. It conveyed the eighteen-year-old's conviction that he was born on another planet and had inexplicably fallen to this forlorn place on the Earth. Icy and mysterious (and done at an earlier age) it lacked the sensitivity and poignance already apparent in the picture-in-progress of Esther. Dorian had never chosen to paint his father.

Karin gazed rapidly over the twenty-odd paintings visible from where she sat. She wanted to gorge herself on the fantastic illusion Dorian had created of Charlestown as Paradise. Two boys discovering a secret pond, a naked Arabian warrior sheathing his sword, a Scotsman strutting the Highlands, an Italian boy struck dumb by a burning bush. So much for the material world. On to St. Michael leaping down from Heaven to expunge Lucifer. Another angel hovered over a darkened country road. A winged muse burst in through a sunstruck window where a boy pondered a blank page. A dove fluttered over three crucified figures whose blood spiritualized the earth below their shattered feet.

Dorian envisioned hell as well. It took the form of a haunted city. A headless statue dominated a city park portending things far worse than muggers. The furnace that powered civilization had a fiendish face and its watchman had fled, leaving an overturned chair the only sign of tenuous life. Card players turned into skeletons, but continued their game while a black cat prepared to pounce upon his decomposed masters to alert them it was long past feeding time. A paranoiac tried in vain to hide from a bold light invading his empty room. A detective was all dressed up but lacked the will to unfreeze himself from his window and its vista of a night city peopled with scraps of fleeting flesh.

Karin escaped to the woods and fields, skies of purple and yellow arching over Charlestown. A mansion and its gazebo with a quiet Dorian-like figure overlooking the lush summer valley. His own house was made to look bloated with prosperity and surrounded by abundant foliage that in reality had long since died.

And a long-since abandoned diner served as day's end reward amidst devouring underbrush.

"Hiding out?" Dorian was back. Karin smiled gratefully at both his presence and the thriving hallucinogenic world she'd enjoyed in his absence.

"Yes. A few moments of peace. Where did you go?"

"I snuck out."

"Oh, did you remember to report those guys' car?"

"No, I forgot. Oh, that's right, the clothed one described it to me."

"The clothed one?"

"I put Jeff in the tub, and all the thanks I got was getting kicked out. Why should I do that guy a favor?"

"Don't worry about it. I'm sure if it was all that important they'd have already left. Dorian, I think they want to be here."

"Really? They must be nuts, but I'm not complaining."

"Ethan picked me up at the hotel. And one look at the other guy—I knew he was your type."

"Thanks. He's almost too easy though, you know?"

"Well, that's probably cause they're from the city. Easy come, easy go in places like that. Everyone getting bulldozed by progress. Rats in a maze. It's a sad thing, really."

"Yeah, people from the city are pretty desperate. Makes me wonder why I want to go."

"I thought you were in such a hurry. School's over and you're just staying put."

"I have work to finish here. As you can see." He momentarily enjoyed the paintings that had provided Karin such a long spell of pleasure.

"You're getting better all the time. But that's not what's keeping you here."

Dorian did not like being rushed or pushed. "Karin, the difference is you don't have your family to worry about."

"What a way to put it." Karin was astonished at Dorian's lack of tact. Perhaps he really was from another planet, one where brazen observation blotted out feeling.

"I'm sorry, I didn't mean it like—. Come on, you know I love Charlestown. That's one of my favorites," he said with a nod at the four evangelists in their landscape. "It makes me want to fly up over the whole valley."

"It's time to fly right out of this valley." Karin remained somber from Dorian's remark about her absent family. "I don't know about you, but I may never get another chance like this. Their father's a doctor. They're well-off."

"Right, doctors must make a mint."

"That's not the point, Dorian. He actually offered to help me get into medical school. Can you imagine?"

"Yeah, tons of blood and sick people everywhere."

"We all have our calling," she retorted, now a little annoyed at his hideaway world of pretty pictures.

"What, so you're going to run off with that rude guy Ethan?"

"I didn't say that. I'm loyal to Eddie."

"You're a saint in that department."

"You should at least talk to him once in awhile."

"I try. All he says back is Brrraaaa, bllllaaaaah, brraaaaa, the thing, the thing!"

"The stroke destroyed the speech part of his brain. If you're patient, some of it will come back."

"That's OK, he never talked about much that interested me."

"You both love history."

"Yeah, but for him that's World War Two. He doesn't know a thing about ancient Greece."

"I know, I know, where men and boys knew their place. In each other's arms."

"Beats killing and maiming each other. Where did Mom go?"

"She's roasting our guests over an open fire."

"You like this new picture of her I started? Wasn't she pretty back then?"

"Looked like Bette Davis. Even better."

"I want to finish it and give it to her on her birthday. After that, maybe I'll leave for Boston."

"Then there will be some other excuse to stay."

"Those guys are awfully cute. Which one did you want?"

Karin laughed with Dorian. Her laughter stopped first and her eyes settled on his picture of the abandoned diner. Its rotting chrome walls in fading twilight certainly offered little hope for a continued life in the country. And as pale night clung to the windows of the third floor, the alarming colors of the "Haunted City" gave her goosebumps of anticipation for anything, dangerous or desirable, that waited around its corners.

CHAPTER 9

Hustled out of bed barely past dawn, Ethan and Jeff were made to carry boxes, barrels and garbage bags. They were given the task of sorting tires and odd parts of an automobile that had died in the late fifties. Esther had them rearrange large piles of junk from room to room, although it was obvious by midday that nothing was getting any more organized.

At noon Ethan found himself up the lone tree that graced the left side lawn. Esther stood ten feet below, ordering him to cut off branches to suit some private notion of symmetry.

"That one . . . aw, hell, now over there. Does it look even? How about that one? No, the higher one. Down there . . . I meant down there!" Esther's corrections came so quickly after her directions that the absurdity of the pruning was soon apparent even to Jeff whose assigned chore was to collect the branches as they fell. Even so, he had no qualms whether the tree was being rejuvenated or destroyed; Jeff viewed any job as the arbitrary way in which 'healthy' people chose to fill their time. He generally did what he was told because, left on his own, he would do nothing and that was plainly unacceptable in the 'up-and—at—'em' world to which he was born. Not that he was lazy. The fanfare of stimuli competing for mastery of his mind exhausted his will only seconds after getting up in the morning. At the asylum he could raise his head, start to sit up, then collapse again and lose himself in the wall. Back in the real world more was expected of him. He was required to participate, to do his share, make a contribution to a wildly overpopulated world where far too many souls were engaged already in doing way too much. Now it was raining Stick Men from

Space and Jeff mustered a dash of pleasure in the knowledge that he was protecting a vulnerable patch of Earth.

Jeff was further amused by the fact that only yesterday he'd been up his favorite tree and Ethan had come along to yell him down. Now Ethan was the one up a tree. If he'd let Jeff alone he might still be down on the ground where he was more at ease. There was a difference of course: Jeff had been allowed to merely nestle in his tree while Ethan was being ordered to hack away at the very branches that maintained him. Jeff felt an instinctive need to be kind to Ethan and not gloat that turnabout was fair play.

While Jeff mused internally on the nature of work, needing a rationale of his own for every move he made or was forced to make, Ethan grunted and did what he was told. Hard work always made him feel good. Something was being accomplished and it was unnecessary to think about a damn thing.

It hadn't crossed either brothers' mind why the crash of their car was not already big news in this town where, according to Karin, little ever happened. They had only gotten about six hours sleep. Ethan woke up too high, Jeff too low, and reality glided somewhere in between. But during the night, back on the Missing Link Road, things were being determined in such a way as to postpone their need to deal with the grim facts.

It was pitch black by the time the demolished police car was recovered and its wreckage sifted for whatever remained of the once male and female officers. A congregation of firefighters and police grieved at the scene, their silent prayers belied by loud profanity.

"They called in just before following the fucking scum onto the Missing Link."

"Shitty road goes all over the place for ten miles. Assholes could be anywhere by now."

Ethan's car had literally flown off the road, leaving no tire tracks as a guide to where it had gone. The green of the Jaguar blended in so well with the foliage in which it was immersed that only a trained naturalist could have picked it out. It was certain that police searchlights sweeping slowly along both sides of the Missing Link would yield nothing all night long.

Not that the Missing Link Road was some forbidding backwoods trail. Less than a decade ago it had been the only avenue from Springfield to Bellows Falls, Vermont, via the forested foothills of Charlestown. Route Five had forged a straighter path, but the Missing Link maintained its charm for people in less of a hurry. There were places where it ran along the river and large houses held fine views from the hill rising above it. A motel on it named for Hetty Green, "the Witch of Wall Street," often filled for the night, especially during foliage season. The richest American woman of the 1920s, Hetty Green had spent so long looking for a free clinic when her son was run over, his leg had to amputated. But Hetty did not haunt the highway, and the people who still lived along it were far less strange and distinctive. There was no superstition or mythology about the road. Its name was merely the result of literal-minded New Englanders referring to its faded usefulness. What befell Ethan and Jeff on the Missing Link had no ghostly benefactor; it originated in the actions of the young men themselves and could not even marginally be attributed to some ancient country curse. But to those engaged in the futile cleanup operation on that somber summer night, nothing came to light to dispel the notion that damnation itself had lured the luckless cops on a detour down the Missing Link.

The moodswinging lady currently dictating the day of Jeff and Ethan had had her own experience on Missing Link Road. Her heart was much bigger than Hetty's, but her fortune was infinitely smaller, so a honeymoon in Quebec was the only respite before a life of frustration in the confines of Charlestown. The weeklong trip in Eddie's car had begun by heading north on the Missing Link, a bottle of Scotch hidden beneath the seat. Once the handful of well-wishers had been left in the dust, the bottle came out and went from Eddie to Esther, toasting each other in merry gulps. The happy couple was tanked before they'd left the Missing Link, but Eddie had hugged the road with a skill that

Ethan would have envied. Esther told him that story, along with many others that made somewhat less sense, while breaking him in on that humid June day of 1972 as the latest in a series of hired hands, recruited whenever and however, for the purpose of helping her maintain the only fantasy she had left—that the house in which she'd been stuck after that week in Quebec was not on its last legs. She considered herself lucky this time around, getting two workers for the price of one. Secretly she held no grudge against Jeff for taking out that upstairs window. It should have been replaced many nasty winters ago.

"Chrissakes," she moaned, seeing that one large branch stuck out like a sore thumb and there was no way left to correct the imbalance. Eager to please the new boss Ethan turned around and around in the treetop, looking for a way to salvage things. His pants were caught by a sharp piece of bark, ripped them open and sent him straight to the ground. Jeff broke his fall. The car wreck survivors bounced right to their feet after such a minor mishap. Ethan's pants were ruined and Esther could see he wasn't wearing any underpants.

"Damn—look at you hanging out all over the place! Eddie has loads of spares, you should've said something." Ethan blushed, but it only took a minute for Esther to re-suit him in saggy boxers and overalls. "There!" she winked and paused for a cigarette to celebrate her ability to dress up the help. Ethan could do nothing but acknowledge that a tipsy old woman had him utterly by the balls.

Eyes off him, Jeff had started to wander aimlessly to the other side of the house where Karin was walking Eddie in a large circle. Jeff paused at the corner and eavesdropped.

"Eshter's—braaaaaggggh—oh, you know, she-she-she'sh cleaning."

Eddie was talking with more difficulty than the day before. Jeff wondered how Karin could understand him. Then again, normally he wondered how anyone could understand anything. Eddie's next utterance was remarkably clear. "The last—last time she cleaned up was before the w-war."

"Which war, Eddie?" Karin only needed to pick up a single word to keep the conversation going.

"I was in, back in, phhh, braaahhghh—you know, that place, that place. I used to cook—oh—things for things."

"Do you miss cooking things for things?"

Jeff winced at Karin's apparent callousness, but then saw that Eddie did not take it that way. Karin was the only one who made the slightest effort to comprehend him; she knew which 'things' were which, so Eddie smiled and kept going.

"Yeah, them things sure liked what I cooked. I made the best stew-stew-stew, oh stop it, stewstewstewstew—"

Stuck in that groove, Eddie reminded Jeff of the rotten stew of Esther's that had been his introduction to life with the Osbornes. Time passed so erratically for him, he suddenly had only the faintest notion how long he'd been there. And Karin's voice was starting to sound as garbled as Eddie's.

Esther had finished her smoke and tossed the butt into a wide hole, pointing Ethan to the next job.

"This hole here has to be at least three feet deeper. I'm planting a bed of roses, if Eddie doesn't fall in it first. In which case I'll have you fill it in real quick. You think I'm kidding? I'd do it for damn sure if the cheap prick had kept up on his insurance payments. Course Karin's doing such a good job keeping him going, it looks like it'll be the roses. So dig! What are you waiting for?"

"A shovel, Esther."

"Oh, I thought it was in there. Dorian's always putting things away, some kind of anal fixation." She got the shovel from a hook in the garage and heaved it down to Ethan. "Make it nice and deep. Hey, where's your brother?"

"You can't take your eyes off Jeff for two seconds. He needs constant supervision."

"He needs work therapy. Boy his age on pills. Pah! I used to be the best psychiatric nurse in the valley. We didn't have all these weird chemicals in my day. Work therapy was the key. You take some guy who's depressed, whacked out, whatever, and you put him straight to work. Work him from sunup to sundown. Work his ass off. The point is you'll get him to the point where he's too damn beat to be crazy. Course if in the end he's still raving, well, at least you got some free work out of him."

Ethan marveled that Esther took Jeff's condition right in stride. She couldn't know where he'd been only twenty-four hours earlier, unless Jeff had inadvertently told her. *She can't have figured it out for real—in her book maybe Jeff's just another loon passing through town. If she was a psychiatric nurse, I'm a brain surgeon on vacation. The trick with this lady is to play along, flatter the fuck out of her.*

"Yessir, Esther, you got Jeff's number. He's my only brother and I love him, but, God, he can lie around all day doing nothing but think. Brrrr! Yep, work therapy, best thing in the world. Whatever ails you."

"Ha! I like hearing common sense for a change. Between Eddie and Dorian, all I ever get is lies from the war days and fancy atheist horse manure about God being inside our heads."

Ethan sent up a hefty load of dirt. "What about Karin? She's pretty smart, huh?"

"Smart ass, more like it. Eddie's gone nuts for her. I could be jealous, but I know he can't get it up anymore."

Leaving Ethan to dwell on that one, Esther circled the house, lassoed Jeff and took him into the black hole of her kitchen.

"I kind of envy you this job," she said, sitting him at the head of the junk-filled table. "Go through and separate whatever's metal from the rest. The fringe benefit's that you get to smell the nice aromas coming from my stove."

Jeff cringed at the mishmash she intended him to tackle. He was relieved when she plucked a rusty old electric drill from the pile. Oh good, she's going to demonstrate.

"Leave this alone. It doesn't work anymore, but it has sentimental value. Dorian's sister Sandra gave it to me as a present before she moved out of the country. Wasn't that thoughtful?"

Jeff stifled a laugh as Esther poked at the air with the defunct drill as if she'd stick it to God.

"What's that? Dorian? Is he trying to slip out?" Esther ran out and Jeff lapsed into panic. *What if I make a mistake? Look at this thing—it's a combination of metal and wood, so where's it go?*

Dorian's head start of a few seconds enabled him to ditch Esther.

"I'm out of red, Mom! Gotta get some at Ralph's, then I'll be back!"

"Fat chance. Out of red, he says. Like that's what this house needs."

Watching Dorian eagerly flee, Esther came back from the porch and plopped down in Eddie's briefly vacant chair. Propped up next to it was his 'hobby,' a bulletin board of newspaper cutouts. One thing to keep a scrapbook, another to make a big sign and share your dull imagination with the world. The current crop of clippings was nothing but horrible headlines. Death, disease and destruction from around the corner and around the globe. U.S. Resumes Bombing of North—8000 Viets Dead. Muskie Finished by Tears in the Snow. Bloodbath in Ulster. Real happy stuff. And to add a personal touch, Eddie interspersed little obituaries, some of people they'd heard of, most who just happened to be in the local vicinity when they keeled over.

Esther picked up the scissors that had assisted Eddie in his demoralizing collage and contemplated using them on herself. Sometimes she was amazed she'd made it so long through life. It had to be three-fourths over, maybe more. Otherwise the possibility of years and years beyond what she'd already endured was as gruesome as any of Eddie's souvenir headlines.

Ethan was making impressive progress in the hole. He had been casting anxious glances up and down the two roads that intersected at the Osborne's. Despite his certainty that his cover story would hold up—virtual prisoners of the town madwoman after being beaten and robbed by the thugs who'd stolen his car—he still wished above all to remain unseen. That one ambition fueled his digging. He was finally deep enough and dirty enough to barely be seen by a passing car.

Yeah, gonna dig my way to Australia. Whole world's crazy. There's a couple billion people less fortunate. Or at least there used to be before I went and joined the club. What a shithead I was to go and—, but it's done, it's done, it's done. Nobody can see me down here. That's good. I'll show Jeff. We can disappear. Mom and Dad must think we're dead. Great. Great! When they find out we're not they won't mind about the car being totaled.

Unbearably overheated, he peeled off his shirt. That gave Karin a show when she rounded the corner with Eddie.

"Oh, look, Eddie, new flowers coming up." And close by, a sexy guy in a ditch.

"K-karin, honey. I have to—I have to stop. My legs, oh you know."

"Just once more around, Eddie. It's what you need," and then to the ditch-digger, "Hey, you know how long Esther's been working on that hole?"

Ethan was pleased she had walked his way, even to make fun. "I'm proud to make my contribution."

"She's just going to have you fill it back in tomorrow."

"Work is work, keeps you fit." Ethan overfilled the shovel and raised it slowly, allowing his muscles to bulge for Karin.

Eddie was jealous already. "Oooooowwww! I'm getting worse, honey!"

"You're making big progress, Eddie."

"It's the same, shame damn t-ting every damn day. Maybe you should, oh, you know, over-over-dose me."

"I don't want to hear that kind of talk."

"I'm just in everybody's way."

"No you're not!" insisted Karin, trying to see past Eddie for a good glimpse of Ethan's sweaty torso.

"Where's the thing? You know, that thing that I use for my— for my, oh, you know, it's late today. Late!"

Karin knew he meant the paper and made up some excuse

about the nasty little newsboy whose older brother paid her the kind of attention she was lavishing on Ethan. She got plenty enough offers in Charlestown and had learned how to fend them off, play them against each other to her advantage. But it was becoming a tiresome activity. Ethan's imaginative style of flirtation was a welcome change. She bent over to pick a flower for Eddie, hoping to give Ethan a good return view. The magnificent curve she created almost made Ethan swoon to his knees in the dirt.

Sensing her success, Karin decided to gather a whole bouquet for Eddie, granting Ethan increasingly wonderful angles on her horticultural pursuits. Eddie agreeably got lost in a wartime reverie, allowing 'those kids' free range in their mating dance. No telling how far the silent seduction could have gone if not for Jeff's eruption.

His private desperation had a way of going public at the least opportune times.

Wood . . . metal . . . rubber . . . wood. . . . there's another combination. Is that rust or mold? There's too many categories. How am I supposed to know? And—and all these things—they're just in my way. In my wall, nothing stayed in my way for long. I'm not supposed to have sharp objects. Who's trusting me? I'm not God—I shouldn't be making these crucial decisions!

"Wood! Paper! Vegetable! Dead rat! Ethan, help! I want to switch jobs! I'm not God! I'm not God!" Jeff didn't know when he gave voice to his misery, but everyone else in the house did. Ethan was out of the hole in an instant, kicking up dirt everywhere as he rushed to Jeff's aid.

Mumbling a string of incoherent laments, Eddie started for the house, longing for the comfort of his chair. Karin found herself alone in the yard, holding a small fistful of flowers.

Jeff's tirade also ripped Esther away from her imaginings of the pleasures of death. Her kitchen mattered more. She reached her disgruntled new employee an instant after Ethan. Some of the junk plunged off the table.

"You O.K., buddy? It's O.K. Don't worry, I'll pick all that

up." Ethan was still holding the shovel and it occurred to him he could just go on digging in the kitchen, scooping everything up and out the windows.

"What the hell did he do?" Esther prevented any but the briefest communication between Ethan's and Jeff's eyes. Jeff knew he had let Ethan down again. *But he's letting me down every second longer we stay in this house. He says he wants to save me, but how is burying us in this junk heap going to do that?* Jeff realized he had answered his own question—nobody in the outside world would ever believe this house existed, let alone want to look for us inside it. *Ethan's a genius!*

"Ethan, I get it, I get it, you're right as always!"

Many other times Ethan would have had no problem accepting his brother's acclamation. This was not one of them.

"Cool it, Jeff. Just like—listen, Esther, Jeff feels a little cooped up. I think we should switch jobs."

"Yeah! Switch jobs! Switch jobs!" yelled Jeff, always ready to do anything to get out of what he was doing.

"Funny, I took him more for the indoors type." Ethan's tanned body against Jeff's pale face and hands would have confirmed Esther's insight if she ever needed objective proof for her beliefs. "How's he as a digger?"

"Twice as good as me," assured Ethan. He handed Jeff the shovel and coaxed him toward the door. The worst thing would be to give Esther more time to study Jeff. If she really used to be a psychiatric nurse . . .

Jeff started talking to the shovel before he was out of the foyer. Ethan talked loud to drown him out. "Don't worry, Esther. I'm on top of all this!"

"Yeah, you're on top of something," said Esther, nudging Ethan quite close to the crotch. "Hey, just you wait. I'll have Clara send over some of those beefy spacemen to help out.."

Wondering if he could compete with extraterrestrials, Ethan set to work sorting things on the table. Not even Esther's absurd instructions about metal, wood and sentimentality stood in his way of astute organization. His efficiency would eventually shut her up. But Eddie's enormous return to his chair caught her scattered concentration and got her off his case even sooner. "Damn! Physical therapy's over already?"

She poked her head through the lazy butler (in that house it seemed more accurate to call it a hole gouged out of the wall) and saw Karin's handful of flowers. "Here, I'll put those in water," she snatched.

"Esther! They're for Eddie!"

"Aw, he'd just cut 'em to pieces and paste 'em on that damn board of his."

"If that's what he wants." Karin came into the kitchen and tore the bouquet out of Esther's wet hands.

"He'll kill 'em like he kills everything else!"

"Do you want him to get better or not? Let me put a little beauty in his environment."

She winked at Ethan as she whipped the lilacs back into the living room.

Esther was not going to let her triumph in front of an outsider. "Eddie could eat them and die," she informed him, heading for round three by Eddie's chair.

Karin definitely likes me. We're safe in her hands. No matter how crazy Esther and Eddie are, we can blend into the woodwork in this house and be safe. For long enough. And their son looked ready to jump in the tub with Jeff. He's not going to complain.

Watching Jeff from his bedroom window, Dorian was indeed far from complaining. With his new tube of red paint, he'd slipped back up to his room via a ladder. Even if his mother hadn't been so preoccupied, she wasn't strong enough to dispose of his 'secret' way in and out. And Dorian could get friends up unnoticed in the middle of the night or whenever. Jeff would be the next guest, but Dorian enjoyed spying on him for awhile first. No complaints at all.

CHAPTER 10

Jeff had gone agreeably into the hole, chattering to the shovel. *They all make small talk, parroting each other's witless remarks. Oh did you? Really! I've always wanted to. What a nice dress. What a great pair of pants. Hot day. Don't mind if I do. Thank you, thank you. Conversation they call it. Killing time's what they like to say. What the hell, I'd just as soon talk to the shovel.*

"I've never dug a hole so I'll just follow your lead. You'd like it back where I was. Lots of landscape for you to dig up."

Watching intently from his bedroom window, Dorian suddenly realized Jeff wasn't talking to himself. That would have made sense. Muttering what a nut his mother could be. But no, Jeff's topic was more far-reaching. He even allowed long pauses for the shovel to offer its perspective.

"The days go by and nobody but me seems to notice that time has stopped and space has imploded. Our brains are so big they won't stay inside our skulls anymore."

The shovel says I'm being too egotistical. "You think your brain can encompass the universe, but really it's just a radio receiver. Thoughts are in the air, the property of all."

"Yes, but are you suggesting brain tissue is no different than the dirt you're grinding? Physical matter can be human or worm, and thought merely deceives us into self-importance? That's anthropomorphic, you Shovel-Head you!"

Dorian was impressed that ideas, no matter how off base, were being discussed. A discourse between a person and a shovel was disturbing only if awareness was lacking, and Dorian did not for a moment entertain those ramifications. Jeff obviously was putting on a show for him.

"Hey, you nut, where did they let you out of?"

"Walpole Manor!"

Dorian laughed at Jeff's spontaneity. "Yeah, right. You must've heard Mom talking about that place."

"I was there before I ever met her!" insisted Jeff.

"Well, that is a coincidence. Cause that's where I've had her put away a few times. Oh yeah, I'm old enough to have her put away. They observe her, recognize incurability and send her home. But by that time she's dried out and Dad's calmed down. Ha! So she would have recognized you if you were really in there. Now come on up here. I want the straight story."

Jeff considered going up the ladder but worried what he'd have to say for Dorian to accept the 'straight story.' He kept digging.

"They ever give you art therapy at Walpole? I bet not. Come on up and see my stuff!"

"I don't want to get fired. This is the first job of my life."

"Oh yeah, Mom's reference will get you real far."

Jeff dug faster and more spastically

"I'm going to have to bathe you again." That was an appealing prospect. But how would they keep Ethan out this time?

"Maybe you should come down here. Hole's big enough for two now."

"I'm not joining the chain gang. Come up for just a little. If you hate my paintings, I promise you can go right back to work."

Jeff conferred with the shovel to see if a break was in order. The shovel had barely said 'yep' before Jeff was out of the ditch and up the ladder. Immediately on going through the window into Dorian's room, Jeff felt the paintings come at him from all sides, their colors and weird images washing over him in ways simultaneously pleasant and frightening. Apparent beyond both extremes was the confirmation of his repeated secret conviction. "I definitely never left the hospital. I've been in the wall this whole time."

Dorian loved when people had a strong reaction to his pictures. He faced Jeff toward his current project, the portrait of Esther as a young woman. Jeff was amazed at the folds in the gown and the texture of the skin. He could barely believe this was the same woman carrying on downstairs.

"This is Mom back in the forties. Wasn't she pretty?"

"The skin is so. . . . people shouldn't have to deteriorate as they get old. Aging is worse than dying." Jeff rarely shared his secret fears. But Dorian's paintings were the perfect conduit. He felt at ease, as if he were directly addressing the portrait. Thus it was less alarming when Dorian shot back, "Death is the last great adventure. I can't wait."

"I'm not suicidal."

"Neither am I. I'm just saying that when the time comes I'll be ready."

"Adventure . . . adventure . . . What do you think happens?"

"I don't think. I know. First your four bodies split apart. Your physical body crumbles—well that part's obvious."

Jeff was riveted on Dorian's voice. Not only was the timbre and level of it absolutely absorbing. These words, these ideas being presented by it with such calm clarity were unique in his experience. How could he be so comfortable with the notion of four bodies? Was that the same as Jeff's six minds? And how come they all shut up for a few moments, actually allowing him to pay attention to what came next?

"Then the etheric and astral bodies split off from the Ego, which is the eternal spiritual part. The first three days after dying, what happens is that you relive all the highlights of your life. After that, it all flows backwards, from old to young, right back into the womb. But everything you did happens like it was done to you. Like if you killed someone, you get to feel what it was like to be killed by them."

"And I make your mother dig a hole?"

"Possibly. It's how you repay all the pain you caused. And that's a karmic plus for your next time around. It all happens in a place called Kamaloka which lasts for about one-third of the length of your time on Earth, and then—"

Jeff shook his head. "You mean it's more complicated than life? I was looking forward to a good long rest."

"It's not complicated. It's exciting. Haven't you noticed the way your body only ties you down?"

"Yes! What are we supposed to do about that?"

Dorian smiled at the eagerness with which Jeff entered his philosophy, which everyone in Charlestown believed was bullshit. He pressed his left palm against Jeff's.

"Are you asking what we can do about the effects of the physical body?"

"Yeah . . . its effects. What did you call those other three bodies?"

"We can delve into each of them, one at a time."

Their palms danced in small circles. Jeff reacted like the slight pressure pushed him backwards, nearly off his feet. Following gravity on an increasingly dizzy path, Dorian gently nudged Jeff around the room, bringing his paintings into Jeff's view like a kaleidoscope, a panorama of pastoral whimsy and urban paranoia. Through haunted castles, mystical rooms, surrealistic landscapes and fantastic settings laden with religious symbols. The widening circles of their palms took them past a painting in which snakes swirled together to form a tree, whose branches formed both a cross and a Star of David. Dorian's art seemed to embrace irreconcilable opposites. But before Jeff utterly succumbed to the spell, the voice of Esther came like a rocket from below, blowing to smithereens everything, including her soft inviting portrait.

"Dorian! You back? I need you down here now!"

Dorian put his fingers first to his own lips, then against Jeff's.

"Shh. Ignore her."

"Dorian! I know you stole that new boy! I just went out and he's not in the hole!

Bring him down here! It's time to move that refrigerator."

"Refrigerator?" Jeff said, as if the weight of the word itself was enough to crush him.

Dorian smiled wickedly. "I told you there's no end to Mom. If you don't stay as quiet as a tomb, she'll have you on a Roman slave ship by nightfall."

"Dorian! Don't make me climb all these stairs!"

"She can't," Dorian confided, "And she won't. She counts on the sound of her voice making me cave in."

Esther called Dorian's name ten times with only a pause or two for breath.

"How can you not cave in?" said Jeff, more than ready to throw in the towel.

"I once ignored her for a whole hour," Dorian bragged. "Just put her out of your mind."

Jeff wondered how to keep so determined a voice out of a place so unprotected as his mind. Dorian brought older paintings out from under his bed, confident that his personal history as a painter was the ultimate distraction from Esther's monotonously operatic pleas.

"Dorian! The refrigerator won't wait! The one down here is about to die and if we don't move everything into the one on the second floor, it'll all go bad and we'll have nothing left to eat! Dorian! Remember eating? Dorian!"

The campaign to enlist Dorian had taken Esther to the foot of the stairs, far enough from Eddie for Karin to restore equanimity in the living room. Through the lazy butler hole Ethan could see Karin from the waist up. The way her lips puffed into a variety of smiles no matter how flustered she got brought him ripples of pleasure. He angled his chair so he could keep sorting objects and enjoy the view of her curving, stretching body, always anticipating her patient's next move. Despite all his troubles, Ethan was able to settle into his life of the moment. Continuous physical work and a flirtation progressing naturally toward inevitable fulfillment—those were the keys to temporarily plugging up the fear.

A thwack at the door off the kitchen did not disturb his fantasy until he heard Eddie say, "The thing! Is the thing here?" From the window, Ethan saw a boy on a bike loaded down with newspapers heading down the road.

Ethan went to the door and got the paper, relieved to see it was rolled up with a rubber band. He could tell it was a local paper, but a headline about a cop crash wouldn't be any less huge. Could he risk a quick peak? Maybe it would be better if even he didn't know yet, make his cover-up solid and convincing. But Karin was already in the kitchen.

"Don't get it all dirty," and she reached out, expecting Ethan simply to hand it over.

"I hate being out of touch." Ethan possessively cradled the paper.

"The Charlestown Times won't change that," she assured him, groping for it.

A tug-of-war ensued, prolonged by eye contact that escalated the unspoken stakes.

"Don't knock local news."

"I'm not knocking it. I just want Eddie to have it so he can cut it up."

"Is it tough losing a patient?"

"Only when I get personally involved. I should know better by now."

"Maybe you can't help it. It's only natural."

"Let me give it to him and then you and I can talk about what's natural."

Ethan waved the paper over his head, a rather unnatural gesture. "I've noticed as you go from country to country, even state to state, you get a totally different slant on the news. You start to wonder what's really going on two miles away."

"Right, the truth hurts." Karin tickled him, he lowered his arms, and the paper was hers. The bundle stayed rolled up until it landed in Eddie's lap. "Here you go, Eddie, a paper full of lies and deception."

"Good, good, good! More for my, more for my, oh you know, that—that thing I do."

Eddie saw that his bulletin board had fallen over out of reach and somebody, most likely Esther, had stolen his scissors. Ethan decided it was best to remain in the kitchen, feigning nonchalance. Now that it was no longer a game, any dire attempt to steal back the paper would look suspicious.

But the rubber band remained unsnapped. Karin propped up the bulletin board and went to find the scissors. Eddie admired his latest work, wondering what was due to come off to make room for new stories of demise and decay. The paper was still a rolled-up secret when Ethan strode into the living room, prepared for the worst.

"Did you see any scissors on that table?" asked Karin. Ethan had paid so little attention to the sorting task, he couldn't have honestly answered. "Scissors?" he repeated, alerting Esther to the fact that something was about to get cut. She bolted back from the hallway giving a last call of "Dorian!"

"No shredding till the rest of us have a chance to read it," she ordered, swiping the paper from Eddie. He looked so desperately hurt Ethan considered taking his side against Esther. Eddie cutting the paper to ribbons was actually a safer bet.

But Esther tucked the prize under her arm; she'd read it when she was good and ready. Right now there were far too many emergencies to consider a leisurely perusal of town gossip. The Charlestown Times was locked in the crook of her left, while her right remained free to commandeer.

"Nice job on the table. Now go on up and you'll see the spare fridge just around the corner. It's got to come down. Not the lightest thing on Earth, but you got your brother and Dorian and I may never have so many men in the house again. Karin, leave Eddie to me and go get Dorian. Tell him the rest of the day's free after this one job."

Karin obeyed Esther because she had also started to resent Dorian's aloofness. Reaching the top floor, she was less than surprised to see he had spirited Jeff up to his room.

"If I have to wait, so do you," she said, poking him in the ribs. This, even though when she broke in, they'd shown no signs of fooling around. And things had not gone beyond palm rubbing.

Dorian was enough excited at Jeff's visceral reaction to each and every painting that the urgency of seduction had receded. Jeff was entranced by a picture of a road winding away through a Tolkein landscape of woods and wondrous hills.

"He loves my picture of the Missing Link." said Dorian because Karin had never given him adequate feedback on that one. He wanted to rub in Jeff's keener aesthetic taste. "I keep reworking this picture. Can't seem to get away from it."

" Neither can I," mumbled Jeff, not giving Dorian nearly enough to impress Karin. She delivered the bad news. "Let's go. You've seen everything. Time for a 'Still Life With Refrigerator'."

"Still life, I wish," rejoined Dorian, nudging Jeff off the bed to follow Karin out.

Ethan had clawed his way to the second floor and looked around all the corners.

"Sorry, Esther, but I just don't see it."

At wit's end, Esther resigned herself to climbing halfway up where she knew she could point right at it. "Don't think I'm old. I just hurt my legs chasing Eddie down to the bar. I caught him all right, but the doc said no stairs for at least a month. Let's see, it was right there." Hanging on to the banister with her left hand caused the tucked—away newspaper to fall from her clutch. It slipped into an open box amidst the rest of the stairway litter, insuring it would at least be briefly forgotten, if not permanently entrenched among the relics of the house.

Ethan gave a nutty look of 'here we go again' as Karin rounded the corner from the stairs coming down from the third floor. Without a word, she pulled at a bedspread and showed him the gigantic old refrigerator.

"Ha! Good work, Karin! I knew it was in there somewhere. Hey, sneaky, when did you ditch my hole? And where the hell is Dorian?" He'd found an excuse to let Jeff and Karin go down ahead of him. "Dorian!"

"Be right there, Mom. I'm just straightening something that got tipped over."

"Eddie's tipping over and you never straightened anything your whole life!

Actually, just need one boy on top and one on the bottom, right Karin?"

"Top and bottom?"

"The bigger brother on the down side and you and Jeff guiding it from the top."

Taking charge, Ethan shimmied the fridge toward the edge of the landing. He indicated where Karin and Jeff should get a grip. The three were able to maneuver the clunky old thing down three steps before it got wedged between the wall and some junk that refused to be kicked out of the way. Using the excuse that Jeff could get hurt trying to jar it loose, Ethan climbed around like an orangutan over the banister. The unplanned but highly desirable result was that Ethan was upstairs with Karin, and Esther was barricaded downstairs even if her legs miraculously healed. This minor triumph somehow obscured the major disaster buried with the paper on the stairs.

CHAPTER 11

Eddie was grumbling about his 'things' as he got up from the chair. He was right to mutter complaints. He had been forgotten by everyone in his house, including Karin. Karin, on whom he'd come to rely completely, whose gentleness was his only respite from Esther's harsh retorts. She kept him on track with his medicines, made it easier for him to stand the frequent injections of (some heart drug), gave him a reason not to smoke or eat harmful foods, hell, she gave him something worth opening his eyes to look at in the morning and all the other odd times of the day when he woke from too much sleep. But now even Karin had deserted him. She'd been drawn into Esther's foolishness, moving some damn thing from here to there. As for Dorian, the kid was smart to stay up in his room, keeping clear of the insanity that ruled the lower floors. Eddie worried about his son turning out strange, being a recluse, not going out on dates even though he was about to turn eighteen. Then again, what was the point of all that if he was likely to end up old and infirm before his time? Or go off and fight for his country, hoping for great adventures, and find himself a premature basket case? What was the point of any of it, if promise was so great and result so terribly pathetic? Maybe it was better not to have lived at all.

Or at least to get drunk and blot out such miserable thoughts. All that damn noise on the stairs, things crashing down, Esther hollering, Karin screaming for her to be reasonable, strange guys snooping, pretending to work, probably planning to rob them blind. To rob what? Was there anything of value left in this house that he'd bought almost forty years ago in hopes of making it a wonderful home? That was the most depressing thought of all.

The home had become a tomb. Perhaps the new fellas were nothing but grave-robbers. Fine, let them steal his corpse. Now off to the bar for a bit of relief. No one, least of all Esther, heard the screen door slam.

"Well, we can't just leave it there," she was saying, pretty much to the refrigerator, since nobody else was visible from where she stood.

"We should've measured first, Esther," came the voice of Ethan.

"Hell, that thing's been up and down these stairs so many times—" Esther dropped off in mid-sentence. That argument would win her nothing.

"Sure, it used to fit, Esther. But now there's so much junk on the steps." Karin was the only one comfortable saying the obvious.

"That junk, as you call it, is a godsend. Ask Dorian. When I was pregnant with him, Eddie and me had one of our worst knock-down-dragouts. He kicked me down the stairs. That's right, poor old helpless Eddie. I could've ended up in a heap here at the bottom if I hadn't caught onto the piles. They broke my fall. Dorian would've never been born if not for what you call junk."

What a horrible thought—Dorian never born. I love all this junk. I'd better go ask him if that story is true. Jeff went back up to the third floor, almost as unnoticed as Eddie's departure from the house. He found Dorian sketching rapidly through the pages of a pad. "Quitting time?" he said, casting a smile at Jeff, ripping off a page and starting a sketch of his new friend. "Hold still," he added, hoping for the impossible.

Esther stared and stared at the fat old refrigerator. For all her excuses, she knew Karin was right. She'd been a lousy housekeeper, the place had fallen down around her over the years. No matter about Eddie being gone in the war, or Sandra moving as far away as possible after that nasty prom incident, or Dorian's brother who'd had even less to do with her, and the illegitimate one who'd come out stillborn, and Dorian's stubborn ways—in the end she could have at least cleaned house. The results plainly shocked any newcomers to the place and made oldtimers shake their heads in dismay that things could actually keep getting worse. Maybe the refrigerator was a sign. No more shifting things around, upstairs, downstairs, inside and out. If that icebox stayed there forever she could point to it and say, "what am I supposed to do?" Short of Clara Muff's spacemen swooping in and zapping it onto their ship, word of the fridge that wouldn't budge might spread and the talk all over town might be "poor, poor Esther." Saddled with shell shocked Eddie and a refrigerator frozen in time.

Esther brooded happily for a few minutes. When her mood changed, as it was bound to, she cursed out loud and declared, "I have just the thing to jar that damn thing loose!" She took off to the garage.

Ethan and Karin had stayed quietly a few steps up from the fridge, waiting for a signal from Esther and that was it.

"Have you seen the second floor?" Karin initiated a new round of small talk.

"Yeah, here it is." Ethan picked up a box of books and kicked the linoleum. " I don't need to use the bathroom, if that's what you mean."

Karin laughed. "My room's just before that."

Ethan dropped the books and followed Karin down the hall. Her bed was covered with clothes, shoved aside to make a space large enough for one person to sleep. She got some things onto hangers, doing what she could to give the space a bit more dimension.

"Take a load off your feet. I know Esther's had you on the go since seven."

"Are we taking a nap?"

"Whenever Esther goes to look for something, that's pretty much the end of the work day."

Ethan was so covered with dirt he was reluctant to lie down even at her invitation. *She told me not to get the paper dirty, and now it's fine to lie in her bed even though*

I'm a giant mudpie. She's almost as nuts as the rest of them.

Ethan took off his shoes as a show of good faith. Karin slipped out of hers as if to say 'that's a start.'

Right above them Jeff had amazed Dorian with how motionless he could become, allowing himself to be drawn. Dorian did not realize it was a short spell of catatonia. Jeff felt a sudden wave of depression, some unknowable mixture of the decay of this house, Eddie's infirmity, his brother's bizarre actions, and most of all, a reaction to the handsome guy who thought it not a terrible waste of time to copy Jeff's likeness on paper. Long used to being ignored, being put on the spot like this was more incapacitating than a houseful of woes.

"You're doing fine," commented Dorian, "I have most of you done. Just hold on a few more—."

With those words of encouragement, Dorian had lowered the boom of self-consciousness on Jeff, who fell flat under its weight. *We're all going to die, the world's full of monsters, these paintings will crumble in a matter of centuries, why does anyone do anything?* Jeff became an empty sack of clothes.

"Oooops. That's OK. I got the basic sense."

Dorian showed Jeff what he'd done. It was very good, but Jeff couldn't bring himself to make comments on the worth of something because at the moment nothing had any.

"You don't have to say anything yet. I know where it's going. Are you O.K.? Maybe we should have lunch." Dorian put aside the sketch pad and stroked Jeff's hair.

"What do you like to eat?" As if asking Jeff about his tastes would do anything but drive him deeper into psychosis. The scalp massage was a more promising approach.

While Dorian used his creative fingers to craft his way down Jeff's neck and back, while Ethan and Karin advanced beyond footsies in the bedroom below, Esther groped her way through the dark garage. The overhead bulb had sputtered out when Esther hit the switch at the entrance from the house. The garage door might be raisable, if she could reach it through the maze of stored crap. There was no car; neither Esther nor Eddie had been able to drive for several years. Naturally a space large enough for an automobile cried out to be filled, and the overflow from the inside of the house rapidly rose to the occasion.

Esther banged a shin against some metal thing sticking out and sat on a rusty oil can to recover. It was stupid to try and make it across the garage with only a splash of light from the doorway, but it was equally useless to turn back to find a flashlight. Esther felt something soft and smooth next to her. A gift-wrapped package emerged as her eyes focussed. Closer inspection revealed once attractive paper, darkened and spotted with age. What was taped up inside? Having had no other treat that day, Esther undid the present. A hardcover book on the human body. Something for a kid under ten by the design on the cover—a cartoonish X-ray of esophagus, heart, stomach and no genitals. Handwriting on the inside of the front took Esther back eight years. "To Dorian on your Tenth Birthday from the Best Nurse in Town." So that's what happened that year, thought Esther. Did Dorian have to make do with nothing on that birthday? Damn shame. Nice book. Maybe he was a little too old for it now. He'd certainly draw in the genitals with ease.

Trying to recall what drunken episode caused the misplacing of an entire birthday, Esther moved on to memories of Eddie. If he'd been around that year, that would have led to a certain conclusion. But if he'd been off in Greenland, shooting deer and selling the meat to stay alive, that would place the blame squarely on. . . . was it Greenland? Or was that the stretch in Germany? Not the first time—when she was scared he'd be sent back in a box—but the second, when he was over there sharing war stories and doing nothing more dangerous than serving up slop for the troops and she was jealous as hell at his chance to travel while she was stuck behind in Charlestown. All, or most, was forgiven during his brief homecomings. They actually used to connect physically without fists leading the way.

Esther sat in the dusty dark and scanned the days and nights of a measure of happiness with her husband. She could not have imagined that her search for a crowbar in the garage would unwind in a dormant sexual fantasy. Nor that in levels above her, such realities would be acted out.

Karin and Ethan were all over each other. It took awhile for the rest of their clothes to follow their shoes to the floor, but once they did, their lovemaking made a huge mess on the bed even messier.

Dorian's persistence in believing that Jeff's withdrawal was more from shyness than illness, enabled him to get the boy face up. And then their actions mostly duplicated those of the twosome on the next floor down.

Esther remembered undoing the buttons on Eddie's uniform. She could taste his lips, almost free from the familiar scent of liquor. She held him and whispered how happy she was he had come home safely.

Ethan covered Karin's stomach with kisses. When she did the same to him, he laughed himself right out of bed. Half on the floor he waved his arms for a lifeline. She catapulted him to softer ground and made a pillow of his chest. She cupped his buttocks in her hands. He got dizzy looking at her face and consumed her nose and mouth. They rolled over and over, never able to settle for more than a few seconds who preferred the top or the bottom.

Dorian kept steadily at work on Jeff until even a catatonic had to respond.

Enveloped in Dorian's passion, Jeff finally understood where his body ended and another's began. Dorian pulled him up to his face and rubbed Jeff's genitals all over his cheeks, in and out of his mouth. And sometimes, doing nothing but just hugging, a breathless embrace that was the most rapturous moment of all.

The lovemaking of Ethan and Karin took a disquieting turn. Ethan's anxiety and desperation were renewed by the passing thought of the damning newspaper on the stairs. He immersed himself in Karin all the more as he acknowledged his disappearing act was unlikely to solve anything.

Esther's head was so full of Eddie she couldn't imagine ever being upset with him again. Life had been good to them on occasion; it was only since the stroke that things had gotten really glum. But now she was sleeping and that put her back in his arms when they'd had strength and were capable of wonderful caresses.

Ethan became awkward in his moves. He gradually curled up into a ball, becoming utterly passive in Karin's hands. Jeff finally returned Dorian's affection, craving more and more of the sensuous feelings he'd been deprived. Dorian put aside his mechanical notions of seduction, showing a wealth of tenderness and patience. When it was over, he and Jeff held each other in the room full of paintings, its vivid colors illuminated by the setting sunlight streaming in.

Karin and Ethan lay kissing and cuddling in the cluttered room she currently called home. The shades were drawn, depriving them of light. Indeed her room, despite their breathing and sighing, seemed virtually airless.

Ethan did not know that Esther had dozed off in the garage and so his fear of being discovered quickly returned. *Karin is so wonderful, but she knows nothing about me. I can blame Jeff's pills and I do and then I can play the victim to the hilt, but what the hell am I doing with this woman? Who is she? What does she expect of me? And when do I tell her who I am and what I've done?*

Jeff's post-coital thoughts were bound to be less specific, but no sane person, and certainly not his precise and pragmatic brother, could have kept up with the volume of his renewed mania in Dorian's total embrace.

There's a road that goes nowhere and my mind is empty. If a road can go nowhere and still take you places, then an empty mind is secretly full. I sat in my room, doing nothing but stare at my wall. The deeper into it I went the further I felt from myself, which was good because when I was inside my body, I was so sad. I was this lump of flesh that somehow had been charged with life, dropped down into the world, and left here to fend for myself. But there was no "my" or "me", only an "it" that looked like someone. Other people have souls, entities that chose to incarnate as bodies, and now they are filled with a mysterious sense of mission—to explore the physical world and make all their in-

ner potential absolutely concrete. But me, I have no mission. Only an awful awareness of the chasm between my own lump of flesh and all these others, running around on their oh-so-serious quests. To have more, to get more, to be more, wanting to want more. But wait—if they need to get more of whatever it is they're after, well, they must have had very little to start with. Perhaps it was me, Jeff, who arrived already full of the substance they all needed to get. That's why I do not need to go questing for it. I was born with my mission already fulfilled! I was complete from the word go and that's why I look around in amazement at everyone who feels incomplete and is still searching. Why be afraid? They're the ones who are fragmented and needy. I am complete and fulfilled. But if my mission is complete, then shouldn't I die and move along to the next phase? Apparently not, or else the desire for suicide would never leave me alone. The urge to be silly because life is so ridiculous is no less absurd than the urge to be serious because life seems so desirable.

If Dorian had the slightest notion what he'd unleashed in the boy he'd just seduced, he might have wanted to pull the bedcovers over his head. Instead he glanced at Jeff's eyes, so blue and full of life, and closed his own eyes, comfortable in the knowledge that the world was sometimes an extremely fine place to be.

Jeff preferred it when Dorian's hazel eyes had been open. Once they closed, Jeff got triggered on notions about death. Dead police in the woods. Death encircling this house that to Ethan seemed such a sanctuary. And behind those serene blue eyes, Jeff's secret voyage went on. *There was a man who lived on a island where he spent years doing nothing but trying to figure out his life. He drove himself insane—if he wasn't already insane when he went to the island with that purpose. I don't have his problem. I realize I was put in the world, which is an island of sorts, and that there is no use trying to figure out my purpose because it is already accomplished by the fact that I am here and conscious of not having one!*

A couple of people lost their lives and it was kind of our fault. A couple, a dozen, a hundred, on into the thousands—what does it matter if millions of people are killed when there are billions of people left?

Because each individual person is a universe, each means the world to at least somebody somewhere. And even those who don't have anyone to care about them, those who drift through life having lost all ties, yes, even them! To live as though everyone is expendable is terribly unfulfilling. That's why we at least have to pretend or make the effort to believe that everyone means as much to themselves as I mean to myself. And that if I can care about someone as much as I do right now for Dorian, then each and every human individual has the potential to be loved and valued to an equal degree. Therefore, even the loss of one life can be felt as tragic and not simply redundant. And so two people who happened to be police, and whose lives took them up to the point of being in a car that blew up—yes, they mattered. To each other. To their families, to people I can't even imagine. It's made-up meaning, a sense of feeling by default. You show up and you're involved. . . . I wish I were somebody else. But then I wouldn't have met Dorian. Knowing him at this moment is a privilege granted only to me. Only to me, whoever I am, inside this strange and sad lump of flesh.

Then Jeff was just as suddenly aware of feeling good. For a minute no part of him hurt. A kind of emptiness in his head, but that was acceptable, even preferable to the horrible things that could fill it. And then he decided that what he had just done with his body, interlaced with Dorian's, thinking none of these thoughts, feeling things which now he couldn't even remember except that they felt wonderful, all that stuff with his body—that was "Jeff" too. He was not his head, but the entire living being lying in the bed. Just as his disease often forced his body up into his head where he became lost amidst all of these maddening ideas, now he could throw his mind down into his body and simply experience life as physical pleasure.

Jeff felt himself running. He was out of the bed and no longer naked. It may have been a dream but that didn't matter. He was running. He started running because the nagging currents in his mind felt like something to get away from, and fast. But after a few moments he was running entirely for the sake of running. His mind was still blank, but now that seemed appropriate, not a cause for alarm. The fact that he was running through woods and that Dorian was running after him filled him with sheer delight. Yes, emptiness had turned into pure feeling and that purity evolved into pleasure, and the pleasure, while it couldn't last forever, was certainly worth something. What an exhilirating thing to finally know! Jeff raced with feet, arms, heart, even head; he raced toward whatever may happen next. It was fun trying to escape and it would be fun once he was caught by Dorian. Jeff's breath flew out ahead of him. He'd have to run twice as fast just to catch up to his own breathing. If Dorian was doing the same, then Dorian's breath was already on top of him, had already caught up with him. Breathing together, they were together. Even though they were still at least a dozen feet apart, rushing headlong out of the woods and into a vast open field.

CHAPTER 12

Karin couldn't keep from giggling as she led Ethan through the second story disaster area in the dark. He hushed her again and again, having genuine cause to worry. Esther was in the kitchen, nourishing herself with nibbles from a cold melted cheese sandwich she'd made an hour ago when she dragged herself in from the garage.

"Damn, I'm getting as bad as Eddie," she'd muttered, dusting herself off and checking for crawling things that could have climbed inside her clothes when she conked out.

She couldn't find a clock with the right time, but she guessed she'd slept for a good three hours or more. Preposterous dreams and twilight replays of epic battles, yearnings for the distant places Eddie had been, her children adrift in a world full of indifferent strangers—such a vast canvas of images had been stretched inside her head that three years could have gone by and she wouldn't have been surprised. Then she'd somehow thrown together this grilled cheese sandwich and had a few bites before nodding off and reawakening to find it half-stuck to the table and her hair.

"Damn if I'm not getting worse than Eddie."

At that point Eddie was waking up in a honeysuckle bush midway between the hotel bar and his house. The sweet fragrance worked wonders on what he'd spewed on himself before falling, and the combating aromas enabled him to suppress most of his pain. That included the unveiled abuse he'd received from old friends in the bar. The cause of their cruelty was folded in his shirt pocket—the lost love letter he'd sent Karin to find. It turned up in a crevice at the corner of the bar and brought loads of laughs to the unimaginative drunks. At least Eddie had once been able to write letters full of sentiment and hope. The guys lashed him all the more because they had never come close to that stage of development. Eddie drank heavily and fought back. They played keep-away with the letter, wanting to deny him the opportunity of showing it to Esther as a peace offering.

"If she says 'so-what?', let her, that's my business!" roared Eddie. He got the letter, got out of there, and got sick. Then came the blackout. Now all he had to do was lift himself from this goddamn perfume bush and give Esther the taste of nostalgia. Once he figured out in which pocket he'd stuck it.

Esther, pulling hairs from her cheese sandwich in the familiarity of her kitchen, had more time to dwell on the negative. She sobered up faster and created an exaggerated picture of Eddie's out-of-house experiences.

"Sneaking off to get smashed and brag about his war days, huh? Leaving me alone in that dungheap of a garage he never cleaned like he promised. Lucky I left the door open a crack. I could've died from lack of oxygen and the town paper would have called it suicide. Well, he's not rid of me yet and he can sleep at the hotel if he likes it there so much!"

For no apparent reason, even while railing against the only man she cared about enough to hate, the question "where did I put the newspaper?" flashed through her mind. She looked forward to news of the outside world, something to focus her longing, to make specific the list of her regrets. And it added sport to their lives. Could she read it before he shredded it? It was a daily clash of wills that sometimes gave her the illusion of pleasure. Now was the time to find it and lose herself in local and worldwide trivia, before Eddie assaulted it with scissors and glue. But her hair was stuck to the cheese and the cheese made a long string to the table. None of which would have bothered her if Ethan hadn't appeared in the doorway. He was loosely dressed and showed enough skin to feel as awkward as Esther in the web of cheese.

"What are you doing up in the middle of the night?"

"Uh, I think it's only like eleven." Ethan buttoned, tucked

and straightened his clothes.

"I thought a bedtime snack would be nice." Karin rounded the corner, no longer caring what conclusions Esther would jump to.

"If I'd known you two were ever going to come down, I'd have grilled a half-dozen of these."

Ethan's eyes, hurting from the light, studied the pathetic sandwich. Esther made the best of his implied insult.

"It's a hat. Put it on your head and make like a moron."

"Go to bed, Esther. I'll make us something." Karin started smashing around among the pots.

"Well, I guess you have a few minutes to eat. Gonna need your energy back soon enough." Esther rustled through some junk and came up with a long piece of rope. She put it in Ethan's hands which seemed eager for something to hold.

"Make a good strong knot around this knob." Ethan took the challenge while Esther ran to the front and side doors, making sure they were locked. She came back, approved of his progress and told Karin to stop clattering for a moment so she could listen. The sound of Eddie's moaning and grumbling, cursing and panting, as he approached the house grew more distinct even to Ethan's untrained ears. "I hear him, Esther! Now what?"

"All you have to do is pull real tight when Budweiser brain tries to come in."

"Oh, God, Esther—."

"Don't God me, Karin. Give your boyfriend a hand."

"I'm not helping out with any schemes against Eddie. He's a got a weak heart."

"And I got a broken one, big shit. I pay you, girl."

Ethan's imitation of an entire junior high team getting ready for a tug o' war cracked Karin up and she got behind him, secretly hoping to make his side lose.

"You'll do anything for money, I see."

"Nah, I just have a good heart."

Karin tickled him, Ethan's carelessly hoisted pants started to fall, and Esther came between them. "Here he comes . . . "

They could see Eddie in the dim light outside the kitchen door. He paused to search for something. Esther feared her team would lose momentum and indeed Ethan was starting to drift. *What am I doing in this whacked-out house, hundreds of miles from home, playing S and M games with country fruitcakes? Just two days ago I owned a great car, was helping my brother, had a real crack at getting out in the world. Now I'm back in the playpen.*

"Now! Pull!" Esther hollered in his ear. "Pull!"

Ethan and Karin yanked hard. Esther dug her feet in, determined to do her share. The three defenders of the shabby fortress were all poised at drastic backward angles when Eddie turned the knob and the door opened inwards. Esther merely dropped the rope and her mouth in surprise. Ethan and Karin went sprawling off their feet and collapsed in a corner.

"Shit, since when does it open that way?"

Karin and Ethan laughed helplessly at her curious tone. They laughed so hard their banged-up arms and legs instantly stopped hurting. Eddie, quite used to laughter at his expense, kept moving and muttering. Rope on the door, people on the kitchen floor, just get in and go to bed.

"I'm tired, sho tired, dear," and he puffed a makeup kiss at Esther. "Thought you'd be asleep. Early day tomorrow, church and all. Holy pie in the shky time."

"Didn't you hear? I turned atheist cause God never answered my prayers."

"Aw, keep praying. Just another few years to go . . . "

"Not for me. I was praying He should put you back to work building bridges up in Heaven. There it won't matter when they come tumbling down. Up there everybody flies."

Karin whispered to Ethan about the time a bridge Eddie had helped to build across a narrow stretch of the Connecticut River fell down. Nobody was hurt, but Esther never let him forget it. Ethan, still chuckling over the pointless job with the rope, conjured an image of all the citizens of Charlestown and all the people back in Jeff's mental hospital sliding off a broken bridge into a muddy river. His laughing fit was refueled.

"Real funny," said Esther, pointing to a pile of shingles, wood and tools right next to Ethan. "He stored up all those things to fix the house, then collapsed in his damn chair for all eternity. Whole house is sinking, but Eddie's in his chair, clipping out obituaries and all's right with the world."

She gave the building materials a good kick and faked hurting her toe with enough style to keep Ethan in stitches. Even Karin was starting to enjoy the misery.

She wrapped the rope around Ethan's waist. He countered by pretending to bind her wrists. Esther grabbed a broom and followed Eddie into the living room so she wouldn't have to see what a great sex toy her old rope could become.

"Yeah, come in here, sweetie. I want to show you shumthing." Eddie was close enough to his chair so when Esther tried to deck him with the broom he was able to fall to the comfort of his musty cushion.

"Bravo, Esther! First time I seen you with that-that thing in ten yearsh!"

"Like I haven't tried to keep this house from falling on our heads. Why are you taking so long to kick off? I had those new boys dig a nice deep hole for you out back."

She swung the broom and whacked him across the face. His glasses fell off and the look he gave her—"you could have blinded me"—did more to make her drop the broom than any force would have.

He pulled some folded paper from his pocket and yowled in triumph.

"Henry found thish. A letter I shent you back in the Air Force. I think I was stationed in . . . in . . . oh, you know, that place, that place over there, you know—"

"Yeah, I know. Only time you ever stayed away long enough to make me think I missed you."

"Jus-just lishen, honey." He got his glasses back on, noticed the letter was upside-down, and recited what he remembered until he could straighten it out.

"Dearest Eshter. . . . isn't that a nice opening?"

"Real clever, where'd you think that one up?"

"Dearest Eshter . . . Well, it's about time I wrote you. I am sorry I haven't wrote before, but I have been so tired and sick I jush can't think."

"This is news?" But Esther already felt a pang of regret for putting down Eddie's noble attempt to read to her.

In the kitchen, Ethan's laughter subsided as his rope games with Karin triggered a sensual response. She slapped him with the rope and motioned to the stairs. Ethan was eager, but realized they hadn't had a drop to eat, the only reason they'd come down in the first place. His self-respect crumbled and he took a few fast bites from the antique cheese sandwich. Karin pulled him out of the kitchen before he did anything more desperate. The late hour and the chaos had gone a long way toward blocking out his disturbing memories when the half-open newspaper on the steps shocked Ethan awake. "POLICE FOUND DEAD ON MISS—"

As Karin kept pulling him along, all Ethan could do was kick bottles and scraps of trash on top of the paper as he went by. Karin was too aroused to notice his abrupt change of mood. Within seconds she had him over the refrigerator and back in her bedroom, inside the sheets. The tension spread instantly all over Ethan's body, making him twice the lover he was earlier that evening.

And while their mouths opened and consumed every inch of each other, just below them the older couple found a subtler pleasure in reciting passages from the recovered letter of long ago.

"I hope we get some help here before long. I worked eighteen hours today,"

Eddie's thick tongue pushed out the words while Esther bore with him. "It was rainy and cold. Looking forward to church tomorrow. Nice and warm in there. I can sleep. Only chance I'll get."

Esther didn't notice her hand letting go of the broom. She

went limp and absorbed the letter right down to her bones.

"I have dreams about you, then I wake up and curse because I'm still here. I mish you so very much, Eshter. Did you get the— the—the ten dollars—the ten dollars—I—I . . . oh hell, it's getting all blurry."

With a mixture of impatience and tenderness, Esther took the letter from his trembling hands and went on reading it aloud.

"Did you get the ten dollars I mailed you? I shot a few deer and sold the meat. It's illegal, but it makes more money than we get for a whole month. My legs and back are hurting again something awful."

Esther unconsciously started massaging Eddie's neck. "I can't wait to see you at Christmas. My dear wife, you don't know how much I think about you. And the kids. I hope you'll tell them be good because their Dad loves them and misses them." Esther stopped reading and seemed to be lost in a fugue state of anticipating that twenty-year-gone Christmas. "Tell a two year old to be good? Boy, you had it easy over there," she huffed.

"Keep going, k-keep going."

"Yeah, let's see . . . loves them, misses them. Hmm. Give my little one a kiss. I am sorry I don't write more, but most days I'm sick and my hand's too cold to hold the pencil. Esther, I love you always. God bless you. We will be together again soon, I pray. Your husband, Eddie."

Esther's glasses had fogged up as much as the letter's author. The Osbornes looked like a pair of unfinished comic strip characters, eyeless goggles floating on figures still dressed for the Depression. Esther had found her way onto Eddie's lap.

He groaned at her weight but enjoyed it. She folded the letter and kissed him on the forehead.

"Yeah. Nice to save things like that."

"Well, we never were much good at throwing things out."

They hugged each other in the only corner of the living room not bursting with the things they'd accumulated in their lifetime together.

Up in the third floor bedroom, Dorian and Jeff were off to a shaky start if theirs was to be a lifetime together. Not out of direct anxiety between them so much as bumpy sleeping habits and chaotic dreamscapes. Dorian 'landed' in bed with a bounce or two after one of his many flying dreams, the sort that most people cease to have past the age of ten. There was hardly a week went by when Dorian didn't launch himself over some Grecian, surrealist, or Maxfield Parrish vista.

"I'm flying over the town! Everything below is pulsating brilliantly! All the living and the dead of Charlestown applaud as I swoop up over the hills!"

Jeff stared at him enviously. "I close my eyes just dreading where I'm about to go."

"You have to say some kind of prayer before you fall asleep. Godhead will protect you."

"But I can't believe in anything."

"What's stopping you?" Dorian nestled closer. "Sleep is an alternate universe.

Our physical bodies alone need to rest. The Ego and astral selves go soaring in the domain which they're from. You're freezing."

"I remember now! I was having my blood dream. A side effect of the pills I take. A huge jet took off. Its engines conked out in midair. Whole thing crashed. When it hit the ground, the earth cracked down the middle. Blood gushed up out of the dirt. It was so real. I heard screaming. Could smell the blood. And that constant roar. I kept thinking—how come I'm lying here O.K., whole, alive—when all around me people are bleeding to death? And then I knew . . . I was one of them! Dorian—I dreamt I was already dead! Don't you die in real life if you dream it?"

"That's a myth. Like when I fall from the sky and the ground's coming at me. Sometimes I land right here, all soft and perfect. Once in a while I smash to bits. But I wake up fine."

"My arms or legs are always falling off. Blood spews from the open ends.

Sometimes my body turns into some chunky substance—salt or pumice—and then crumbles bit by bit."

"Maybe you should go off those pills."

"I may have to. I lost them. But I better get some more and soon."

"Tomorrow I'll show you all of Charlestown. The town of my dreams. You'll forget all about that junk."

Jeff hugged Dorian but his inner cold was barely affected. It would take many nights before the Charlestown lad's body heat would penetrate his own badly bruised skin.

CHAPTER 13

And so three couples in that dirty isolated old house reached sufficient exhaustion to lose consciousness. Whether by the culmination of chaotic lust, or the weight of hideous memories made bearable by the distance of time, or simply the heat of wool blankets forming a cocoon over wounded young bodies—sleep came. Karin and Ethan held each other tightly while above them Dorian and Jeff did the same. And on the first floor Esther and Eddie dozed off in the closest proximity of all, that of their hearts. Lights had been left burning; at four in the morning the house was far from dark, but it was stone silent.

Until Esther woke with a full bladder, could not see a clear path to the first floor toilet, and headed up the stairs only to run smack into the barricading refrigerator. She recovered from the fright of its heavy door swinging open in her face and sat on the steps before daring to make another move. "Damn fool Esther, you'll break your collar bone or worse. Lucky the damn thing didn't fall on top of you. Everyone would wake up and see hands and feet sticking out from under the fridge and go, "Yep, that's Esther on ice.""

She looked for a cigarette so she could take her morbid fantasy further. Her sweeping hand motions caused the newspaper to emerge from hiding amidst the stairway junk. A lighted match gave Esther her first glimpse of the previous day's headline. She let out a scream that woke the house.

Dorian's astral body and Ego returned to his resting physical form; Jeff came to with a brief rush of pleasure. Ethan was confused by strange surroundings; when that passed he shuddered with a fear he hadn't known since he was very little. Eddie belched and knew it was best to fake continued sleep. Only Karin actually got out of bed to see what was the matter. From the top of the stairs she saw Esther flailing around with the newspaper.

"Are you OK? I thought you fell."

"There was a big accident on the Missing Link!"

Esther stood up to make eye contact with Karin over the refrigerator. "Listen—'Policeman and policewoman found dead in their exploded car.' It says their bodies got burned to a crisp. Pretty awful, huh? Course it makes you wonder what they were doing. I remember all kinds of hanky-panky between the nurses and the doctors."

Karin edged around the blockade and took the paper from Esther. "Let me see that."

"Sorry to scare you. Eddie's sleeping like a ton of bricks. I didn't want to be depressed all alone in the middle of the night."

Karin heard Esther, but the headline so absorbed her she went back to her room, leaving Esther all alone again.

"Hey, did you ever report your stolen car?" Karin nudged Ethan roughly.

"Why? Didn't Dorian?"

"It says here they radioed in they were in hot pursuit of a green Jaguar."

Ethan grabbed the paper. The headboard light was so covered with crap it barely helped him read. "Those creeps! Karin—they're going to think it was me."

"Wasn't it?" Anger and disappointment got the better of her strongest craving to believe him.

"No! If cops were tailing me, I'd pull over. I swear I did not, did not do this!"

"Well somebody did."

Karin's wish that he was telling the truth took flight even as she balled him out. "Where are your feelings? Two cops are dead, and one of them was a woman. A twenty-five year old rookie woman cop. Dead!"

"God, I'm lucky there wasn't a baby cop with them too. Then

you'd really think I'm a heartless bastard." *What the fuck was I thinking, leaving it up to that flaky guy to make the report? But I didn't dare leave the house.*

Ethan's lifelong mastery of self-justification wasn't going to fail him now. "What are we going to do?" Though spoken like the soccer captain he once was, his urgent plea did not immediately impress her.

"I'm going to have to turn you in."

"You don't believe me? You've got to!"

"Look me in the eye and tell me you didn't do it."

It was dark enough for Ethan to take the challenge and look into her eyes without seeing his own conscience. "I had nothing to do with it."

Then came one of Karin's erratic mood shifts, so often frustrating, now a blessing beyond Ethan's deserving. "It's kind of exciting. You guys on the lam from God knows what. Probably criminals since your early teens. Outrunning the law and ending up in my backyard."

"Those hitchhikers were so out of it. They had a gun. I wouldn't put this past them."

"Ethan, even if I believe you, how will you ever prove it to anybody else?"

"It says here the car hasn't been found. The cops drove through an oil slick, veered off into a tree and the Jaguar kept going. You're our witness that we showed up here before this happened."

His voice was so achingly persuasive Karin felt her mind go blank and any chronological sense of the past few days was lost. "You did? That's right, you did."

"Thank God," whispered Ethan. It miraculously came out sounding more like a genuine prayer than an obvious expression of relief. Karin brushed her hands against his cheek and shoulder, offering more than a trace of reassurance. Then she darted from the room. "I should ask Dorian."

She did not expect to meet anyone on the steps going up, certainly not a muttering schizophrenic. Jeff had wandered out of bed once Dorian started to fall back asleep. Moving carefully down a step at a time, he talked to himself, trying to straighten out the past day. "Work therapy, art therapy. All day, all night, nothing but this therapy and that therapy. Why fight off the inevitable? This is me. Me, me, ME!"

The barrage of "me's" came at Karin in the dark and she almost fell backwards.

"Oh, fuck, it's you! Dorian's up there, right?"

"If he hasn't flown off someplace." There wasn't a trace of irony in Jeff's tone.

Karin let him pass, figuring she was lucky to get Dorian alone. When Jeff paused on the second floor landing to consider the innumerable ways around the refrigerator, Ethan heard him and wondered if he should call him in. Jeff oddly sensed Ethan nearby and the two stayed transfixed for a long moment. The sibling telepathy ultimately led to avoidance. Ethan didn't even rustle the paper. Jeff made his way down, believing there was immunity from his strongest critic if he made it past the refrigerator.

In the kitchen he got a fright from Esther that repaid his sputtering attack on Karin.

"What the hell are you doing up?"

Jeff panicked and ran twice around the table. Esther pushed him down into a chair. "Stop making me nervous!"

Wow, do I have that kind of power? I'm always thinking people exist to fuck me up. But I can do it to them just as much.

Esther didn't allow him a moment to relish the notion. "Hey, what's this I hear about you being in a mental hospital?"

She knows! Ethan will kill me.

"It's no big deal. I cornered Dorian, pried it out of him. Getting him to spill secrets is just about the only entertainment I get these days. Besides, it's important I know the kind of people I hire."

"He—he said you and me have a lot in common."

As jumpy as he was, Jeff realized he could be himself around this woman. She had taken off her glasses and he could see her eyes contained pain, mirth, bewilderment and "I'm gonna do whatever I like" all at once. He couldn't recall when he'd last met someone so utterly free of duplicity.

"Lot in common, huh? Maybe cause I used to be a psychiatric nurse. Hey, I bet I could freshen up on you and come out of retirement. Trust me, I've had worse cases."

People worse than me? I love you already! Please tell me, describe them. It's great hearing about helpless psychotic losers. Nothing made him forget about his own problems faster. Jeff was the sort of guy who called a graphic movie about the ravages of war 'escapist entertainment.' A frothy musical or light comedy could send him over the edge in seconds. The sick story Esther was about to share normally drove people from the room. Not Jeff.

"When Dorian was growing up I had to take in boarders to make ends meet. There was this one called Babyface. She'd been a drifter, but something about Charlestown caught her fancy and she settled down as the town whore. She was old as me, but she had some kind of skin disease that made her look twelve. All puffy and white. She was the dirtiest thing on two feet. And she didn't take precautions!" Esther cupped her hand demonstratively over Jeff's crotch. It made him giggle.

"Yeah, you know the type. She just kept on having kids. She already had five when she moved in. Nobody else in town would have rented to that menagerie, but I'm such a softie at heart. There I was—living underneath all them screaming, shitting brats. Eddie was off to one of his wars and I liked having the sound of life in the house. Dorian's sister bitched about it, his brother moved out to become a mechanic in Michigan, and Dorian was too small to complain. Never saw a baby that cried so little. Just stared a lot and made insect-type sounds. It wasn't up to them who I rented to. Besides, I had to feed 'em, right? Right! But boy oh boy did I have a shit fit when I heard that Babyface's number six was on the way. Her kind of life, all that abuse—I kept thinking, that kid's not gonna make it. Well, I got my wish and now I could kick myself for thinking such mean things. Babyface got syphilis and hepatitis and you name it. Raging fever and covered with blotches right during delivery. She was miscarriaging and bleeding and when the poor little thing finally came out, he was born in pieces. Arm. Half a head. Three toes. Took half the night to make sure he was all out."

Jeff was riveted. What a wonderful example of life's random cruelty! Esther took note of his bizarre smile.

"Oh, we know it was a 'he' for sure. Little pecker came wriggling out all on its own like it was looking for something, anything to rub up against. We gathered up all the different parts in Glad bags and went right from the birthplace to the graveyard for a quick ceremony. He's buried in the Hillside Cemetery that Dorian likes so much. Babyface didn't bother to give it a name or anything. The marker just says 'Babyface's Baby.' She was completely nuts after that. All her other kids had to be shuffled off to foster homes. Business fell off. She tried to do herself in a few times. I was making a special cake for Sandra, I come in and Babyface is practically crawling into the oven, inhaling the fumes and chocolate crumbs. Yeah, try to top that in your fancy pants 'mental facility'."

Jeff raced through his personal assortment of lunatics. He couldn't wait to share anecdotes with Esther!

"But wait, wait, I haven't gotten to the point yet. Picture Babyface in a pit of misery, so far gone not Sigmund Freud himself could imagine pulling her out. That's when I started her on intensive work therapy. You guys ain't seen nothing yet. I worked Babyface's butt off. Talk about your sixteen hour days. I had that woman on her hands and knees, scrubbing things to the bone. And it worked! Damn, I saw the proof—you wouldn't have recognized this place. The Ritz had nothing on me. I got a clean house out of the deal and Babyface collapsed with the biggest grin you ever saw. Died one month later but I'd given her a real sense of accomplishment."

Jeff all but burst into applause. Even Esther was taken aback that he rejoiced at the fate of Babyface.

"Anyhow, if working for me cured Babyface it'll do wonders for you. And for your smartass brother. Even if he thinks he's so normal."

Jeff wanted to believe Esther was some kind of proto-psychiatric witch who brewed rural potions undreamt of by pharmacologists. He knew he was incurable and that Ethan certainly was unchangeable, but neither of them had ever encountered someone so unorthodox in her approach to treatment.

Or maybe I'll still in my wallworld and she's just some drunken country woman looking forward to another binge. Jeff never ruled out the rational explanation. He simply knew better than to trust it entirely. There was only one thing he felt a certainty about at the moment.

"Dorian understands. It's not that he sees the world the way I do. In fact, it's the complete opposite. He even believes in reality. And yet there's something about him that just cuts right to the heart, sees through the garbage—"

"Well, he's had lots of training in seeing through the garbage," Esther admitted.

"Plus you really don't mind how he is."

"Oh, that. Why the hell should I? Half of history's greatest have been queers. Alexander the Great, Tchaikovsky, Lawrence of Arabia—they all went for guys. Loads of kings. Richard the Lionheart, Edward—I think number two—King James, that's right, the one who turned the Bible into English. Told his scribes, 'Finish up Genesis by Friday,' then went right back to bed with his dukes. Don't think I'm sacrilegious, no sir. You won't meet a holier person. I'm the only one in town makes it a point to go to all five churches on Sunday. It ain't easy, but I got some of them to stagger the services. God loves drunks, he loves homos, hell, he adored Babyface. While I'm on the subject, I bet you never heard we've had a gay guy in the White House. Yessir, a queer for president!"

"Really? Which one?"

Esther leaned over and whispered her naughty secret. "Taft."

Then, realizing there was no reason the whole world shouldn't know, especially the night after two cops were senselessly killed in a car crash, proving that life was at best a crap shoot, she belted it out. "Bachelor president, my ass. William Howard Homo Taft!"

She spat out "Taft" with such vigor Jeff ducked, Eddie was startled to his feet, and even Ethan clutched the newspaper against his thumping chest.

Jeff's down there with Esther. She's seen the paper and he's probably filling her in on the details like he's some genius who can predict tomorrow's headlines. I have to go break it up.

Back on with his shirt and pants. He nimbly jumped the fridge, proud that he was the only person in the house for whom it was of no consequence. But at the foot of the stairs was Eddie, his night-time crawl taking him smack into Ethan.

"Dorie, my boy, shtop and talk to me."

"Uh, it's me, Eddie. You feeling better?"

"I n-never shee you no more. Wh-what are you going to do now that you grad-gradu—gradata—oh, you know, out of that place?"

"I'm not Dorian. I'm not your son," and under his breath, "Thank God."

Eddie was still in the dark. "Promish me you-you—you'll make shumthing of your life."

Ethan realized he couldn't see and tried to spell it out. "I'm Ethan. The new help. Remember?"

Eddie gripped Ethan by the wrists and shouted in his face. "Promish me! If I die, I want to know you turned out all right! Promish!"

Fuck, he's back in the war and he's gonna kill me! "O.K., O.K. I promise! I'll do something really great . . . Dad." Spared broken wrists, Ethan gave Eddie a quick hug to move him aside. Suddenly the old man realized it was not Dorian.

"You don't fool me. You're not—not him!"

"I tried to tell you—"

"You been sh-sh-shooting deer!"

"Huh?"

"I killed 'em, but I had to! You shoot-shoot 'em for fun!"

"I hate hunting."

"Stupid kid. How you gonna shupport a, you know, a braaaagggggh, a—a—a framily?"

"Not a problem for me yet, Eddie."

"Who are you? I don't like strangers in my house! Who are you!"

I can't be Dorian, I can't be myself, who does he want me to be?

"Ethan. My name is Ethan. From Boston. Just passing through and offering my services around the house. Took some time off from medical school to, you know, figure things out. Life can sure seem complex when you're just starting out. But I'm keeping a handle on things. I've been wait-listed at several great colleges, so as soon as I make up my mind I can go back and decide which one would be the best for—"

"You don't have time to wait! I was jush—jush starting out too and look at me. And look here!" Eddie pulled Ethan into the living room and shined a flashlight on his bulletin board with its paste-up tragedies, obituaries and horror headlines.

"Yeah, it's nice work, Eddie."

"Nice! Nice, you shay? Read it! Read! I shaid read!"

One more attempt to be diplomatic and then I clobber the old fart.

"Bloodbath in Ulster. Muskie Finished by Tears in the Snow. U.S. Resumes Bombing of North—8000 Viets Dead. Harvard students seize Dining Hall. Trapeze artist mauled by Gift Tiger from Delhi. De Gaulle's Mother Dead in Botched Liver Operation. "

Ethan was getting into a rhythm; none of it was so bad he couldn't humor the poor guy. Until Eddie pulled the current newspaper from where Ethan had tucked it halfway in his pants and read the headline like a circus barker. "Two Police Found Dead on Missing Link!"

Getting his nose rubbed in his own place in history gave Ethan enough adrenalin to finally shove Eddie away. He sent him plunging into the chair and knocked the bulletin board a few feet the opposite way. "What a sick hobby! Karin should trash that thing!"

"You bum! If you hurt her, I'll beat the, oh braaaaaggh! I told Eshter—you keep letting strangers in and you—and you'll be shorry. You thing! You goddamn thing-thing!"

Esther and Jeff had been rattling off famous queers, drunks and psychos, hoping the situation in the living room would take care of itself. But Esther soon acknowledged her peacekeeping tactics were sorely needed.

"Eddie! Your goddamn blood pressure is the only thing to worry about! Now calm down!" She heroically put herself between the wildmen.

"Bloodbath!" cried Eddie, straining to recover his big board. "Bloodbath! Bloodbath! Bloodbath!"

The flashlight's beam bounced off the walls, Eddie's and Esther's screaming lost all coherence, and Jeff caused a crash in the kitchen when he dove under the cluttered table for safety. Ethan forgot why he'd dared venture downstairs. He was up and over the refrigerator and back in Karin's bed like his life depended on it. Luckily Karin had returned also, so there was something for him to cling to besides the covers.

"Is Eddie O.K.?"

"He loves that fucked-up bulletin board."

Karin looked for the paper and realized Eddie had finally gotten his beloved headlines. "Good, that should quiet him down. By the way, I just asked Dorian. He never did report the car stolen."

"What? Holy shit!"

"Well, why did you count on him? It's not his car."

"You told me I could count on him!"

"If you report it tomorrow, it'll look very suspicious."

"What else do you suggest?"

Karin paced her small room. Downstairs things had not quieted down, but they were being drowned out by the approach of the long freight train's nighttime pass through town. The blaring horn warned of its imminent arrival and within seconds the whole house was rumbling. The engine's headlight cast a wide arc that invaded the windows and made Karin look like a restless ghost.

"We should sneak off right now."

"I'm totally wiped. Got to sleep." He buried himself in the covers.

"Ethan! It's almost dawn. Esther will grab you, put you back to work. You'll never get out of here."

"We owe her," came Ethan's muffled response. "What if she goes for the sheriff? And how can Eddie get along without you?"

"Don't start me thinking like that. I'll never leave."

"We'll plan it out tomorrow. Or the next day."

Karin would have accused Ethan of not talking sense if the train's hurtling noise wasn't unsettling her far more than usual. Peeking out from the covers, Ethan offered sympathy. "Wake the whole town, why don't they? You live with that every night?"

"Yeah. Normally I don't mind. They have to keep the horn going as a warning. There was a terrible accident a few years back because a car didn't see it coming."

"What, there's no stoplights or anything?"

"Charlestown couldn't afford them. Never a problem before or since. The car stalled on the tracks and they didn't get out fast enough. The whole family was killed in an instant."

Ethan watched her face in the quickly fading light as the train's dark series of cars trundled along for what seemed like a solid ten minutes after the initial stark beam of the engine. She looked so haunted by even the memory of distant disaster he knew he could never tell her what really happened to him. He had to stick to his concoction. The crash must seem as big a shock to him as anyone else. *I have to believe that. I was robbed, beaten up and thrown out on the side of the road. Those hoods cracked up the car and it looks bad, but it's clearly not my fault. Not our fault. God, but how can I control what Jeff spews whenever he feels like it?*

He reached out and gently coaxed Karin back onto the bed. He kissed her on the neck several times and whispered, "I'm telling you the truth. Please don't think what you're thinking about me."

Karin said nothing, but what she was suddenly thinking would have eased Ethan's mind. She was finding him more alluring than ever.

The train finally faded away. Esther had soothed Eddie and now was talking so quietly even the hypersensitive ears of a mental patient couldn't make it out from his nearby hiding place. If he had come out from under the table, Jeff would have heard her say, "Come to bed now, Eddie. I just want to hold you and be thankful you never got blown up in the war."

CHAPTER 14

Most of Charlestown was asleep while the Osborne house was percolating on all three floors. But a group of five teenagers was also making the most of the night, carousing in the woods on a beer-drinking romp. One had his underpants on his head as he went tripping through an overgrown glen in search of the perfect spot to pee.

When he banged into something low and hard, he grabbed his wounded dick and kicked the thing that hurt him. The clanging sound told the young naturalist he was not dealing with a tree or a shrub. He felt his way around the large manmade object, but was too drunk to identify it. He shouted to his friends and soon five shitfaced philosophers were trying to determine the make and model of what he'd unearthed.

They flung open the only door that would budge and scrambled over each other to check out the interior. One found a Coke can on the floor, crushed it and tossed it away. The only guy who chain-smoked kept lighting matches to follow the trail of pills and capsules scattered over the seats. While the pantless kid pretended to drive the dead auto, a shirtless buddy untied the dangling pig from the rearview mirror and pocketed it.

The great time they were having was not the least undermined by the discovery of dried blood on the windshield and seat. They christened it the Deathmobile and shouted plastered theories on how many died and who stole the bodies.

The light of dawn crossed Dorian's face. He sat up, saw Jeff back beside him and tenderly nudged him. "The way things were going last night, I'm kind of glad you ended up here."

"Esther told me us nuts have to stick together."

"Figures. Quite a night.. But the day's going to be even better."

Karin awoke to find herself alone. Had Ethan already made his decision? She felt relieved, then depressed, and finally convinced herself it was nothing. For about five seconds. Then she got up; moving quickly was the only way to fight off a wave of heart-wrenching pain.

Fleeing her suffocating room for the pleasant aroma just outside the house, she sensed something odd about the sheets and towels on the clothesline. One had been pulled down except for a corner that stuck to its clothespin. Beneath the shield of whites and blues, Ethan lay sleeping. Karin unclipped the sheet so it fell over his face. When he didn't budge, she undid more clothespins. Only when he had come to resemble a pile of fresh laundry did Ethan begin to stir.

"Felt like camping out, huh?" Karin laughed at Ethan's wrestling out from under the linen. "It's as good a hiding place as any."

"Hiding . . . oh shit." Ethan had mercifully blanked out on his dilemma for a few hours.

"But listen—Esther will find you soon enough and put you back to work."

"I don't mind ... whatever she makes me do." And he instinctively began re-hanging the laundry.

"I figured things out last night," said Karin, playfully fixing his hair.

"You did?"

"You know how your car was stolen right before those cops were killed?"

Ethan stuck his face in a flapping towel in case his expression showed too much alarm.

"Well, that makes two weird things in a row. And they say things come in threes.

First I just happened to be at the hotel. If Eddie hadn't lost something we'd never have met. Then comes that newspaper about the big crash on the Missing Link. And now I know what the third thing's going to be."

"Um . . . yeah. That's two strange things all right."

"And now... the population of Charlestown is about to go down by one."

She found his face amidst the terry cloth and kissed him on the lips. Ethan was encouraged to throw his arms around her. They held each other in the entanglement of bath and bedclothes waving like celebratory banners in the light of the new day.

The cloudless sky continued to emerge as Dorian and Jeff hiked down to the river. The young painter had herded his new friend out of bed and down the escape ladder early enough to evade Esther's wakeup howl.

"Dorian! Breakfast is on! Don't waste the best hours of the day." Her mind was full of lists, more things than a lifetime could achieve, let alone one morning's energetic surge.

But the boys were even out of range of Dorian's extrasensory contact with his mother. Still, Jeff was panicky.

"Ethan's going to be mad I went out."

"No business of his," Dorian shrugged. "It's another perfect day in Charlestown!

Look up that way."

He pointed Jeff at the Connecticut's northern course. A thick mist over the trees made for a spooky effect Dorian loved. He couldn't yet perceive the depths of discomfort that eerie weather patterns produced in his unstable companion.

The trees are being strangled! Dorian doesn't see the poison in the mist. Doesn't he notice how there are fewer leaves than last year? One of these days winter's going to kill everything permanently. Spring is so much shorter than it used to be. Everyone runs around fucking everybody else for like two weeks, and they don't care that the birds and the bees are lying sick on the ground. Maybe one more year, maybe two. Charlestown may last slightly longer. But all the wild places of the world are doomed. The plague of the future will strangle it from the roots on up, drain the sky of all color. Dorian's eyes are so happy. I won't tell him yet.

"So many beautiful things left to paint here. Karin's crazy to want to leave."

"Where would she go?"

"Ask your mad brother."

Jeff was delighted that someone was calling Ethan nuts for a change.

"He's so cute too. Is he completely straight?"

"I think so. We don't talk about it much. But we tend to look in opposite directions most of the time."

"Oh well, dream on. One out of two ain't bad."

Dorian put his arm around Jeff as they strolled along the river bank.

"Caravaggio was gay. So was Leonardo. Raphael was straight as a board, but he's my favorite. So it just goes to show you can't dismiss straight guys as insensitive.

Just the ones at my school. By the way, what artists do you like?"

So many names and images crammed Jeff's brain he froze up. *What if I name someone he hates?* Jeff found a good answer in spite of his doubt. His arm shot out and pointed at Dorian. Dorian was tickled at Jeff's attempt to butter him up. It made him want to take off his clothes.

Jeff was startled. *We've been at it all night. He's awfully horny.* But Dorian was only stripping for a swim. In an instant he was splashing around in the river, beckoning Jeff to join him. "Come on in! It's not deep here!"

The depth of the water was not the problem for Jeff. And he could swim just fine, although he'd only learned at the age of twelve after a prolonged fear of water that had even made baths an ordeal. No, the immediate obstacle to swimming with his new favorite person was the simple fact that everything had been transformed into breakable glass. Jeff dared not move or the entire landscape could shatter. In a way it was beautiful, like a huge pane of stained glass. The trees were cut out in jigsaw shapes of ten shades of green. The sky was etched in blue deepening to purple the higher he looked. The river was done in blues and grays with the merest highlights to give the impression of flowing. But it was the amber and sienna of hills across the waterway in Vermont that proved Jeff's insight that the world had turned to glass. Nothing real was done in such alluring colors.

Dorian is splashing and jumping. Why isn't the whole thing getting smashed to bits? Dorian was unusually nimble and graceful. It had showed in the way he scaled the ladder and tap-danced through the disaster area that was his home. Even on the short walk to the river Jeff's ankles had given out for no apparent reason and he'd stubbed his toe against an aboveground root. *Sure, Dorian can swim through a world of glass. But if I try, it's bound to shatter.*

Jeff's head felt as heavy as if it too were made of solid glass, a shimmering crystal ball condemned to foresee the future. And then it changed into a bowling ball, beyond that into a medicine ball, eventually becoming heavy as a brilliant ball of a star that had imploded and become the densest matter in the universe. Jeff's head was so burdensome it was remarkable he could hold it upright. Only the beauty of Dorian swimming a perilous course through the glassy river made it worth the trouble to keep it balanced on his neck.

The "stained glass" Charlestown burst into a million shards as another human being intruded on the boys' Eden. It was only a park ranger patrolling the river campground in search of stray trash, but to Jeff it may as well have been a brigade of warriors thundering onto the scene. The sound of a bottle hitting the bottom of a trash can had the deafening force to send Jeff scurrying for cover behind a wide oak. Amazingly, in the wake of all that carnage, the newcomer and Dorian were able to carry on a conversation.

"Hey, Dorian! How's the water?"

"Just fine! What are you doing out so early?"

"Nobody in town appreciates how I'm down here every day at the crack of dawn to make sure it's cleaned up." The park ranger was right at the edge of the river, enjoying Dorian's butt bobbing out of the water. "I'd love to join you, but there's all this work."

Dorian thought, yeah right, so get going and get on with it. He was impressed with how fast Jeff had hidden. He'd explain this guy later. First experiences—there's no getting rid of them.

"Where you been keeping yourself?"

"Painting!" and Dorian dove deep, hoping the ranger was gone when he came back up.

"Should get out more often," suggested the ranger, perhaps to the fish. "I'd like to see you sometime!" He marveled at Dorian's lung capacity and walked away. A temporary defeat. Charlestown nights were long and dull. Dorian would be back. In the meantime there looked to be fresh prey behind a tree.

"Hello there! Always nice to meet a budding explorer." The park ranger had his man. How dare Dorian keep such a find a secret? He stuck his sunburnt face over a limb into Jeff's safety zone.

"You'll be interested to know you picked a Quercus rubera to hide behind. And that little creature down there is a herbivorous Marmota monax." He loved impressing attractive youngsters with his knowledge of the local flora and fauna. But Latin was unlikely to smooth communication with this particular newcomer. "Our whole valley is a symbiotical system where every creature feeds and thrives off each other."

"So that's why people chew me up and spit me out?"

"Ha-ha! Never thought of it that way. I'm Fred Simms, Chief Park Ranger. See this stick? Carved it myself from genuine Juniperus Ashei." He rotated his walking stick like every angle offered a thrill to the trained eye. Clearly Jeff was not a country lad. "Listen, you can go on in too. Swimming hours don't start till eight, but I'm kind of loose with Dorian. What's your name?"

He hasn't answered my question, I won't answer his. "It's a—it's another perfect day in Charlestown."

"Yeah? Perfect? Guess it looks like we're off to a good start.

Early summer's deceptive though. Can still snap down to freezing at night."

Jeff shivered at the mere mention. Ranger Simms noted the response, taking it as approval to gab on.

"You know, I always say those who get hooked on one time of year are never quite at peace with themselves as those who appreciate the beauty of each passing season."

"You didn't make that up."

"God damn, a smart one! I pick up lots of snazzy quotes so I can explain things to tourists. The Greeks, Dante, Neil Diamond, anyone's fair game. 'Gimme a crisp October day in New England—and a warm puppy! If you get simple beauty and nothing else, well, you get about the best thing God invents. Folks, an early snow surprised us in our autumn paradise. Like a country gate that's always open, welcoming all who wander by, our hearts are open to the faith that calms and stills.'"

Fred swung open an imaginary gate and crossed into Jeff's private space. Closer, closer—his uniform was the excuse for innumerable intimacies in the open air.

"Yessir, always open, always open! Our hearts like country gates . . . "

"I'll take the warm puppy. You can shove the rest up your ass."

Jeff ran down to the river and jumped in, fully clothed. Fred muttered in disbelief at how close he'd gotten only to be brushed off. There had been an astonishing stillness to Jeff, fooling the ranger into presuming an easy conquest. The sudden Olympic dash into the Connecticut left the forester at a loss for everything except words.

"Why, that cagey little creature. I bet him and Dorian set me up. Look at them go." He watched the two guys in the river with a sleazy grin. His only regret was that Jeff hadn't stuck around for a more detailed description of his stick.

"Take care, smarty pants." He gave a backward wave as if he could outdo Dorian at the casual game and headed up the hill.

Dorian knew well enough to give him a good ten minutes to ensure he wouldn't be back. By that time Jeff was thoroughly saturated. Water therapy had not yet occurred to him or his keepers back at the hospital. It was his first swim in nearly two years.

Out of the river Dorian stayed naked, letting the sun do its slow job on his pleasantly exposed skin. Jeff's drenched clothes stuck to his body and the pair would have made a curious study to the birds had any of them been as prurient as the park ranger. "So your hunky Harvard brother is a liar," said Dorian.

"What's real and what's not! What's real and what's not!" Jeff blurted out any phrase he'd recently heard in response to a situation or remark that caused anxiety.

Dorian was getting used to Jeff's non-sequiturs and would not be easily driven off track. "Can't you remember the car being stolen?"

"I'm still back in the hospital staring at my wall."

"What more could I do to convince you you're not?" With most other guys, Dorian would have slid his moist hand onto the available crotch, but something about Jeff told him to exercise restraint. For the moment.

"I've always been this way. Ethan will tell you, he can tell you everything, cause we're only three years apart and he watched me growing up all the time I was watching myself growing up and—and—."

"Karin's sure crazy about him. But you should see the guys she's had to deal with. The collective IQ of this town is nothing to brag about."

"If Ethan's so smart, how did we get in this mess?"

"Mess? I thought I was your favorite artist, all that."

"I'm worried about the future." It was as succinct an admission as Jeff was likely to make about his terror before the fractured personalities loitering in his brain.

"Everyone from the city worries about the future! When's the world going to wake up and see the spectacular beauty of infinity?"

That's a solution? Give me the future over infinity any day. And when's he going to get dressed? I can't control myself forever.

Dorian jumped up and pulled on his pants, timing the tease better than he knew.

Jeff got back on his feet, but Dorian made shifty foot moves so he'd fall again. "Ha! I learned that from a soccer player I once dated."

"I'm not bad at sports, unless it's for competition."

"Yeah, always having to win, that kind of stinks, but once you really get to know soccer players, you start to see the appeal."

"There was more than one soccer player?"

"I'm really not trying to make you jealous. But Charlestown can be heaven."

And he tackled Jeff as a prelude to exaggerating past contacts with football players.

CHAPTER 15

None of it would have fazed Esther who assumed Dorian had inherited her sense of teasing, that vital weapon she frequently wielded to offset Eddie's ever-wandering eye. And she was certainly wise to Ethan's game plan with Karin. Thinking of all the potential hanky-panky in her house, Esther determined to channel all that randy energy. No matter that Dorian had slipped Jeff away; Ethan was a handful by himself. So down into the backyard hole with him and make sure he stays there all morning long.

"Do it real deep," she instructed. Ethan was already digging with enthusiasm.

A convertible drove by. Ethan practically buried himself in the soil. When he looked up at Esther he was all but unrecognizable.

"You're getting the idea. A little dirt never hurt anyone. So it stands to reason that a lot of dirt can actually do some good. My grandmother's second husband used to take baths in a tub full of worms. Maybe that's pushing it. The point is—hygiene isn't everything. Keep digging. I've got to figure out what to do with your brother when he turns up."

"I know exactly what to do with him," grumbled Ethan. *Just take off, leave me to do all the work, as usual. I don't know, just cause someone's diagnosed insane they get a free ride. Esther's right. A long hard day's work would do Jeff the world of good. If Mom and Dad hadn't pampered him, giving in to every ridiculous mood, he might have been forced to knuckle down.* "We couldn't afford to take the chance he might get all moody and try to shoot the President or someone." *Come off it, Mom. If only Jeff were that disciplined. I'm happy he and Dorian hit it off, but Christ, guys, stick around and do your share.*

Ethan came to a stubborn stone and tried to uproot it from all sides. He became something of an artist himself, scraping away the dirt and noticing the changing patterns across the face of the rock. It gave him a bizarre little thrill he didn't understand. After all, it was an obstacle hindering his work. Why be so enthralled with swirling globs of earth sticking to a stone? *Oh God, I've having flashbacks! The damn stuff hasn't worn off yet! Jeff has no right to desert me after leaving me that little surprise in my coke. Oh, I'll see things the way he does all right. Geysers of dirt and everyone's face looking like something out of Mardi Gras , no masks needed. What fun! Everyone should be insane for a day. Whoooa . . .*

Ethan lost his balance and ended up sitting on the immovable rock. He was so woozy it had to be from the unknown medication. Then again he hadn't gotten much of a night's sleep. And maybe there were strange chemical fertilizers he was unwittingly inhaling. *Bath of worms, here I come.*

Esther was running water in the kitchen. When she forgot what for, she looked out the window and was pleased with Ethan's progress. "He's already so deep I can just see the top of his head. Well, one good worker anyhow." Then back to the sink to stare at the water and wonder whether she wanted it good and cold or nice and hot. Either way she'd have a long wait.

Karin was grateful for the time alone with Eddie, to get in a good dose of physical therapy and offer encouragement before Esther got back in the mood to hurl abuse. Having cleared a decent amount of space, Karin was able to walk Eddie in a circle without tripping over anything. Perhaps it was one more losing battle and Eddie would go the way of her last five patients, but this time she would be defeated by Nature and not a spiteful spouse.

"Oh, honey, it hurts!"

"You're doing fine, Eddie. Just once more around and we can sit."

"I can—I can't—I—I—I, ooh—"

"There you go—one foot , then the other. Left, right, left—each step is a plus."

"You—you think so?"

"Sure. Isn't it obvious?"

Not to Eddie who stared longingly at his chair, praying for this session to end. He'd never move again the way he used to, so what was the point of this half-assed creeping along? Sitting was still something he could do in fine form, so let's cultivate that. He wished he could say 'cultivate' to Karin. Impress the hell out of her. But less than half the word would get out, she'd start the guessing game, and they'd go down a road of hopeless miscommunication. There were better ways to pass the time. Today's paper would soon be on his lap and he'd cut and slice, sprucing up his board with fresh news of death and decline. That board contained everything he wished to say to the world. Besides a thing or two to Dorian.

Karin glanced out at Ethan's head barely popping up from the hole. He certainly wasn't digging and whatever he was doing was caking on layers of crud that would take hours to scrape off him till she got down to the skin, his lovely skin. She couldn't remember when she'd last looked forward so much to that late afternoon time when Eddie slept and Esther miraculously disappeared. Normally she had to rest too. Some rest—stare at the ceiling, dwelling on her sadsack life and kicking herself for not moving on. Today at least there was this guy to bathe. And he'd pull her into the tub on top of him and her breasts would press against his handsome face . . .

"Ow!" Eddie had taken a sudden left turn and hurt his hip. Karin massaged the side and offered words of comfort while her mind was still in the bathtub with Ethan, rolling around so naked, covered only with Camay.

Ethan was climbing out of the hole as if to inhabit her fantasies, but it was too soon. He'd clean himself off and she'd miss out. Karin had Eddie back in the chair in seconds. He didn't mind at all. It gave him one more thing to love about Karin. She was merciful about cutting short the physical therapy if he begged her enough.

"Give me—give me—" The word 'cultivate' was still trying to come out, and Eddie's hand was reaching in the opposite direction, but Karin knew to hand him the bulletin board and any piece of the day-old paper. Better to turn Eddie loose with a pair of scissors on that stupid headline about dead cops and car crashes than leave it lying around for them all to dwell upon. Nothing to be done about it, and nothing to do with anyone she knew.

"Ethan, not in there!" Karin tried to stop him but Ethan was rapidly drawn past her by the sound of running water. She'd have to train him in the art of avoiding Esther.

When she peeked around the corner, she was happily confused to see Ethan by himself at the sink, making use of the conveniently running tap.

"You're lucky. You just missed Esther."

"She doesn't bother me."

"Get in the tub, you're getting mud everywhere."

"I've got the whole day ahead of me. No point getting totally clean."

"No?"

"Just got dirt in my eyes. Tell Esther the hole's done unless we can scoop out solid rock."

"Oh yeah, Dorian told me about that rock. Now Esther will have you fill in the hole and dig someplace else."

"Oh, no, no, no. I am going to make something of that hole."

"If it kills you."

"If it kills me, then you can fill it back in and we'll have accomplished something together."

"You're not what Esther wants in the hole."

"I'll tell you who I'm ready to put in it. Where the hell did Jeff go with Dorian?"

"How should I know? You expect him to stay cooped up with Esther and Eddie? He's not the one who's strange."

"I think I get through to him and he pulls this stunt."

"Just rinse out your eyes and we'll go look for them." Karin was already helping Ethan clean his hands. It paled beside her imaginings of what she'd hoped to be rubbing, but their interlocking fingers felt pretty nice. "Esther might even buy it as an excuse to go out."

"No way. We wait right here till they come back."

"How come?"

Ethan ducked his head under the water so he wouldn't have to answer. Karin wiped her hands and goosed him from behind. He knocked his head on the nozzle, water sprayed everywhere and she spanked him. "Hey, come on, I'm trying to—ow!"

Wiping water and dirt off him with towels and rags, she whispered, "Let's leave town."

The rubdown felt good, but Ethan was getting annoyed with Karin's hyperness.

"We'd better way a few more days."

"But your parents must think you're dead!"

"Great—when they find out we're not, they won't mind about the car being wrecked."

"Your parents are not so weird they'd trade a Jaguar for a dead son."

"Probably not, but the very fact that I'm worried about that proves that I shouldn't make a decision till my head is absolutely clear."

"If you're innocent, that doesn't matter. Who would blame you? Mugged, beaten up, left on the road, your schizophrenic brother out of control. Look, I know you're embarrassed and—and—ashamed. You fucked up really bad. But Jeff can go back to the hospital, the car's probably insured—"

"Too much time has passed! I haven't come forward and it's gonna look terrible.

If I had gone straight to the cops—"

"Yeah, we know what you should've done. But you were doped up and trapped here."

"Right, right, that's my best hope. Or the best thing for Jeff anyhow. Non compos mentis, ha, pre-law comes in handy."

"I can say I found you conked out by the side of the road and brought you back here. Even once you came around, maybe you had kind of amnesia."

" I did. In a way, I still do."

"No, now that you remember everything, you have to come forward or go backward or whatever you would have called it in pre-law. I thought you were in pre-med."

"You name it, I've been in pre-whatever. I intend to sample everything before making the fatal choice."

"Uh, the fatal part has already happened. I think your best bet is to go right home and get help from your family. I'll even drive you there."

"What? No, I have to fix things up before bringing them into this. If Jeff ends up back in that horrible place I'll never forgive myself."

"What does this have to do with protecting Jeff?"

Ethan was getting confused about how much he'd worked out with Jeff versus what exactly he'd confided to Karin in the midst of last night's serial passion. He knew damn well that Jeff's guilt for what really caused the accident was something that would certainly seem to prove the need to send him back to an asylum for good. But if Karin was to be brought no further than the story of hitchhiking thugs, then why indeed continue to hide out, for his sake or Jeff's? He just knew he was not ready to face police and put the best face on malleable events. Time and amnesia were the best course. Emerge in a week or two and be baffled as everyone else what happened to the car and those crooks. And that's what he chose to tell Karin. He added that it wasn't fair to Esther for him to run off after agreeing to help her and pay off the damage.

"Listen, you could stay here five years and not work off that stupid window."

"Yeah, maybe we could," he said, blaming everything on the vestige of pills in his bloodstream. His hands and face were no longer a mess and he just wanted to kiss her. So he did. She smooched back and may have been derailed if Ethan hadn't whispered, "I've always been curious about real country living."

He considered that a nicely erotic thing to say, but she pulled back and said with surprising disgust, "Please don't be another guy going nowhere."

She impulsively went back to the living room. Ethan caught up with her and tried to ease things with a hug.

"Not in front of Eddie," and she freed herself again.

"Hey, I've seen so many idiots going places, 'nowhere' starts to look appealing."

"Then it will appeal to you alone." She went out the front, pushing the screen door so it would slam extra loud. The scissors flew out of Eddie's hand like he'd heard a gunshot. Ethan gave them back and was rewarded with a close-up of the headline that had nothing to do with him: TWO POLICE FOUND DEAD ON MISSING LINK.

"Th-thanks," said Eddie getting back to work. *Christ, it's all he has. What a jerk I was to yell at him.* Ethan caught himself feeling more remorse for Eddie than about the people that had chased him to their deaths.

"You—you—going to th-th-war?"

The question made Ethan wonder what had happened to Esther, not the conflict in Southeast Asia which he'd heartily protested even after he drew a lottery number that safeguarded him from the draft.

Esther had obeyed a sudden impulse to attempt a sneak invasion on Dorian's room. She'd forgotten the fridge on the stairs and her plot was aborted early. Then she remembered the running water and cursed her haphazard consciousness. Noticing a convenient soft object, she cozied up to the refrigerator and soon found sleep. After all, she'd spent the previous night roaming the house, getting no peace. Water ran, Dorian slipped away, the new boys robbed her blind, Eddie enjoyed a bit of lascivious therapy with Karin, and Esther could give a damn. A few minutes of blessed blackout.

Karin refilled Eddie's prescription and prowled the drugstore. She flipped through magazines from glamour to trash, Vogue, Tattler, U.S. News and World—Flash! Playgirl has made it to Charlestown! A cocky redhead languishing behind the steering wheel wore nothing but a seatbelt. What had Ethan said? "Whenever I'm tailed I pull over." "Oh, you get tailed often?" should have been her response, if she hadn't been wanting to lick what was under that seatbelt. Karin was getting too turned on so she wisely closed Playgirl and dwelled on the most downbeat headlines of the tabloids. The lives of the grotesque and hopeless held her attention only slightly longer than the movie stars and studs. She rejected the entire wall of newsprint and glossies and returned to the street. Ah, the torpor of Main Street, already heating up to maximum mugginess. The occasional swoosh of cars played off the silent houses, their proud wealth and stability facing away from the squalor of Charlestown's back streets. No matter how bored she became, Karin found something soothing in the easygoing repetition of the life here. So what if she escaped to the world being exaggerated by all these magazines? The people out there were no less crazy, no less desperate than the Osbornes or the other families she'd nursed through their ups and downs. They just had more distractions along the way. Hell, they probably read things like Yankee magazine and fantasized how lovely it would be to spend their days in eternal autumn solace. There was no escape, only the building blocks right in front of her (or piled at her feet, thanks to Eddie). To look to Ethan or any other handsome thing in a car as a way out made her feel foolish. But only for a moment. It struck her that Ethan's flesh was real, that his body could get dirty and bleed, and it contained a mind complex enough to upset her fantasies as often as it fulfilled them. Karin headed home, already thinking of her next beautifully unpredictable encounter with Ethan.

 The police car in front of the hotel bar gave a sharp nudge to her thoughts and she walked faster.

CHAPTER 16

It was time to force Ethan's hand. There was nothing to be afraid of. She went in the side door, hoping to catch him off guard, but it was Esther who surprised her, waking from her stairway nap with a loud snort.

"There you are! Go get those guys and tell 'em to finish moving this damn thing out of the way."

"I just got Eddie's meds. I don't know where Ethan is."

From her vantage point, she could see him kneeling next to Eddie. He was getting the hang of real country living all right, helping her patient figure out which way was up on the want ads page. The newspaper won the struggle, Eddie noisily pushed it away and returned to mute admiration of his world tragedy callboard.

"Shum people have it worse than me, yessir."

As if she'd been dreaming about the headline Eddie was staring at Esther said, "Them cops, it's a damn shame, awful for their families and all, but you gotta put it in perspective."

"Perspective, Esther?" Karin anxiously balanced the Osbornes and Ethan, anticipating the worst.

"Yeah, look. The whole planet's crawling with too many damn people. Every tragedy's kind of a plus."

"Well then, I've definitely done my share. Lots of pluses wherever I go."

"Aw, Karin, you'll get the hang of this nursing thing. Most of 'em all you can do is make them comfy on their way to the boneyard."

Eddie heard that. "Blah, blah, blah. Motormouth keeps going

all day long, blah, blah, blah, put a sock in her in her m-m-m-m—"

"Karin, come here. Eddie's getting kind of—you know—." Ethan's plea was intercepted by Esther, already on her feet and careening toward him.

"So you finished up the hole, huh? Good, cause there's plenty to do indoors. That fridge is becoming a pain in my butt."

"Esther, maybe it's best to leave it there so we can focus on clearing out the first floor without moving everything to the second floor for a change." Karin wanted Ethan to see she was trying to help. Vain attempt, and Esther deeply resented the implication of a flaw in her cleanup routine.

"I know why you want it to stay. Big fat fridge is better than a locked door. Somebody can hide up there all day doing God knows what."

"Dorian needs a little privacy."

"I'm not talking about Dorie, I'm talking about a certain loose girl who I just might let go so she can be completely loose. In the streets!"

Ethan came to Karin's defense. "Esther, I'm happy to help. Karin just means I won't be much good if I get a hernia moving that thing by myself."

"I'm not putting up with an employee revolt! I don't know what kind of weird ideas you're putting in her head. Or Eddie's!" She pushed past Ethan to make sure Eddie was as defenseless as ever. Ethan immediately took Karin by the arm.

"We have to talk."

"Up to the guest bedroom then."

"No! I mean talk."

"We can talk lying down."

"We can stand on our heads, but I have to figure this thing out."

"Oh, I figured everything out coming back from the drugstore."

Ethan glanced at Esther and Eddie to make sure they wouldn't hear whatever Karin was about to say.

"Who took my-my-my chigarettes?"

"You can't smoke! Doctor's orders." Esther lit up.

"Give 'em back!"

Esther puffed smoke rings down the hall toward Ethan and Karin.

"It's bad enough you eat those five-egg breakfasts! They'll kill you if these don't."

"I'll shtuff 'em down your throat!"

Eddie sprang from his chair with astonishing strength. Scared at what could happen, Karin coaxed Ethan, "You grab him, I'll get her!"

Esther escaped Eddie's first lunge and connected with Ethan. "Get me that pickaxe from the front yard! I ain't facing him unarmed!"

Her mania was irresistible; Ethan went flying out onto the porch where he spotted the axe across the lawn. Karin yelled, "No, no, no, you two! Ethan, don't you dare!" But Ethan realized he'd better grab the pickaxe if only to stop Esther from getting her hands on it. Then he saw the police car crossing the train tracks down by the hotel. He was back inside as if a giant hand had swept him off the porch.

"Help me!" Esther was crying even as she smacked Eddie who had managed to seize her from behind.

"Pull them apart!" screamed Karin, grabbing at Esther.

"I ain't doing nothing! Get him off me or I'll turn you out in the street!"

"With my back pay? Gladly!" and Karin left the prying and pulling to Ethan while she moved anything breakable from their path. Ethan shoved Eddie back in the chair and Esther went down on his lap. Ethan flung himself up the stairs and went headlong over the refrigerator. "Karin! Get up here!"

"I can't leave them!"

Eddie's and Esther's flailing arms were impossible for her to stop alone. She ran after Ethan to get him back. "Ethan! They're killing each other! Where are you going?"

"Karin, the cops are right outside! You have to hide me. I'm not ready!"

"Ready for what? Oh—oh, go in my room then! Everyone's gone to hell! I quit!"

Esther actually heard her. "Hear that Eddie! Your girl friend quit you! It's just me and you again and I ain't taking your shit!"

"Bashtard, woman, you thing! You thing! K—Kar-Kar-"

Later she would hate herself for seeming to desert Eddie, but Karin was lured up to the second floor by Ethan. His problem at least struck her as solvable.

Two cops knocked hard and the screen door opened by itself. Seeing Esther wielding a pair of scissors and Eddie about to bash her with his board, they immediately restrained the wild pair. Eddie sputtered his gratitude.

"Thank God you're here! Jush the two of you? How you gonna ho-hold her down?"

"Well, it's about time!" Esther let the scissors drop. "He's all yours, boys."

The cop who'd squeezed the scissors from her grip looked from her eyes to Eddie's. "I, uh, hate to disappoint you, folks, but we're not here for either of you."

"Come on! Lock 'er up!" Eddie wailed as Esther said the same thing about him.

The cops held them till they quieted down. The one holding Eddie told them his name was Officer Sokol and, "we're looking for two fellas, late teens, early twenties. We think they caused a bad crash over on Missing Link Road."

"Yeah," said the other one who identified himself as Officer Orcan. "They told us at the hotel they came here with a young woman who works for you."

"Ain't no young woman works here anymore! I gave her the sack!" Esther shot back without a moment to think.

"What, you mean she never came back here?"

Esther paused to catch her breath. Her normal instinct was to dislike cops and not tell them anything. Her uncle was a cop and he had done nasty things to her when she was a little girl. Ever since then she felt discomfort in the presence of police, if not outright revulsion. But cagey friendliness was the best defense. "You guys like a beer?"

"No, ma'am, and if you don't mind, we'll have a quick look around."

"O.K., but be careful. I just cleaned."

"P-put a gag in her mouth and shend her up the river. Ha-ha-ha, bon voyage, Eshter shweetie!"

Sokol was impatient. "I'll check the back. You go upstairs."

Esther and Eddie were deposited at opposite sides of the room. Eddie was too exhausted to stalk his wife, and she was happy to make a good impression on the cops. It would come in handy in the future if she had to press charges. They were witnesses that she was a battered wife despite appearances that he was a helpless husband. She looked for another cigarette to smoke, hoping her first one had gone out and would not burn down the house. Eddie's glasses had fogged up so he couldn't see Esther if he'd wanted to. How could she embarrass them both in front of the police? He'd never believed Esther's tale of child abuse and maintained a considerably more favorable attitude toward men in uniform.

Orcan took barely a minute to make it up the obstacle course. That old couple of kooks made a refrigerator on the stairs no sweat. The doorway to Karin's bedroom was wide open and he went in. He was prepared for the wild disarray, but saw no immediate need to dig through what looked like a mountain of clothes that covered the bed and everything for three feet around. If someone was lying in wait for him, Orcan would make himself a sitting duck getting bogged down in that mess. Down the hall, he found the door to the bathroom locked and knew he'd made the right decision.

"Hello in there! Could you come on out now please?"

Karin's voice came out peevish but sexy. "You want to give a girl the chance to finish what she started?"

"Excuse me, ma'am—police. We got some questions for you." He could hear suspicious sounds of things getting knocked around. He broke down the door. It was so old and rotting it caved in with one kick.

Karin was wearing nothing but a ragged purple towel. She screamed and threw a roll of toilet paper at him. Orcan flushed with embarrassment and hid his eyes. Karen let loose a tirade.

"That uniform gives you license to be a Peeping Tom? I'm calling your boss! I'll sue the whole damn department! Esther, watch out! There's a rapist in the house dressed like a cop!"

To prove her wrong, Orcan rushed back down the hall to the landing above the stairs. "Sorry, sorry, sorry! You can come down when you're ready." His heart was pounding. She was ravishing and if that towel had ridden up about half an inch—.

There were perks to this job, yessir. And hazards. He tripped over a rusty toaster and tumbled down the steps. He dislodged the refrigerator and sent it crashing down.

Sokol had come to the bottom of the stairs when he heard the screaming. The fridge nearly flattened him. He leaped aside and his gun went off. Esther cursed and Eddie went into a shell shocked reverie.

"Look out! Things! Hell! Them things again!"

"You almost killed me!" roared Sokol at Orcan who shot back, "Goddamn place is booby-trapped!"

"You're the only boobs I see! Where's your warrant?" Esther was back in charge. "It's only an old fridge, didn't do nothing! What are you shooting it for?"

"These guys we're after are dangerous. I had to be ready."

"Ready to give Eddie his third heart attack? He fought for his country but I guess that don't rate a little peace in his own home."

"You don't understand. We're after fugitives and they were seen with that woman!" Orcan pointed straight up as Karin appeared in a long shirt at the top of the stairs.

"Don't listen to them, Esther. They're perverts just dressed like cops. Did you get a good look, Mister?"

"I'm sorry, miss," lied Orcan, struck by her pantless attire, "but we heard you met two bloody guys at the hotel and left with them."

"Hey, I thought you said there was no woman here," exclaimed Sokol, trying to stick it to Esther.

"I only just now fired her. She had to dress and pack before getting out."

Esther folded her arms like she was the only person present with a grasp on reality.

Sokol was on a roll. "You fired her cause she brought back some strange men?

Weren't you scared? Especially if your husband had a bad heart. Where are they now? Orcan, you saw everything up there?"

"Not quite," Karin continued her flirting as the best decoy.

"Finish dressing and come on down, Miss. It's a crime to cover for fugitives."

"Fugitives from what? Yeah, I met some guys. They'd been beaten up by hitch-hikers who stole their car." Karin slipped on a shift making no effort to do it in private.

"Hold on, Karin. Let's make 'em describe who they're after." Esther wanted to think the best of her new help.

"We don't know yet. They only just now found the car in the woods. By the time they run a check, we could lose them. There were two of them. Young males. And they drove like maniacs when the officers hailed them."

"Yeah, we saw the headlines. But by that time, I'd patched them up and they were on their way."

"They ran out on me?" Esther fell for Karin's ploy.

"Why did you hire people you don't know?" demanded Sokol.

"They looked nice. Better than most of the types you get going through Charlestown. I had this one boarder called Babyface, the dirtiest thing on two feet. Five screaming shitting brats and still she didn't take precautions—"

"Ma'am, we'd like to hear from the young woman you said you fired."

Karin had come down and looked at both officers with open-faced sincerity.

"I'm a trained nurse. They'd been beaten up. I couldn't leave them bleeding. I did first aid while Esther tried to talk them into working for her. They weren't about to fall for that. I mean, look at this place. The last I saw of them they were planning to hitch out on Route 12."

"Hitch?"

"Yeah. Their car was stolen. I suggested they hitch to Bellows Falls and catch a bus from there to wherever they had to go."

"You didn't find out anything else about them? Just took their story at face value and sent them on their way?" Sokol found it almost as hard as his partner to believe that this vulnerable small-town nurse would make anything up.

"Well, not immediately. They were kind of in a daze and really weak. We let them nap and it sort of turned into all night, but by early morning they took off."

"Wait a second. Didn't I just see one of them run out of here five minutes ago?"

Esther was about to ruin everything, but Karin was ready for that. "Don't listen to her. She's drunk."

"I'm stone sober. Take a whiff." Esther helped prove Karin's story with one puff in Sokol's face.

"Come on, this is pointless," he said to Orcan, opening the side door. "About how long ago since you left them hitching to Bellows Falls?"

"That was at least eight or nine. But the hitching's pretty slow around here. They might have ended up walking all the way."

"Thanks for your help, Miss. Come on, let's radio down to Bellows Falls and check all the connecting bus stations."

"But I don't think they're the ones you're looking for, " insisted Karin.

"We'll get 'em and question 'em ourselves. Thanks! Sorry for the trouble."

Sokol and Orcan were gone almost as abruptly as they'd arrived. Esther reached for Karin as she headed back upstairs. "Hey, Karin, you didn't tell me those boys are criminals."

"They looked nice," Karin echoed Esther's own justification.

"Yeah, like Eddie once looked nice. Now all's I got is a pile of regrets taking up a perfectly good chair." She saw Eddie slowly coming out from hiding his head under both arms, realizing the 'bombing' was over. Fine, those boys were typical drifters, in trouble with the law, but now they were gone. Whatever they'd done they were out of her hair, so now she should make sure Eddie didn't wet his pants during the scare. But wait! Dorian was out of his room and the only thing still keeping her from getting up there was her own troublesome pair of legs. The first flight of stairs hadn't been this clear in months. Dorian was too preoccupied with the new fellow to keep up the usual defenses. All those paintings begging to go up for sale. She started upstairs not thinking that it would be harder to come back down carrying canvases. Then she glimpsed a boy just out the side door. "Georgie!" she hollered to the neighborhood kid. "You want to earn an easy buck?" Georgie, an easily distracted ten-year-old, responded to Esther's offer faster than a hungry pup.

While Karin had been covering for him, Ethan had dug to the bottom of the ton of rummage and bedclothes that Orcan had mercifully sidestepped. The aroma at the bottom of the pile was so insufferable, Ethan didn't have the slightest doubt why his hiding place had worked. His mind, only recently starting to recover from the unknowable overdose, had plenty else to go over.

Nobody will find me in here. It's safe and warm and dark.... What, am I nuts? They'll rip up the place. Damn, they must've spotted Jeff out on the town with Dorian and followed him back here. But it doesn't sound like they have him. All I hear is Esther and Karin. Unless he's back in some kind of catatonia. Fuck, they better not beat him just cause he can't answer their questions. He's so fragile and now this. And what if they didn't find him? He's out there on his own, unprotected. I've got to get away—at least for his sake. If I can still save him, I won't be just another guy going nowhere . . . Karin's going to want an explanation after they're gone. If I'm innocent, why didn't I just talk to the cops, tell them what happened? Why don't I? I could make up a description of what those hitchhikers looked like. Jeff really would be put back in the asylum forever if they figured he was to blame for the crash—which he was. And maybe it would all come out in court as involuntary manslaughter, cause I wasn't responsible for being under the influence, and Jeff definitely wasn't responsible—the insanity defense was never more true than with Jeff—so, where does that put us? I didn't stay in law school long enough to know what the sentence would be for involuntary manslaughter plus my own temporary insanity caused by an accomplice's long-term insanity—what am I even thinking about it for? We are not turning ourselves in! That would be the stupidest move of all. No, those guys, the three fucked-up hitchhikers, they dumped us in the woods, we made our way to the nearest town and met Karin in that hotel bar. Jeff was completely whacked by that time and I was disoriented, maybe a touch of amnesia from hitting my head against a tree. I think that's true—I was out of it for at least one whole day. And then getting sucked into this weird house, Christ it's like falling into a time warp and all the accumulated crap of the last hundred years coming down on our heads—nobody could walk into this house and not acknowledge extenuating circumstances. Esther's out of her gourd, Eddie thrives on obituaries—he shreds the paper every day, we never even saw it! Dorian's probably good for my brother, but it's too much too soon, a country kid's not gonna know what to do when Jeff throws a fit. And Karin, poor Karin, she's had to get used to running this place like a hospital, so when two wounded guys show up, what's she to do besides put them to bed in her hospital? Days and days go by, we wake up and gradually get back into circulation and find out, oh my God—my car's been involved in some disaster! And at that point—at that point I—wait, wait, wait—O.K., it works out that I didn't report my car stolen and in my delirium I told Karin to report it and she told Dorian and he just didn't do it.. And Karin wouldn't let me up out of bed—"you have a concussion, you're going to rest if I have to tie you to that bed!"—so I had to trust her that Dorian absolutely positively reported my car, and I conked out and waited for Karin to tell me I was better. So then when I finally do follow up with the police and ask if my car's been found, they detain me and grill me and I tell them the whole hitchhiker story. They start a big manhunt and—and—they never find them. Cause they don't exist! It's just my word and as time goes by, people will stop believing me because nobody else will ever be found. The hitchhiker story falls apart and it looks like I lied for exactly the reason I am lying—to save Jeff's neck if not my own. Fuck! That's why I can't come out and deal with the cops. Especially not right now when it's on their terms, when they've hunted me down and I haven't gone to them of my own free will. It looks horrible. It's bound to come off as a made-up story. And even though nobody will trust Jeff's account, if it conflicts at all with mine that makes us look bad. He'll get all confused and say—'what hitchhikers?' He might even tell the truth, which screws me and then himself even worse. So the hitchhiker story is out. It bought me time, that's all. I can bring Karin in on the truth. She'll stick by me cause she'll understand why I had to lie at first. She may even like me more cause I'm a decent guy and not an idiot who goes around picking up mangy hitchhikers and getting beat up cause I have zero judgement. She cares about the Osbornes the same way I care about Jeff. She'd lie for them, do anything to keep them from killing each other. Yeah, good, good. But . . . then what? Real country living. We stay here forever? No way will Karin go for that. What am I thinking? Like I would? Just choose to never go home, disappear forever and make the most of the new direction my life's taken? I am nuts, maybe I did bang my head into a tree or those drugs are so powerful they're still screwing up my brain. I can't even slow it down. Just breathe deep and calm down and get logical. Shit, the deeper I breathe the more noise I end up making. Stop breathing! Stop thinking!

Now one thing at a time. Once the cops are gone, then—then I make my plan. The accident was a disaster, sure, but, but—it was also an opportunity. Every bad thing that happens to you can only destroy you if you think like a loser. For instance . . . I'm not a dropout. I'm *taking time to make the right decision. I could be a doctor or a lawyer or a businessman and make lots of money and have a so-called successful life. But thousands of guys in my position end up doing that. They live out their rich, successful lives and they die and so what? What kind of difference did they make in the world and were they even happy for following all the rules? That crash may have saved me from making my decision too soon. Or not making it at all. Every disaster's an opportunity. Every disaster offers an alternative. Well, this is worse than most disasters, but if it was any less enormous I wouldn't be forced to decide anything new. I certainly wouldn't be hiding under a mountain of dirty laundry. If this isn't a unique opportunity I don't know what is. It's a terrible thing to make Mom and Dad worry, have them think we got killed or mysteriously disappeared, but if we show up after a month or two they'll be so thrilled they'll help us out of any jam. Oh, so I'm gonna rely on their money, keep running and hiding and in the end bring on the big bucks and resolve everything. Real new path. Another rich kid gets away with murder. And then out of deep gratitude I'd never want to let them down again. Boy, would I go for the straight and narrow. But that's not the worst of it. Dad will give it to me good. "So, Ethan, you did your best for Jeff and that was pretty lousy. You left him alone in the car so it was your own fault he put pills in your Coke. You betrayed our trust, you made the wrong decision whenever you had the chance. Now perhaps you'll listen to me. Jeff's incurable. You leave him to us. Your only job is to get back into a professional program and stay there until you're the best in your class and ready to make a name for yourself, like I did." No way am I going to listen to that. Like I don't know how bad I fucked up and let everyone down.*

Disaster into opportunity, disaster into opportunity. I can break the mold. I can become whatever I want now. The old Ethan is dead. Maybe I wanted it that way. Maybe I'm actually jealous of Jeff being able to be outrageous and unpredictable and say to the whole world—fuck you, I'm nuts and there's nothing you can do about it. Not that he's happy, not that anyone would want to trade places and be cooped up in a mental hospital . But to not always have to be so perfect, so well-dressed, so popular, so cool and appreciated. There's a million ways to be and a million more combinations and everyone I know is so predictably well-behaved or predictably rebellious. They all think they're so unique and they're such obvious types. I've been given the opportunity to be more. Two people are dead. I'm not saying they were just cops, so no big deal. I should have stopped. But they didn't know I was wired on something, and they should be used to chasing speeders. And they ran off the road. So did we. Jeff and I could be dead, the cops could've survived and everything would be different. Nobody in the world would give a shit if the tables were turned. "The mental case must've caused it. Or the dropout bit off more than he could chew. The family should've known better, but the mother was sick and the father couldn't leave her side. What a pathetic family." Ultimately, nobody cares. We have to make our own way and it's nothing you can decide in a couple of days. So that's it. We disappear for awhile and see what opportunities turn up. One more lucky rich guy going nowhere. In the end that at least won't be my story. Disaster into opportunity. Nobody knows what it's all for. Jeff, the road, everyone sick and dying, everything blowing up . . .

The whole pile was churning, scoops of clothes were lifted from his head and the ordinary world opened up again. Ethan's heart was thundering; all the rational and crazy thoughts equally evaporated in an instant.

"Karin!"

"You can come out now—fugitive."

A pair of panties dangled from Ethan's left ear. He gulped the relatively fresh air and tried to read Karin's expression. Did it contain more love than hate? At least more compassion than resentment? The way her hand touched his lips and received his thankful kiss was a positive sign. The rush of thoughts ballooned out again and he wondered which part of it he should now share. All of it, every shred, came another internal voice. Tell her everything or you're dead.

CHAPTER 17

"I want a bacon burger with cheese. Get yourself whatever you like."

Dorian had just emerged from the woods behind the diner. Thirty seconds sooner and he would have seen the patrol car containing Orcan and Sokol speed down Main Street in the direction of Bellows Falls. Twilight was descending and he would have enjoyed the bright blue spinning lights against the deeper, more mysterious blue creeping over Charlestown. Instead, he beheld a silent boulevard and didn't wait around for any more cars to spoil it. He ducked behind the diner and gave Jeff some money. Jeff didn't move, so Dorian repeated the order.

"I can't go in there alone," pleaded Jeff.

"You have to. Mom has spies everywhere. One of them spots me, gets on the phone to her, and the fun's over."

Jeff weighed the argument. It had been a fun day, extraordinary really. Swimming with Dorian had given him an actual enjoyment of water, a substance he'd lived in terror of through most of his teens. Hiking and exploring what must have been an area a hundred times larger than the grounds of Walpole Manor. The woods around the institution's pristine acres had been too foreboding to venture in alone. But Dorian was more than a trailblazer. By sharing with Jeff his fantastic interpretations in every grove, at each bend in the road—extraterrestrial launch sites, ancient burial rites, this twisting path was the route of Alexander's conquests, that rock a gateway to the underworld home of elemental earth beings—Dorian filled him with an eagerness to endure what could have merely been tangled vines and daunting hills.

And finally the talk, never forced, never making him feel self-conscious, or at least less so than most others made him feel. Even the silences were appealing. That was important because otherwise Jeff would have been overwhelmed by the excess of pleasurable activity. Too much of a good thing could have easily tipped him over the other way. Dorian's blithe acceptance of Jeff's abnormalities (indeed, he reacted to the strangest actions with an equanimity bordering on obliviousness) made it easier for Jeff to participate or withdraw. Yes, this day had contained many things that had not disturbed or tormented Jeff and that was the best way he knew to define 'fun.'

"You did have fun, right?" he heard Dorian say, and he was able to nod, ever so slightly. Jeff looked at the ten dollar bill, wishing it would fly out of his hand.

"Don't make me, Dorian."

"Oh come on, you have to get over this shyness of yours."

"I'm not shy, I'm insane."

"Jeff, it's just takeout!"

"People will stare. They'll think terrible things about me."

"Now listen, people did terrible things to me all through school. If all you get is bad thoughts that's pretty lucky."

Jeff's bad thoughts suddenly threw him into a battle zone in the midst of the Second World War. Vivid pictures he'd internalized from his father's stories of survival at Guadalcanal and Pearl Harbor. A peaceful Sunday morning on the island of Oahu and the soldiers who weren't in church—that being the majority—were sleeping off Saturday night hangovers. Dr. Leblanc was crossing a field, heading into town for some groceries, when he saw planes coming in the distance. Jeff became his father and there is no one who can say he did not feel the oncoming rush of events with as much intensity as if he'd actually been there thirty years ago.

What are our planes doing coming in now? All the ships are back in the harbor. The command was to stand down. No planes should be out. Unless—is it possible they're not ours? Can't make out the insignia. They're—no, it can't be—Japanese! A huge wave of them advancing over the island! The only thing at hand—big canister-guns of insecticide. Perhaps the clouds of spray will at least give us some cover. The green torrents are gushing out into the sky. The planes are turning aside. They're going up, turning back! They must think these are secret weapons—walls of poison gas coming up at them. Keep spraying! Vollies of bug spray for a surprise infestation of Japs. But it won't be long before they realize it has no effect. Some are turning back toward us already. Run! Dive into the foxholes! It gave us time to take cover. Sunday morning and all the ships pulled back into harbor. We're sitting ducks! We're as good as dead!*

As much as Jeff was able to thrust himself into the running figure of his father on the open fields of Pearl Harbor, he could instantly swap identities with his mother, walking in the yard of their bungalow, hearing the planes, getting news of the surprise attack over her garden radio.

Oh my God—Andrew! Out there unprotected, without his gun or his gas mask! He's on the road between here and the store. I have to find him! Have to help him! Who moved my bike? There it is! Gas mask dangling from my belt. Pumping the pedals faster, harder. He has to be on this road, he wouldn't have cut across a field, he better not have! But where? Where! Bombs! They're about to hit! Just look straight ahead, they're not aiming for me! Oooh! I'm down, I'm bruised! I'm under the bike! But Andrew—Andrew could be killed! Soldiers everywhere! "We're confiscating this gas mask, Ma'am. We need it immediately!" "No, it's Andrew's gas mask! He'll suffocate in the poison!" The soldier she didn't know put it on and he was the one who almost suffocated. In her haste, Rachel had grabbed a defunct WWI gas mask. It was not only useless against the fumes—it allowed no air in at all and the soldier was choking, gasping, dying! *What if that had been Andrew? Thank God I didn't find him! But where is he now? More bombs are falling! Blood and bodies everywhere! Corpses all around me in the mud!*

Jeff came back to Charlestown after several nudges from Dorian. "Jeff! Hey!"

Just keep thinking how good that bacon burger's gonna taste."

Next came a hefty shove in the direction of the diner's front door. Jeff still had one leg in Pearl Harbor and the green mist from the insecticide guns obscured Dorian's ducking back into the forest. Jeff was alone. The image of his mother's ill-fated bravery spurred him on. The diner's name in a sharp dash of neon dispelled the last bits of insecticide. "Trolley Stop" shimmered above his head, as clear as the insignia on those enemy planes. Someone left and held the door for him. When Jeff didn't move, the old man shrugged and let go of the handle. Jeff darted through the narrowing space. He had penetrated enemy territory and left no fingerprints! Now for the hard part. Takeout.

Inside the diner all the voices sounded like mumbling and muttering, now low and malevolent, now high-pitched and silly. Improbably, everyone in the place turned and stared at Jeff. The heads at the counter swiveled in a single motion. A burst of laughter was caused by his very presence. It shook him up; he dropped the money and bent to get it back. A passing waitress loomed hugely over him and almost dropped a tray of food on his head. Jeff cringed at the foot of the counter.

The waitress kept walking and the heads were simply eating and talking. Hardly anyone had paid Jeff the slightest notice, but he was already enervated. The will to make an entrance and endure that harsh inspection had sapped his strength. A long rest was warranted before attempting to order anything. A little boy whose feet were swinging near Jeff's head was the first to initiate genuine interaction.

"Hey, Ding Dong, what didja drop?"

"M-m-money."

"Yeah? Gimme a quarter?"

The boy was sweet and Jeff would have happily indulged him if he had change.

"I only have this."

"Wow! Ten dollars. Just for lunch?"

The mother intervened. "Don't bother that person, Sammy. Sorry, mister."

Jeff wanted to tell her he didn't mind, but his throat lumped up. The woman continued to reprimand her kid. "You don't ask strangers for money. You ask me."

"Can I have a quarter, Mommy?"

"Nope!"

Jeff regretted the torrent of emotion he'd caused between mother and son. What if she started beating the boy and he ran away from home? Jeff saw his face in the chrome of the rotating seat and had the disheartening thought that he had personally unleashed all the hostility in the Osborne home. What a happy family they had been before he barged in on them! *No wonder I've been locked up for so long. Eventually I'll be caught and put back where I belong. But till then, I'd better do what Dorian says. At least he'll vouch for me. I did my best while I was loose.*

Slowly standing up, he shut his eyes and pictured Dorian waiting for him behind the diner. He smiled, determined not to let him down. "I'm with Dorian. We're in the woods." The fantasy eased his nerves; it would have mortified him if he knew he'd said it out loud.

"What can I get for you? Hello?"

Jeff opened his eyes. "I'm just—taking a break."

"Boy, I wish I could."

Jeff smiled. His abrupt defense had struck empathy in this good-hearted middle-aged waitress. All she wanted was some time off and all he wanted was to be free from his burdensome task. Instant camaraderie. "You and me both, kiddo. A nice long break. I am sick of this place. Sometimes I'd like to shoot myself."

"I hope you have better luck than I did." Jeff had only picked up a gun once and it jammed when he aimed at a wall and pulled the trigger. Apart from that, an attempted overdose of pills was his only half-assed attempt at suicide. Still, it was a fond memory and he always offered encouragement and guidance to anyone seeking a way out. But was dying truly a way out? Dorian painted death as an ascent, full of surprising encounters. Inadvertently, Jeff again verbalized a thought he meant to hold secret.

"Death is the last great adventure," he told the waitress who started to write 'death' on the top line of her pad.

She scratched it out with a casual, "Come on, sweetie, what's for dinner? Ain't got all night."

The pressure was on. "Uh-uh—wait, I know, I know! I'm supposed to be a whirlwind of decision-making! I know what he wants, but he , but he , but he—"

The waitress looked all around with her big eyes, curious where "he" was.

She realized it wasn't fair to expect an out-of-towner to operate without a menu so she handed him one. That did not speed things along.

"God, so many things! You could spend the rest of your life just sampling the beans, onions, sprouts, six kinds of cheese, your choice of two or three egg omelette, with any of the above, fifty cents per item—"

"Listen, cutie, the place is mobbed, so maybe I'll come back after you finish lip-synching the menu."

"Don't go!" Jeff leaned over the counter and nabbed her shoulder. "Bacon burger with cheese! And the same exact thing for me! Make mine a double! Two to go! And don't be stingy with the bacon. Or the burger! Or the six kinds of cheese!"

Snapped to attention, she scribbled his order. "And to drink? Come on, doll, you have to speak up in this nuthouse."

"This is not a nuthouse," Jeff corrected. "It's a—it's a—a—a kingdom of fine dining. And you're the queen in the sizzling land of grease."

"Yeah?" For an instant she basked in his imagination. It was always a pleasure to have her royal descent revealed. Jeff was not an obvious knight in shining armor, but perhaps he was travelling in disguise. "So do me a favor and free me from the lords of the castle. They're always trying to shove their sticky hands inside my dress."

Jeff was outraged. "How dare they touch you or even look in your golden face which is like the sun, like the sun." The rows of sunnyside eggs sizzling behind her were no doubt to be forged into a crown.

"I'll get you large Cokes, O.K.?" She considered giving them to Jeff free of charge for brightening her day. He insisted she not go just yet.

"If I could have just a month or two, maybe half a year, with no distractions, I could figure things out, then come back and know the perfect right thing to do in every situation. I could have a clear impact."

The waitress put both his roving hands back on the counter top. "Dear, you have had a clear impact already." She went into the kitchen. Jeff chuckled to himself and spun the seat like a roulette wheel that had paid off big and soon would again. The little boy caught the inspiration and started spinning his stool while his mother turned aside to pay the bill. Jeff had blocked out everyone else in the diner while wooing the waitress. To be suddenly reminded of the crowds and thrust into a competition provoked anxiety throughout his body. The seats whirled and the volume of the restaurant cranked up to an overbearing pitch. Faces shoved food in their mouths, chewing and chomping with grotesque slurping. Voices became a cacaphony of "Yep, sure is, yep, know what you mean, nope, can't say," until Jeff's head was whipping around nearly as fast as the seat. When the mother grabbed the boy away with "wait till we get home!" the second seat kept going with a life of its own. Jeff was reminded that what came effortlessly to others was for him a nonstop struggle. He whipped his seat along, but had no illusions it could ever surpass the self-propelling stool next to him. The heavy hand that crushed it to a halt was welcome until he saw whose it was.

"Don't say hello or nothing." Jeff didn't know what to say to the jerk from the park service. It seemed ages ago that he'd eluded him and his big stick and here he was making like an old pal. "Better watch yourself with Dorian. He's trouble." Fred Simms winked and Jeff gave him a nauseous smile that satisfied the man's dirty mind. "I don't know how long you're staying in town, but make sure he brings you over to my house. I'm not going to say Charlestown's a big party town, but you'd have to go to Monte Carlo to find wilder poker games." Another wink and a clicking sound in the back of his throat and Simms was out of there, leaving Jeff's stomach feeling like one more spinning stool. *Party town, cocktails all around, nonstop phony people, card sharks, crap shoots, insiders on a roll, losers tossed out in the gutter, streets full of wildmen, it's safe inside my wall, but if they make me go to Monte Carlo I'll never find my way back . . .*

The only thing that kept Jeff from losing it completely was the hallucinating of Dorian's face in a variety of places around the diner: a licked-clean plate, a glass of water, the clunky old clock on the wall. A better reason to survive the humiliations of a roadside diner was not yet known to Jeff than this: Dorian was outside waiting for him.

The waitress returned with burgers in a bag. It was a gift from a long-vanished friend. He opened the bag and inhaled. Gone was the threatening mob of townspeople, the clang of silverware, the pounding of plates globbed with food. The scent of the cooked sandwiches took Jeff far from anything he feared, back to some rare uncomplicated moment in his life. Other people were not a horror; they wanted nothing from him, and he owed them not a shred of his composure. Everyone, everything around him existed in the purity and simplicity that were denied him almost all of the time. The aroma from the bag set Jeff free for less than five seconds, but in those five seconds he relived long-lost moments of harmony and happiness. As worn down and helpless as he normally felt, those brief flashes held out the hope that he had within him an energy and power that were capable of emerging. Madness was a veil, a dark shroud that lay in heavy folds upon his face and body. Sometimes it was briefly lifted, perhaps by the skillful hands of a unique sympathetic soul, and then it gave him room to breathe, floating as much as an inch from his skin. He could almost see light between the tiny weaves of cloth. There had been many such moments on this strangely wonderful day with Dorian. A few of them came close but could not match the irresistible sensation of freedom contained in the fragrance of those bacon burgers which he had gotten all by himself.

"What is it, Whirlwind? Have they gone bad already?"

She doesn't understand. There is nothing bad in this bag. She is a sweet and generous soul and her kind will one day set free the entire world. And when we're free we won't interfere with each other. The fields inside are vast and we can wander forever without bothering anyone else, and all of them will leave us alone too . . .

"I'm with Dorian. We're back in the woods. In a thick glen of trees. Nobody can see us. We're lost in the Charlestown nobody else knows."

"Me, I always bring a compass when I go in those woods. You can joke, but some people have gotten lost forever. That's seven fifty nine, cutie," and she whispered, "The Cokes are on me."

Jeff handed her the ten and ran out the door shouting to himself. *I did it! I survived the war, just like Mom and Dad! I did it! I did it!* Over and over until the words exploded in Dorian's face. "I did it, Dorian!"

"Yeah, yeah, keep it down. Nothing to it, huh?"

He gave the first burger to Jeff, then hurriedly took a bite of the other.

"Mmm, I love these things. I guess there's no change."

"She deserved a good tip."

"You didn't give her a hard time?"

"No. We kind of . . . hit it off."

"Uh-oh. Did you tell her much?"

"I explained her entire life. I helped her see the diner for what it was."

"That's good. As long as you didn't try to explain who you were."

Dorian savored his burger slowly while Jeff, unable to calm down after such an exciting victory, consumed his in six or seven bites. Dorian wiped the grease from his lips. "Messiest eater I ever saw." Jeff took it as a compliment and hugged Dorian while he tried to keep eating. By the time they finished their picnic at the edge of the woods, twilight was gone. The night was theirs. Jeff knew it couldn't top the day, but for a change he felt no evil forboding that the darkness had come to stay.

Jeff thought of his parents in the war again; it had ended for them and perhaps it would one day end for him. He tried to picture them, not as they were—sick, worried, despondent over his unalterably failed existence—but as they might be had they inhaled the happy aroma of his burger bag.

* * *

For their part, his mother and father could have had no idea what progress their younger son had made, but they knew there was no point in getting hopes up. Ethan would soon be in touch with a full report and in the meantime Dr. Leblanc was superb at diverting his anxious spouse. If his attempts to find the right mix of medications to relieve her agonizing nausea frequently failed, his silly humor always made her giggle in spite of herself. He was impressing her with astonishingly stupid answers to "Jeopardy" when the phone rang.

"I'll take it in the other room. Now pay attention to the game and learn something."

"I know all the answers, darling. I'm just too damn slow to win the money."

The show was no fun with Andrew gone, but Rachel hung in there, calling out wrong answers with enthusiasm. She started to gag and grabbed for a glass of water. Damned if she wasn't going to regain her composure by the time he came back. It was demeaning to acknowledge she only felt well when he was close by.

"No, that seems very unlikely," the doctor was saying in a deliberately lowered voice on the phone. "Well, yes, it is, but . . . actually, it would be better if I came to the station. My wife is very sick and I don't want to upset her."

He hung up, smothering a spontaneous curse. A photo of Ethan and Jeff as little boys was on the table next to the phone. He shook his head at the smiling boys and wondered if he could cover up his dismay while making up an excuse to leave Rachel alone.

"What would upset me?"

"You've got big ears."

"I was coughing and I knocked the phone off the hook."

"So what did you hear?" He turned down the sound of Jeopardy.

"That it was the police. I hope you're not giving more money to their silly functions."

"Stupid traffic tickets," he said with perfect annoyance as he put on his shoes.

"I could've sworn I paid them."

Mrs. Leblanc almost dropped her water glass. "Have they booted your car? Oh my God!"

He leaned back and kissed her, wondering how mild his excuse would have to have been to not incite an anxiety attack in his amazingly sensitive wife. "Do you really have to go there right now?" her voice cracked.

"Well, like you say, I don't want to wake up with a big yellow boot. If I end up being more than an hour, I'll call."

"Why should you be an hour? Write them the damn check and leave."

"Oh clerks, bureaucracy. When is it ever easy?" He prayed he'd be able to spare her any semblance of the truth. Not ever easy to get the details of your son's car crashed and totaled, the boys vanished, and two police dead from the chase. It was hard enough to keep it to himself. That news would jeopardize his wife's uncertain progress. If it didn't kill her.

CHAPTER 18

The hands shifting the ladder to a slightly better angle outside Dorian's window did not show the expert facility of a regular user. Karin had never felt the need to leave the house any less than proudly, defiantly, angrily by the front door. Esther could yell and threaten, Eddie could howl with real or pretended agony—Karin always came and went exactly as she pleased. She did not agree with Dorian's constant subterfuge. Avoiding and deceiving his mother would have become unnecessary if he simply confronted Esther and had things out. Of course, Karin had not grown up in a place where combat was the daily business; Dorian had learned avoidance was the best policy. To fight with Esther, to explain himself to Eddie wasted energy he wanted to put into painting. His inspiration for the most part lay outside the house, in the woods, fields, hills and secret places of his unique town. It was important to have a direct pipeline between the wellspring that was Charlestown and his safe haven of oils, acrylics and other mediums of beauty. The ladder was that pipeline.

And now Karin had reason to follow Dorian's example, leaving the house so the Osbornes wouldn't know about it. Eddie and Esther were remarkably sharing the living room. Esther watched a religious television show and Eddie alternated between admiration of the day's additions to his bulletin board and musing over photos in a book about World War II. He blocked out the obnoxious preacher's voice and the wail of choir singing; she tolerated his steady humming and coughing. That was their way of forgiving each other for the day's indignities without having to talk things over. It was the perfect time to sneak Ethan up to the third floor and away. Karin knew Esther had actually climbed the stairs to rummage through Dorian's room, but since the lights were out she couldn't really tell what damage had been done. Dorian had a lot of paintings ; even with Georgie's help, Esther had not been able to take more than a third of them. The urgency of enacting her own creative plans kept Karin from making incriminating observations. Get Ethan out of the house and help him so he could help her change the likely outcome of her life—that was plenty preoccupation for the evening at hand.

She went down the ladder first and steadied it at the bottom so Ethan could follow. He was carrying her small suitcase and had to come down a bit slower. Karin had convinced herself the suitcase did not mean she was running away. Even if this turned into a one or two night escapade, a change of clothes and her favorite books would be welcome. Indeed, she had several volumes' worth of contingency plans. Her mind worked in overlapping layers, uniting contradictions in ways that would baffle most people, certainly Ethan once he got to know her better. For Ethan's part, the only thing he'd decided (beyond agreeing to flee with Karin to avoid the law's inevitable return to the Osborne house) was an abstract notion of 'disappearing for a long time.' It was a comforting thought; whether or not it made any sense, at least for the next few days. The discipline that had kept him jumping from one career goal to another, exuding equal enthusiasm for them all, enabled him to fake himself out and believe that 'young man on the lam' was a viable long-term profession.

"Oh, I'm going to miss Eddie," said Karin, embracing Ethan like it was her farewell hug to the old man. Ethan didn't know what to say, since her words at the top of the ladder had been, "Thank God I'm finally getting out of this rathole." Even if Karin's every word conflicted with her last, as long as she was physically leading in one direction, Ethan would follow. He tested her by suggesting, "I still think we should have stayed put for another few days."

"You're not thinking straight, Ethan. The longer you hide out, the worse it looks."

"It looks pretty bad, doesn't it?"

She hushed him as they ran down one road, then another, skirting the back streets of Charlestown for safe passage. Only once they were out of earshot of any house did Karin start laying out her approach. "You were covering for your brother. Nobody will blame you for trying to help Jeff. I'm kind of worried about him being alone with Dorian."

"He's not dangerous."

"No, he only puts pills in your drink while you're not looking. I know those drugs. A normal person can't take them. Losing control is a natural side-effect."

"Kind of extreme for a side-effect. Sounds like a main-effect to me."

"Are you telling me you had any idea what you were doing? Cause if you are I don't know why I'm helping you."

"Yes, you do. It comes natural to you. Look what you've done for Eddie and Esther."

"Yeah, and now I might be deserting them." Karin took Ethan's hand, proving his point in the same moment she contested it. *What does she mean 'might'? Would we really ever go back there? I'm fine putting myself in her hands. But I'd better have some idea of what to do if she changes her mind.*

"Jeff didn't mean to do anything. And why did that doctor have him on such pulverizing drugs?"

"Because he's schizophrenic, honey."

"Where are we going?" said Ethan.

"A certain house. I have to go a roundabout way to avoid street lights. We shouldn't stay on foot much longer."

"I'm not sure I'm ready to drive just yet."

"I can drive. You'll give me directions and we'll get to your parents' house before the night is out."

"That's where we're going?" Ethan was so alarmed only Karin's rapid movement kept him from stopping dead in his tracks.

"Well where else? You have to tell them what happened. They

had Jeff put away out-of-state, for God's sake. They know how impossible he can be."

"Yeah, but I let them down. I talked them into letting me pick him up and then I blew it bad. I'd rather fix things up before bringing them into this."

"Fix things how? They're your parents, they have money, they know lawyers, we have to start building your defense."

"Oh, so I'm going to fall back on their big bucks."

"If that's all they are to you."

"I don't want to hurt them! I can solve my problems without crawling home."

"You promised me I'd meet them. Your Dad can get me into a great medical school."

"Eventually, Karin, eventually. But it takes hard work and—and—years of staying undercover while things blow over." He laughed even though he'd been almost serious when he made the remark.

Karin did not have long to puzzle over his curious behavior before they reached the house she'd been looking for. There was a pickup truck parked in the drive. She directed Ethan to hide next to it while she went into the small ranch-style house. When the door opened, the music and voices of the religious program that Esther had also been tuned to came out into the driveway. Ethan had the odd feeling he actually hadn't moved. Worse, the resounding admonitions to the faithful seemed pointed at him personally.

"And just when your hopes have dried up like prunes rotting in the sun, along comes Jesus with a bunch of fat, juicy grapes!" The preacher was really cooking. "They surely are delicious. You can taste each luscious drop as you press them against your tongue. But hold on! Are you going to sit there and hoard all those grapes for yourself? Or will you look around and see which of your brethren needs them more than you? I know, I know—you're thinking: I need my energy, I need to eat these grapes to get the strength to help others. If I fall down and am laying all weak and helpless in the gutter, what good am I to anyone then?" The door got closed, the demanding minister less loud, but the words still made it to Ethan. "I tell you, brothers and sisters, the strength you need is already there, inside your heart. The nourishment comes from the Lord Himself and not from those juicy-tasting grapes he dropped on you. Give the grapes away and you'll have ten times the strength you thought you'd need! Help others first and you'll come home to five thousand bunches of grapes! Pick up and love the rotting prunes around you, even when you're starving to death, and you yourself will become that juicy grape, squirting out the juice of hope, the morsel of comfort, the food of wonder, the abundant seed of hope! Kneel to your sister! Help up your brother! Don't let them down! Amen!"

I was helping my brother. He was the one who let me down. I ate the rotten prunes, every last one of them. They made me sick to the point where I didn't know what I was doing. Act when there's no strength left, huh? Well, you'll see what happens. You can save one person—and kill two others. You can only save so much and then—and then—I don't know. I should have been fending for myself, then I wouldn't be in this mess. The whole world lets you down and if you're not fit enough to stand on your own, what the fuck good are you to another living soul?

Ethan's mind ran on ahead of the gospel show, matching its every singsong high and low. The sin of pride possessed his ego and he believed his rationalizations to be truer than any possible 'higher truth'. Certainly they were more pertinent than all that packaged salvation blaring up and down the streets of a town in the middle of nowhere.

Ethan could see Karin's silhouette behind the patterned curtains. Whatever she was saying was drowned out by the preacher and hallelujah chorus. He couldn't make out who she was talking to, only that it was some seated woman who held their fates Buddha-like in her lap, waiting for Karin to finish so the answer could be 'no.' Ethan wasn't sure when this sense of pessimism had crept over him. Stay focussed on the good. A disaster had befallen him, but he'd been lucky in every respect after that. Jeff and he had survived without serious injury, they'd worked up an alibi, they'd even met a couple of guardian angels. The phrase actually occurred. Karin and Dorian, what else to call them? Even when Jeff was relatively normal, he and Ethan had never found likely candidates for double-dating. But here in this place called Charlestown, minutes after dodging death's door, was this pair out of some teen dream magazine, wasting away in a wreck of a house, with little better to do than escort car crash victims to safer terrain.

Ethan's head was pounding and he bopped it several times against the roof of the truck. Karin swore she'd help him. She must know this person and expect a favor to be possible. So why such bleak expectations? She was taking an awfully long time, for one thing. She had to be pretending she was alone so what kind of inane responses was the other person making to stall things? Ethan first hurdled his most paranoid consideration: that Karin was abruptly betraying him, confiding to a volunteer fireperson that she was running with a fugitive who's right outside, just dial that phone and have the cops surround the area before he realizes what hit him. No, no, no, she'd had ample opportunity to turn him in. No matter how mercurial her moods and erratic her desires, it made absolutely no sense to help Ethan escape Esther's watchful eye only to entrap him on the other side of town.

A more troubling possibility was that she was incompetent. By her own admission she'd lost five of her last six patients. Her training may have been so inadequate, some rinky-dink nursing school kind of place. No matter how old or terminal her previous cases had been, to rapidly go through five? But wait, why assume it was rapid? Karin could have been at this nurse thing for any number of years. He didn't know her exact age, had assumed she was twenty-five at the oldest. She probably had an LPN from when she was eighteen. One patient dying a year was not such a bad average, and she truly seemed to care about Eddie. *Until I showed up, that is, and she ran right out on him, even though I wanted to stay. Who else did she run out on when the chance came up?*

Luckily the choir reached a new crescendo of Hosannas which effectively purged Ethan's wayward thinking. Nervously, he joined in, humming the familiar hymn. He even uttered a prayer, unique in someone who'd long ago abandoned what vague religious upbringing he'd received. "God help me. God help Jeff. We didn't mean for those cops to die or even get hurt. I was out of my head. I'm not making excuses. I only want what's best for Jeff. Do with me what you will."

Karin's hand came over his mouth and he jumped against the truck. "You're not supposed to be singing out here!"

"Oh! Hi, hi—was I singing?"

"Yeah, hopefully no major arias for the neighbors. Anyway, she let me have these." Karin showed him the keys to the truck. What a miracle!

"No questions asked?"

"She was a former patient's wife. He died and well, she's eternally grateful."

"Really? So what was all the talking about?"

"I had to go on with some confusing story about driving to Bellows Falls for some errand for Eddie and Esther and telling lots of lies so she wouldn't get right on the phone to Esther when I walked out. I said I got them both to bed early for the first time in weeks and not to dare wake them."

"When do you need to have the truck back by?"

"I told her I'd park it here late tonight after she's gone to bed. She won't know something's up till she sees it's not back by morning."

"And where will it be? Where will we be? By morning?"

Karin had loaded him in the passenger seat and didn't respond before going around to start the engine. "You tell me, honey. You tell me."

She backed the truck into the street. Since the roads were devoid of traffic she was able to put it in neutral at an intersection and deal with his perturbing silence.

"Ethan? I wasn't being cute."

"You weren't?" Ethan tried to chuckle and pinch her cheek.

"You'd better make the most of us having this truck."

"What do you want—directions to my place?"

"That would help."

Ethan stared straight out at the dark forms of trees and houses. "What if the cops find Jeff and he tells them some twisted story and it gets back to my parents before we make it there?"

"In the end, it's you they're going to believe."

Her declaration made him look more worried than ever. He maintained a silence that she was forced to break.

"You don't want to leave him, that's what it is."

"Karin, I just can't. Maybe you're right that we should head to my house, but we have to find Jeff first."

"I'm not too crazy about driving all the way to Boston with someone on a short fuse."

"Where would Dorian have taken him all day?"

"I'll try the usual places."

She released the clutch and rolled forward against her better judgement. Slowly down one street, more quickly to make it over a hill, seemingly aimless, but that suited Ethan just fine for the time being. The truck crossed Main Street and chugged past larger houses into an area bounded by woods. On the right appeared the Hillside Cemetery.

"It's partly my fault for trusting Jeff like a normal person."

"It's not your fault at all!" Karin had had enough of Ethan's miserable muttering. "I'm not going to be trapped in Charlestown my whole life, feeling guilty about everyone getting old and dying. It's time I started thinking about myself."

Ethan wondered what that had to do with the accident not being his fault.

"Why are you turning into a graveyard?"

"Dorian might be in here somewhere. What, don't tell me you're afraid of ghosts."

"Not at all. Just psychotic country killer types."

"You already know Jeff. He's the only person fitting that description we might find in here."

Ethan eased up until a van full of drunken rowdies shot out of the cemetery from a road they'd just passed. The sudden noise from behind and Karin's accidental gunning of the truck jolted Ethan back to the crash. The light in the rearview mirror became the doomed police car swerving off and exploding. Ethan slid down in the seat as images of bodies pulled from the wreckage unavoidably crammed his brain. Reflections of tombstones riding up the windshield triggered imaginings of funerals for the two officers. Weeping families, hysterical spouses, whole towns shrouded in black to mourn its fallen heroes. All in that instant of fear as a few hooligans careened away.

Karin turned off the headlights and drove slowly along, hitting potholes, cruising carefully past monuments in the dark. "I killed the lights in case there are other idiots partying in here. I can tell Dorian's shape."

The aura of the cemetery was indisputably distinct from the rest of Charlestown. Despite Karin's matter-of-factness, Ethan felt engulfed by its strangeness. He was adventurous in many locations; burial grounds did not fit the bill. They seemed divorced from potential. The surprises that could pop up other places had an unwelcome aspect in places like this. Jeff had once chattered glowingly about a cemetery he loved to walk in near one of his previous hospitals. It was a sign of Jeff's sickness that a place that harbored death and nothingness made him feel right at home. Actually it was completely plausible, had Dorian brought Jeff to this garden of the dead, that Jeff would have suggested an overnight picnic.

The truck jerked down and up out of another pothole; Ethan thought he heard something scrape against his door. A chasm opened and a skeleton flew out, clutching for the door handle. "Jeff, Jeff," the words formed on his lips and he didn't care that Karin heard his lament. "Where are you now? Why did you leave me?"

CHAPTER 19

Ethan was far from Jeff's thoughts. His stomach was full and his imagination still sated with the victory in the diner. To accomplish such a mission entirely on his own!

Dorian had been with him at all other times to divert him from the usual barrage of self-doubt. But throughout the day he'd remained aware of his essential helplessness, that it was only the presence of this unique, kind and fascinating person that guarded him, for the time being, from the formless fears. Only the astonishing awareness that he had walked into as scary a place as Pearl Harbor—an eatery full of strangers—and walked out with sizzling trophies—that alone enabled Jeff to enjoy the fruits of sanity, ever so tenuously.

"It's time to go home," Dorian announced, facing his own more tangible fears.

"She may be passed out by now. I want to touch up a painting before it gets too late. You can watch."

As the guys neared the house at the end of their day of hooky, it was clear that Esther had not passed out. She was pacing the front porch and seemed quite steady on her feet. Dorian stopped to reconsider his decision. He couldn't see the pair of beers Esther had polished off, or the third bottle she'd put behind a post for a moment. Jeff waited, willing to spend the entire warm night outside in search of new challenges.

Esther called to Eddie. "Come out here. Don't make me wait for him all alone."

"Oh, h-h-honey, you know, you know, my legsh, my legsh—"

"They got you to the bar and back. Please come out here. Such a nice night. Mmm, smell those lilacs."

"What's the—what's the—oh, you know, brrrraaaaaaagggghhhhhhh! Dorie, Dorie, Dorie—he comes and he goes and he, oh you know—"

"Yeah, yeah, still it'd be nice if when he comes we can show him he's got two parents that give a shit."

"Blah, blah, Esther, Esther, two parents, yeah, yeah, yeah . . . " Eddie's bold attempt at conversation declined into the usual helpless repetitive moaning. Esther kept up the vigil, peering down Southwest Street, then crossing to the other end of the porch and squinting as far as she could down Dell. After another few moments, she was rewarded with familiar laughter and whispering. Happiness and anger fought for possession of her facial lines as Dorian and Jeff came up the steps onto the porch.

"Oh hi, Mom." Dorian was as casual as if he'd been gone five minutes.

"I thought you'd left town for good." Sadness overcame the other emotions in Esther's demeanor.

"I love Charlestown. I'm really not planning on leaving."

"It's impossible in that house with just Eddie."

Dorian gave her a surprising hug. "Don't forget what I told you. Keep praying to your inner God."

"Inner outer, in-between—wherever he is, ain't done much for me lately."

"Not 'he', not 'she', cut the anthropomorphic junk. The real God is not up in that sky. It's inside your brain. And mine. And Jeff's. Even Dad's. It's our collective consciousness of all the amazing stuff going on in the world. All around you."

Esther was hearing nothing new. "Whenever I get conscious of all the amazing stuff going on in this damn house and have the most natural response, you have me put away."

"Did you read a single one of those books I gave you?" Jeff knew nothing about the reading list that Dorian felt would do a much better job than he could to win over souls as lost as his mother. Apparently, Esther knew very little of them either. She looked away and felt embarrassed, despite her stubborn assertions.

Dorian tried to regain eye contact. The pain he glimpsed was too much even for his own inner god.

"I'm going upstairs. Want to do a few things to a painting before I turn in. Jeff?"

He headed inside and up to his room as soon as he realized Jeff was enjoying clinging to a porch post and swinging rhythmically round it.

"Yep. Us nuts sure have to stick together. What else we got?" Esther felt more at ease watching Jeff spin than trying to chase Dorian around the house.

"He loves you no matter how he acts." Jeff was so startled by his thoughtful comment, he stopped moving and tightly gripped the post like the whole porch might break off from the house.

"That's a good one." Esther lit a cigarette.

"He doesn't hate you."

"Now that's what I call progress." They were both more comfortable now that the talk had lurched away from the sentimental. But before they could get any further down to brass tacks, Dorian burst back onto the porch.

"Where are my paintings? Half of them are gone!"

"What?"

"Don't play dumb, Mom! How'd you get them out?"

"I have my ways."

"I'll kill you! My best paintings!"

"You never let anyone up there. Yeah, Georgie helped me. Lucky I don't have to count on a couple of new hired hands to get everything done."

"My paintings are not your problem!"

"Oh no? But getting through the winter without heat or food sure is! Those paintings might just be worth something. We put 'em up in store windows, maybe some tourists passing through town will make a decent offer. Remember heat and food? They come in handy during these winters, each one worse than the last!" She aimed much of her speech at Jeff, hoping she had an ally by now.

"Nobody in Charlestown's going to appreciate my paintings. The last time you did this some creep smeared manure all over them."

"So? Can't you stand up to a little honest criticism? I said I was aiming for out-of-towners, not locals."

"I'll decide when people see my work."

"Oh, then I guess we'll have to wait for your posthumous recognition."

"Yeah, you'll like me being famous and dead!"

"I don't know about the famous part. Except maybe among maggots."

"First they're good enough to sell, now they're food for maggots. You don't even know what you're talking about!"

"I sure as hell know you prefer the Hillside Cemetery to your own home."

"That's it! Come on, Jeff. I'm packing."

He tried to pull Jeff along, but his grip on the pole tightened and Dorian had to leave him on the porch again. Esther made a last ditch effort.

"Don't let him leave me, Jeff. You can move in here permanent."

"I might like that."

"Course you would. You can see what potential this place has. Cleaned up, it's a regular mansion. Plenty of space for you and your brother."

"Esther! Let's let's chelebrate the-the-the thing! Dorian's home-homecoming!"

It only took two passes of Dorian through the living room for Eddie to realize his son was back.

"It ain't a homecoming! It's the time I been dreading and damn if I'm gonna face it sober!" Esther drank the rest of the third beer. Jeff twisted his hands down his pockets, fighting the urge to grab the bottle from her lips and throw it as far as he could. He had no idea if Dorian would make good on his threat. He only knew that the long day of wandering free in summery bliss was about to climax in that dingy claustrophobic hole of a living room. The seemingly boundless paradise that he'd come to know as Charlestown was going to fall into a dark fissure, demolished by the earthquake at home.

Esther drew Jeff into the mine field center of the living room to make departure harder. Dorian came down with a single hard suitcase; his right arm was free to manipulate Jeff toward the front door.

"Where are we going?" cried Jeff as if going back outside was suddenly unthinkable.

"Your place."

"They won't—I can't—we'll never—!" Jeff couldn't get out the specifics, but his disdain for that plan was clear.

Nothing would cut Dorian's momentum. "If I wait till I'm not mad at her, I'll get stuck again."

"Hear that?" Esther seized at his vulnerability. "He knows it's wrong to leave."

"I'll have nice memories. Go on and drown your sorrows, Mom."

"Hey, come on, stop it, Dorian. Please, Esther—." Jeff had to face that his words had no impact on the Osbornes. But why not his booming, screaming, raging thoughts? It was true—he had sometimes altered the mood of a room just by walking in and thinking bleak things. Project that power deliberately. So far, nothing... nothing... Wait! At least Eddie was beginning to rattle around in his chair. Now aim for Esther.

"Why don't you ever give your Daddy a temperance lecture? He kicked me down those stairs when I was eight months pregnant with you!"

Jeff's brain waving effort to make peace was clearly not working and it dawned on him that the insane are often unable to screw things up any worse than they already are.

Dorian had heard the story of his near-miss at being born once too often. "I'll be sure to tell everyone in Boston what a martyr I've got for a mom."

Esther worked on Jeff. "If I hadn't caught hold of all that junk on the steps, Dorian would never have been born!"

"That's horrible! I love all that junk! And this junk!"

"Yeah, well, trust me—you'll stand by Dorian a lot longer than he'll ever stick with you."

"Don't listen to her. She'll try anything." Dorian knew he had to make the big push for the exit. Esther's tactics were starting to get to him. The reasons to not leave home were piling up. Then Esther blew her advantage.

"Your clothes are a mess. Go on and leave, but you'll change into something decent before I let you out that door."

"Yeah, I actually had fun today instead of sitting in the laundry room having all two pairs of pants recycled."

"Is it my fault you keep getting too big for your britches? Sell a damn painting! That might buy you trousers! Sell two! One for each leg!"

"Nice to know your real opinion about my paintings!"

"She likes them, Dorian. All she means is—"

"You get those filthy things off or there's gonna be holy hell around here!"

"Back to basics, huh?"

"Do it! Strip right here! We'll see you get on that bus stark naked!"

"Better than wearing these cheap rags you buy me!"

Esther was just bombed enough for the insults to trigger the worst in her while still agile on her feet. She went for a shingle laying on top of the pile of building materials and attacked her son with the rough-edged slate. Holding him by the shirt collar she scraped at his shirt. He was too flabbergasted to move away or resist.

"They're coming off! I want my cheap rags back!"

"Let go, Mom! Let me go!"

"Off! They got to come off!" She wasn't connecting with his skin, but the shingle had snagged a piece of cloth and she ripped ferociously. Dorian flung his arms in a defensive gesture and Esther hid behind the shingle, grabbing for the rest of his shirt. Jeff had fallen backwards over the junk he loved, which kept him out of the fray for a few moments. Eddie's eyes opened wide at the sight of his wife and son on the verge of killing each other.

"Stop her! Get that-that-that thing! The thing! The thing! Braaaaagggghhh!" He tried to stand up, but his legs failed him.

With both witnesses down, Esther went on tearing and scraping, mostly at the air, Dorian squirming and trying to keep her off balance without actually hitting her.

Jeff was back on his feet and his protective drive for Dorian overcame his terror of the conflict. "Stop! Stop!" he screamed, grabbing Esther's wrist to knock away the shingle.

"Aw, save your goddamn pity! You probably have a hundred wardrobes back in your fancy Beacon Hill mansion!"

"I've got nothing back there! Nothing! Nothing!" He'd gotten his body between them. Esther kept swinging and he took a hit meant for Dorian.

"Mom! No! You're hurting Jeff!"

"Once a psycho always a psycho! He don't feel a thing!" Jeff hadn't much felt the force of the blow, but it did shatter something inside his head. Caught up in that chaos, he flashed onto a vivid image of his own family seated with perfect equanimity in their pristine dining room. A rage hung over the table but everyone ate dinner as if the cloud of hate would rise up and evaporate. Ethan and his older sister Catherine kept their cool, but Jeff felt like his face was going to disintegrate. The memory radiated for a split second, more real than what was currently happening.

Dorian shoved Esther, she grabbed his arm, and both went down on top of Eddie. Grateful they'd brought the fight to his level, Eddie joined in. Their yelling and clawing pierced Jeff's fluctuating awareness. The Leblancs at dinner and the Osbornes on the floor melted into each other.

"Yeah! Go! Do it! Let it out! Mom! Dad! Ethan! Catherine! Don't hold back! Smash him! Smash her! You want to! Yaaaay! Smash it, smash it, smash it!"

His bizarre enthusiasm was so energetic it made the three fighters stop and look at him. Karin, the local cops and neighbors had often been there to interfere in their knockdown-dragouts; nobody had ever cheered them on. The battle stopped and they all stared at the strange person leaping exuberantly above them.

"Come on, you nut!" Dorian was up and pushing Jeff out the door.

"You let it out! You all let it out!"

"Yeah, great achievement."

Jeff's big smile instantly faded with his last glimpse of Esther and Eddie still on the floor. His final impression was one of deep anguish. By then he was off the porch, urged down Dell Street along with Dorian's frantic flight.

"How can you leave them lying on the floor?"

"It's their most familiar position."

"Dorian, stop! My arm hurts!"

Dorian kept pulling. How many times that day had Jeff complained about some outer or inner hurt that Dorian could see was trivial? The guy had potential, but he had to stop focusing on the wrong things. And sure enough, Jeff stopped yelling and allowed Dorian to set the pace. They ran in tandem for perhaps a half mile, made it across a field and through a patch of dense undergrowth, then over and down a sudden hillside. They scrambled to the bottom where it was so dark and secluded Dorian felt it was fine to stop for a breather.

Already Jeff was uncertain what he had seen. It was possible he had not participated in that flash of homespun violence. The summer stillness fully claimed his consciousness as they lay at the bottom of the hill.

Everything's happening so fast. When did Ethan take me out of the hospital? I was sitting up in my favorite tree, I was falling toward Ethan's amazed face, we were driving and driving, the smell of gasoline and urine and smoke, sick early morning rotting trees, something about dead people, something about fire and being lost, Ethan was with me, he was deserting me for that woman, left me alone and Dorian took his place, then Esther, then no Esther, then Esther again., sick sad old people and happy noisy eating people, weird people who know nothing about me, feeding me, inviting me over, treating me like there's nothing to worry about, I love being with this guy, Ethan vanished, something's wrong but it doesn't seem to matter, then I'm all right and everyone else is upset over—Dead people, who were those dead people? Why were we running? I sat still for so many years. I had my wall and inside my wall there were all those places to go. Now I'm always running, always moving, always going somewhere. I think I like the old way better. Where's everyone running? They'll only end up like those dead people. Even Dorian. He's so quiet now. Is he dead too? No, he's kissing me. Soon we'll be running again.

"There's a bus that passes through town at about three in the morning."

"What?"

"And I want us to be on it. But there's no money unless you still have some."

"I never needed money. Either my parents had it or I was someplace where they gave you everything you needed for nothing."

"I checked my room. Mom found my hidden stash and took that along with the paintings."

"We should find them, huh?"

"Once I'm settled in Boston, I'll come back for all my paintings. And the rest of my stuff. Nothing I can do about it now."

"I thought you wanted to stay in Charlestown forever."

"I'd rather, but there are a few too many problems. Boston's OK."

"Don't ask me. I barely remember it."

"Your parents will be glad to see you. I'll make them a painting. Anything they like."

"They have too much already."

"How nice for them. I could use twenty lousy dollars for our bus tickets."

"Ethan might still have some money."

"He and Karin could be anywhere. I think I know where there's money."

Jeff was starting to get hungry again. He'd used up a lot of energy in that fight he now realized must have been real. He was dirty and uncomfortable. The night air was warm, but too muggy. And all the stars made him feel horribly lonely. He could hug Dorian but could not close out the queasy anxiety that the world lacked substance and he was falling through it, desperately wanting to hit bottom, but worried about being dismembered when he hit. What good would money do? Didn't Dorian realize they could have all the money in the world but they'd still be alone in the dark and falling into infinity?

"Fred Simms, that park ranger, owes me close to fifty bucks. We'll get it from him and be all set."

Nope, Dorian doesn't realize we're alone in the dark and falling into infinity.

Jeff tried to enjoy the few remaining moments of stillness. The sound of the freight train blowing its horn passed through a distant part of the valley. There was life elsewhere besides Charlestown. Jeff feared he'd eventually be forced to experience it all.

CHAPTER 20

Eddie and Esther had only stayed silent till the screen door slammed.

"Esther, no!" he sobbed, drawing the 'no' out longer than any word he'd said in the last year.

"No what?" Esther's arm was caught under him, she was slowly checking the rest of her body to make sure nothing was broken, and the house was quiet. Nothing was happening anymore except for Eddie and his big "no."

"Why did you, where did he, what can we oh-oh-oh—"

"Why'd you get up, damn fool!" Esther freed her arm and got as far as her knees.

Eddie's no's and oh's turned into gasping for breath and a hideous sound came from him.

"Eddie, Christ! Somebody help! Clara! Help! Eddie, Eddie! Please, God, don't, don't—"

Eddie's eyes were closed and she wasn't sure she could hear his heart. She hit him at the right spot on his chest, but her hands were too weak. She considered the two broken halves of the shingle and almost passed out in self-revulsion. She slapped Eddie's face and tried to recall CPR through her beery high.

"I was only joking about putting you in that damn hole! Dorian didn't mean not to paint you! None of us wants you gone! Eddie . . ."

But her efforts to prevent him from ending up in the cemetery that was Dorian's favorite place were proving ineffective.

* * *

Ethan was finding out more about the Hillside Cemetery than he'd care to know in several lifetimes. Karin stopped the truck at the center of the road that traversed the top of the hill. It was the most secluded and creepy part of the place, according to Dorian who was a connoisseur of such things. While the engine clattered into silence, she got out, leaving Ethan alone to feel the full effect. *It's not fucking ghosts! We are in the middle of a place where kids deface headstones, people dig up bodies for medical experiments, and disturbed guys hang out waiting to cut loose. I'm not getting out of this truck. Jeff and Dorian wouldn't stay two seconds in here after dark, I don't care how weird they are.*

Karin opened his door and pulled at him.

"I'm not getting out."

"We'd better stick together."

"So get back in and drive out of here."

"You're the one who wants to find Dorian."

"Not Dorian—Jeff!"

"Same thing. There's only a few places they'd stay all night to avoid going home. Besides Devil's Glen and the old woolen mill, this is pretty much it."

"I can't wait for Devil's Glen."

"Right, see? It can only get worse. So help me tiptoe through the tombstones."

"Hey, how shitty do you want me to feel? I've been psycho on those prescription things for almost two days and just when I start to come down, you drag me into—into-"

"I would just as soon have hit the road. We're only in Charlestown cause you have to save your unsavable brother."

There was something about her incisive logic that struck Ethan as ridiculously funny when applied to his brother. He giggled and snickered and soon was laughing out of control.

"While you're being silly, there's a dragnet closing in on you. Now you can either choose a nice dark place like this cemetery or go where spotlights zoom in on you, they'll nail you, do a strip search and throw you in the back of a padded van. Which is it?"

She had already talked him out of the truck and past a moss-covered mausoleum. Ethan acknowledged he'd rather be with her than by himself in the truck. Searching a graveyard in the pitch of night was no crazier than anything else he'd put up with that day. After a minute of walking through lanes of the dead, Karin thought she could take him the next step. "It'll be faster if we split up and meet back by the truck."

"Fuck, no." He heard something scurry behind some tombstones and froze up.

Karin let go of his hand and took several large strides to investigate. Trying to keep up with her, Ethan rammed into another stone. On the ground, he rubbed his bashed shin.

"Karin! Wait! I—oow . . . "

He thought he heard laughter. Karin wouldn't be that cruel, but the alternative was somewhat more disturbing. His face was practically flush with a low stone and he could make out the etched words. 'Babyface's Baby. 1962-1962. He left this world in peace.' *Poor little kid. He never knew why he lived or died.* He hadn't heard Esther's graphic account of the birth and death of the infant, but he did have an eerie feeling of knowing the deceased. *Perhaps something Jeff mentioned back in the house or ranting in the bathtub. Or maybe the song was playing in the background. Some forties radio station of Esther's. Babyface, you've got the cutest little baby face, bop, bop, bop, bop, there's no one else could ever take your place, babyface—*"

Animal snarling! Ethan hadn't even considered wild animals coming out of the woods. "Karin?" he uttered, too quietly to expect her to hear. Slobbering, groaning, probably something ravenously hungry. Or thirsty. At the clinking of bottles Ethan was almost relieved. Kids drinking in the cemetery was preferable to a wild dog crouching to attack. Until a strong arm grabbed him from behind and a body bigger than his pinned him on the ground.

"Leave 'em alone!"

Ethan looked up into a seventeen-year-old's drugged-out face.

The kid had a flashlight which he used both to blind Ethan and to make his own features dance in a demonic glow.

"Leave who alone?" Ethan gasped. "I didn't see—anyone."

"You're a liar! They're right there!" The hyper teen shone the ray on a boy and girl in a gully about ten feet away. They were virtually naked, writhing in the churned-up dirt of an unused plot. Ethan knew what he was looking at, but the light's arc and the low angle at which he was held against the ground made the white dirty skin resemble some rutting night creatures from the forest. The assailant illuminated his grunting friends as if to whet Ethan's appetite. He bit Ethan's ear in a mock passionate gesture, then spit in his face. "Fuck you, don't get any ideas."

"Karin!"

The kid roughly pressed down on his mouth. "Scream again and you're dead."

Ethan stopped all resistance. Even if he had briefly started to listen to Karin's common sense, the sudden shock and maniacal face shoved up against his had shot him over the edge. Anything could happen in this place and probably would. He felt something nudging his gut. The kid was about to stick him with a knife.

The boy was too high to follow through. He laughed and waved his arms, playing Ethan's torso like bongos, then like clay that could be molded into freaky shapes. He rolled halfway off and Ethan tried to escape. He sat up and tried to catapult the kid. "Man overboard!" shrieked the kid, rolling down the hill into a huge headstone. Ethan had barely stood. Two more teens seized him.

"You leave us alone, motherfucker!"

"I'm not doing anything!"

"Let's bury him alive!"

With the two guys holding him up, Ethan got a better view of the lovemaking pair in the ditch.

The first kid was back on his feet and waving a knife recklessly like it didn't much matter who was on the receiving end.

"Tony, watch it!"

"Get that fucking knife away from me!"

While the three kids got embroiled with each other, Ethan began to move away, spun on his ankle and landed atop the naked couple. They stopped kissing, looked straight at him and both said, "Hi."

"Uh, hi. I didn't mean to interrupt your, uh, party."

The girl, no more than fifteen, stuck her breasts in Ethan's face. "You're cute."

That unhinged Ethan even more than the knife. Her boyfriend pulled her away and offered an apology. "She's not normally like this. Liz, stop making like a tramp."

"Don't call me that!" Liz was back on top of the nude boy in a flash.

Ethan didn't know if he dared move. Every step he took made things worse. There they were, groping each other again, fucking in his face. Ethan laughed and cried at the same time. Helpless, he waited for Karin to come rescue him.

It would take her almost five minutes to aid him, having gotten absorbed in a particular headstone in another part of the cemetery. She was in earshot of the teen orgy, but so preoccupied that the sound of laughter and muffled shouts held no fascination and little threat. She picked up a flower pot that had spilled, restored it, and placed it next to the grave. Nestling against the stone, she seemed to take comfort and forget anything around her. She hadn't been sure whether she'd separate from Ethan for her ritual. She was glad it had worked out this way. Things were strange and tense already; letting Ethan in on her secret could have an adverse effect on their mutual hopes. She wasn't sure why. She needed to know more about him before sharing an intimacy so much deeper than the things they had done in bed.

It was wolf-like sounds from Tony that alerted Karin that perhaps Ethan needed her. There were no dangerous animals nearby (of that she was fairly certain), but in his wired state of mind Ethan could bring out the worst in a big dog bent on protecting his master's grave. She whispered something to the names on the marker and brushed herself off. Even once attentive it was hard to know exactly which way the voices and animal noises were coming from.

The wildman Tony would stop at nothing to outdo his friends in gross, unpredictable behavior. He mooned Ethan, did an astonishingly graceful imitation of harikari, then offered the knife to Ethan. "Now that you've seen our secret rites, of course you can never leave." Ethan gladly took the knife and scrambled away, only to find that the 'knife' was a plastic bottle. The other boys tackled him and nailed him to the ground, squeezing his hand so he'd drop the bottle.

"There's still a few left," announced the shaggier of the two, shaking pills into his gaping mouth. Ethan was just relieved the kid didn't bite him.

Tony, envious of the attention, was back in Ethan's face, leering and drooling.

He initiated a staring contest that escalated Ethan's feeling to pure hatred. At any other time Tony would have seemed a pathetic clown, but the crisis in Ethan's life made such foolishness seem cruel in the extreme. Another moment and he would have let loose a fit of profanity that could have gotten him killed. Karin appeared in the midst of the commotion, stopping the prank just before it had lasting consequences. "Hey! What's the matter with you all! Get off my friend!"

Tony was sent rolling again while the shaggy boy cried, "Hey, guys, look! It's Karin!" and there came an echo of heys and hellos. Ethan clung to Karin to get back on his feet. He felt more disgust than relief—why had she left him with these creeps for so long?

"You know this guy?" said the other boy, whose face was painted six colors. "He's kind of weird."

"I said he's my friend and you guys are shits to beat on him."

Tony was rubbing his back against a tombstone and thrusting his hips up to hump the sky. Ethan saw something dangling from his belt buckle. With Karin apparently in charge, he was emboldened to look at it closely. The pig! The fucking dancing pig! He grabbed it to make doubly sure. Tony showed his ambivalence about another guy grasping around his crotch by shoving it against Ethan and simultaneously yelling, "Get off of me, you fag!"

"That's my pig!" Ethan shouted him down. "The thing from the mirror in my-my-my-my car." He gestured to Karin to come see. Tony was whacking him with his open hands, but Ethan held on. "Where did you find this?" he demanded of Tony.

"That's my magic pig! You like it?" Tony oinked and squealed the role of the little pig.

"It's from the Jaguar, Karin!"

"Your car? You mean—?"

"Hey, was that your car we found, man?" injected the shaggy boy. "Coolest thing. Guess you were in a wreck, huh?"

"Let go! My magic pig! The source of all my amazing power," said Tony, collapsing in drugged-out bliss. Ethan was able to unhook the furry ornament to show it more closely to Karin.

"There's the proof! This was on my rearview mirror!"

Before Karin could ask him what the little pig could prove, the naked girl in the gully became aware that another woman was present and was instantly mortified. She started kicking her sex partner and groped around for pieces of her clothes.

"Oh my God! I can't believe you forced me to do this in here! This is a holy place! I told you it's a holy place!"

"Honey, it's all right. Stop the big act. Karin won't tell anyone. She's always been cool."

But the girl brushed up against Karin and her breath and eyes revealed it was no act. "I couldn't help myself."

The naked boy added, "The stuff is oozing through our brains and it's so amazing."

"What stuff?" Karin asked everyone, but especially Ethan who said, "It must be Jeff's pills. He lost them in the car, he told me. Oh fuck, what's in those pills..."

Tony was straddling a tombstone of the perfect height. "Man, I could fuck the whole world!"

"I didn't want to take it," continued the blitzed girl. "Tony said he knew what it was, but he lied!"

"Hey, I took more than any of you! I was like a—like the—you know, taste-tester.

Now gimme back my pig!" Tony lunged at Ethan. Karin stuck her foot out and sent the clown sprawling.

"Everybody, just leave him," insisted the girl. "He took too much. Did someone force you to come in here too, Karin?"

Tony defended himself while trying in vain to stand. "Oh right, I found the stuff, was generous enough to share it, and you guys come in here and start fooling around right in front of me. You know she used to go out with me, Karin! You know that!" Karin seemed unmoved so Tony implored Ethan, like the recent events had made them fast friends. "What would you do with friends like these, man? Huh? Tell me what to do!"

Ethan was in no condition to give advice to the lovelorn. But he had to get through to these kids. He could persuade Karin or lose her, depending on what came out in the next few minutes.

"Where did you find my car? Who was in it? Did you tell anyone? Was it a total wreck?"

Tony said something incoherent. The painted boy chipped in, "Over in the woods. Just off the Missing Link."

"Of course we reported it, what do you think we are?" said the naked boy, his hard-on finally going down. "But first we scooped up all those pills from the seats. Wow, I can see why you crashed, man."

"Why did you take pills without knowing what they were?" asked Karin.

"Tony took some first and he was hallucinating and laughing his ass off. It was tempting."

"And where was this thing? On the mirror?" Karin took the small pig from Ethan and waved it in his eyes. He was riveted on the innocuous item. "Stupid little dancing, jiggling pig thing . . ."

Tony loved how weird Ethan got. He snatched the pig from Karin and kept waving it in Ethan's face, hitting a smooth rhythm that seemed to hold him mesmerized. "My thing . . . in the mirror . . . it was dancing . . . and Jeff all the time . . . "

Tony snickered, "This guy's a complete loon."

Ethan made himself stop talking, but the hypnotic pig unleashed a frenzy of uncontrollable memories. *Mom loves tiny animals, she's so sick it'll give her some relief, it's for her, but Jeff obviously likes it too. Hang it on your rearview mirror, make it jiggle, he tells me, and how could I refuse? Lockjaw, why do I feel lockjaw, I've had a tetanus shot, had all my shots, never once had the flu, got dosed up and traveled all through Europe and Asia, the pleasure dens of Thailand, amazing how close you can get to Viet Nam and not know there's a war, steady, man, steady, who's driving this baby? I gave the valedictory speech and insulted the parents—how could you throw that sarcasm at us?—"It's a great big world and I'm gonna put on my fanciest shoes and walk all over it." And so I did. While my brother sat in a five by eight room, staring at the wall. Not fair, but nothing's fair, so just let it go and move on to the next fuckup. The Buddhists had the right idea. That bunch I lived high off the hog with in Paris. Get off the rollercoaster of pleasure and pain, pleasure and pain. Hey, I jumped the tracks and stopped cold turkey. Bam! No more pleasure, that's for sure. But then I would've never met Karin . . . how about pleasure inside pain, what would the Buddhists say about that? Nam Myoho Renge Kyo, I can't fucking believe I remember that stupid phrase—"Keep chanting it and you'll get whatever you want"—maybe that's why things screwed up, I stopped chanting for a few months and Bam! But what did I hit? And who are these people that know all about it? They're on Jeff's pills. Just like me. All of us in the same boat. That was your boat we found, man? Coolest thing. Guess you got shipwrecked in a storm, huh? Yeah, but it sure wasn't on a desert island. I've met more weirdos in the last two days than six months on a Eurailpass. But what was the thing with that pig? Why am I all bent out of shape over a stupid stuffed little . . . Karin's so pretty I could just stay here all day, she gets a kick out of that pig, it was a great choice for a gift. Mom, Jeff, Karin, they all got something out of my pig, my pig, my piggy wiggy figgy—*

Karin had been standing right behind Tony. She let him keep dangling the pig before Ethan's eyes because she was equally fascinated at the effect it had on him.

Plus she knew Tony and all these kids; they were harmless and she was tired of Ethan overreacting to everything. She returned to her protective manner only when Ethan's knees gave out and he fell to the dirt. She knocked the pig from Tony's hand and sent him laughing back to the arms of his friends.

"Ethan! Are you OK? What is with you?" She looked over at the teens. "He's out cold. I don't believe it. Tony, where'd you learn hypnosis?"

"I just jiggled the pig like he told me to. Damn little hog must mean a lot to him. Here, for when he wakes up."

Tony retrieved the pig and tossed it to Karin. She examined it to see if it opened up or was anything besides a baby's toy. The girl, still mostly naked, went to Karin with weepy eyes. "Please don't get the wrong idea about what was going on here."

"I won't, Liz. I promise I won't get the wrong idea."

"We can trust Karin," said the boy who'd been porking Liz. "She's helped tons of people in town."

"I'm glad someone remembers. Guys, my friend won't wake up."

"I didn't touch him, Karin," insisted Tony. "I was just kind of tickling him, goosing him, stuff like that."

"You fag, Tony."

"What am I supposed to do when you start fooling around with Liz right in front of me? She used to be my girl."

"Yeah, used to."

"Lay off it, Tony. You were the one made us follow them in here."

"Guys, guys, listen, I need a hand here," Karin broke in. "Help me carry him back to my truck."

"Karin, could we die from those pills? Tony made us take an awful lot."

"You won't die, Liz," Karin stroked the girl's cheek, once more the comforting nurse. "Now please shut up and let me take care of my friend."

Liz felt relief that she had nothing to hide from Karin. She straddled a monument and rode it like a hobby horse, enjoying the feel of her wet thighs against the smooth carvings. Tony and the other boys all grabbed parts of Ethan, lifted him over their heads and followed Karin to the truck.

"Karin, do you think there's Satanists in Charlestown?" wondered the boy with the painted face.

"It's possible, James. I hear they're all over. "

"Cause we figure if we ever find any defacing the graveyard or something, we'll fucking kill them, but you know, you're a nurse and all, is it true they can come back from the dead?"

Ethan was being maneuvered onto the seat and Karin made sure the boys didn't drop him at the last moment. Her silence made James think she was giving serious thought to his concerns. As she shut the door and went around to take the driver's seat, Karin felt mobbed by the horny boys, shaggy, painted, naked and bonkers. "Just always proceed with caution, James. Around the dead or the living. That goes for all of you. And I'm a nurse so you can be sure I've studied the problem a lot."

"Karin, what's the Latin name for the pills we're on?" asked the naked kid. "Just so we know what to watch out for in the future."

"I think you should watch out for moving trucks." Karin slammed the door and released the brake, started the engine and rumbled along the upper slope of the cemetery. The boys dodged aside and raced back toward Liz like whoever won got to be her boyfriend. All except for Tony who ran after the truck. He was feeling omnipotent and tried to outrun it. Since Karin had to go slow at first, it was no contest. Tony quickly outdistanced her, then found himself far from his friends, in a remote corner of the graveyard. His cockiness turned to paranoia and he decided to call it a night, meandering cautiously down the hillside and out of the graveyard, back onto the slightly less malevolent back streets of Charlestown.

CHAPTER 21

Ethan snorted in his sleep and Karin nudged him. "Hey, come on, what went on with you back there?" Ethan slumped over, unable to respond. Karin looked at the little pig lying on the seat between them. It was hard to believe that a small stuffed pig might ruin her most promising relationship in years.

It occurred to her that the kids in the graveyard knew where the car crashed. She kicked herself for not probing more; even if the police had since towed the car, there might be clues left around it that could help Ethan's case. Yeah, right, she corrected herself. Like those guys could remember how to put on their pants. She braked hard when a wild apparition streamed into the road. The jolt did not stir Ethan. Lucky thing, because the apparition was Tony. Not a good idea for those two to meet up again.

"Get in, Tony," she said, meaning the back of the truck.

"You giving me a ride?"

"Yeah, provided you're going to the Missing Link."

"Oh, you want to go back to the pig-lover's car, huh?"

"You remember where you found it?"

"Uh, yeah, yeah. But the car won't be there. Larry took a few seconds out from screwing Liz to call the cops."

"Just the area around it. Maybe there'll be more things like this pig."

"Or like those pills! Let's see, you should cross the river at the north side bridge and then . . . it'll come to me, it'll come to me."

Karin kept her window down so she could hear Tony's directions as he bounced around on the flatbed in the open air. She certainly wouldn't have had him squeeze in next to Ethan, and riding out there made him stay alert. She was pleased with her efficient handling of an otherwise disastrous encounter. Her two years of training in the Osborne household was paying off.

Tony got her onto the Missing Link via a rarely used offshoot. If you didn't watch carefully you could miss the turn onto the Link and wind up on the highway to northern Vermont. Once on the old road Karin went slowly so Tony could pick out the exact spot where he and his friends had emerged from the woods. Backtracking on foot they could find the locale of the missing car. The main trick would be to prevent a showdown between her two passengers. When Tony got excited and pinpointed the entrance to the destination, Karin pulled off the road. Unknowingly, she almost duplicated the path of the Jaguar off the Missing Link to the edge of the woods.

"Yeah, yeah, we came out right here and everyone was all bummed because we wanted the woods to go on forever, you know, we were getting off on being in like the Lost World or something. So we went back in and whoa, there's this green machine! Definitely not prehistoric, but kind of extinct."

Tony jumped out and led Karin into the woods. She had let Ethan go on sleeping, hoping to make her own discoveries, get rid of Tony, and then bring Ethan in.

But the desolate spot revealed nothing under the fading beam of Tony's flashlight.

"Cops must've took every last scrap, Karin. You gotta believe me. It was right here." Broken branches, tire tracks and an unnaturally open space in dense surroundings made Karin sadly believe Tony.

"Yeah, well, they were bound to be thorough. Don't know what I expected to see. They didn't ask you guys if you'd taken anything?"

"Bad enough Larry reported it. I told him I'd kill him if he said we made off with those drugs. I mean, Christ, they might've thought we stole the car and crashed it while we were on 'em. Or something."

Karin made a noisy search through the underbrush so Tony wouldn't realize how seriously she took that last part. Could Tony and his friends have been the hitchhikers and was that exactly what had happened? No, she was starting to confuse the facts with her own wishful thinking. Ethan had told her he drank the Coke doctored by Jeff. But Ethan had a huge memory loss from the shock of the crash. And then he was taking Jeff's word that the pills had gone into that Coke. She was trusting the word of a victim in shock, based on the ever-changing perspective of a schizophrenic. It made sense that Ethan would had invented the hitchhikers—but was it pure invention? Here were Tony and his friends, higher than all get out, with a pig from the crashed car. Was it really the pig that drove Ethan crazy, or the boy who was manipulating it? If the teenagers had come upon the car in the woods, how did Tony know so well how to find the spot from the road?

Questions continued to form like one of Mrs. Muff's monstrous patchwork quilts. It was Karin's nature to think this way. Indeed, it was the mentality that kept a smart, ambitious woman from venturing outside the narrow bounds of Charlestown. All the questions that kept bumping into one another. What if I did such-and-such and then that happened? What's the point of trying that when blankety-blank is the likely result? It was a self-destructive skill that a less intellectual person would have easily unlearned. To be paralyzed by possibilities—that was the unfortunate byproduct of a subtle, far-ranging mind. At least in Karin's case.

And now she turned this over-analytical ability loose on Ethan. She had been so instantly drawn to him, even bruised and bloody. Especially bruised and bloody. The arrival in town of someone so handsome and intelligent, yet not stuck up and with a natural predisposition to help others—what a terrifyingly rare opportunity! Whatever had been keeping her rooted to Charlestown—especially after the worst thing imaginable had happened—it had to mean something that a chance encounter in the hotel bar would be the only thing in the world that could shake things up. Karin's inner voices went to war. "Oh right, he looks and seems great, but of course under all that, he's really a loser with a psychotic brother. The family's rich but so repulsive he's not inclined to turn to them for help in a crisis. No, no, no—that's the appearance, all the bad stuff. The truth is that he was leading a charmed existence—and meeting me was a natural result of that—when this freak thing happened. Either crooks on the lam or an accidental overdose, nobody will ever know which, and a car crashed and cops were killed. I mean, it's their job to chase speeding cars. And there's a good chance that one of those chases won't go so well. It's a terrible thing, but when you have a dangerous job, you can get killed when you don't expect it. Look at my job. People die on me when I least expect it. If I were a scientist or a figure skater, a nun or a poet, the hazards would be different. Things go wrong in life, and there's no point in blaming yourself or suspecting people you like. Ethan doesn't remember a thing and that just might be for the best. Worse comes to worse, I'll visit him in prison. The previous disaster nearly ruined my life, this second one's going to save it. It's not like two strikes and here comes the third, I'm down and out—that's just too cruel and sick and God would not work that way."

What would have left most people in a stew of self-doubt had the opposite effect on one so peculiarly perceptive as Karin. Perversities and inconsistencies pointed the way to salvation in her relentlessly strange world. For a few moments the troubled nurse felt vindicated. Then she heard Ethan scream from the truck.

She ran back to him without bothering to take stock of Tony who had strayed out of her sight. The scream sent Tony the opposite way. Coming down from his high, he had no desire to have a face-off with Karin's friend. Christ, the pig-lover was probably a drug dealer and was pissed they'd stolen all that stuff from his car. Karin could take it from here; it was time for him to make amends with his friends and get some sleep.

Karin found Ethan crouched in the seat, his knees pulled up to his chest.

He flung his arms around her when she opened the door.

"This is where it happened!"

"I know, shhh, I know. We're on the Missing Link."

"How'd we get here?" Ethan had to be physically coaxed out of the truck. His feet on the ground, he gradually stopped trembling.

"I got directions from one of the—" Karin looked around for Tony. As she led Ethan into the woods, she realized he must have bolted. Good, good. Tony's presence could only muddy Ethan's reactions. She needed perfect clarity from him, now if never again.

Ethan stared with indecipherable glumness at the site.

"We could wait here for awhile. In case, like you said, Jeff brings Dorian here."

"Did I say that?" said Ethan in barely a whisper.

"Well, let's say Dorian would take Jeff to all his secret spots. At some point, Jeff might want to return the favor."

"Jeff couldn't find his way out of the bathtub, let alone through these woods at night."

"See, so those guys found it and reported it, cops came and towed it away. Not long after that they showed up at our place. They'd find out who you are from the license plate. Hate to tell you, but your parents must already know."

"Know that their forty-thousand dollar car's a scrap heap, but not a thing of what happened."

"Just that you were transporting Jeff. That should lead to some conclusions."

"It wasn't his fault either! That's why I need time to—to—"

"Whose fault doesn't matter now, Ethan. Even those kids in the cemetery are implicated. You don't remember a damn thing and I don't think anybody's ever going to get to the bottom of it. It's a shame and I know you feel guilty, but there's a way out of this. For both of us."

"What's that?"

"I'll say I found you two in the woods, bashed up and out of your minds. I'm in and out of the hotel bar every day. The word of a few drunks isn't worth shit. I took you home to fix you up, Jeff slipped away with Dorian, we looked, couldn't find them, and finally turned up in Boston."

"We don't turn up without Jeff. Do you get that? I fucked up once, I'm not going to do it again. I went to bring my brother home and that's what I'm going to do. He doesn't crack up the car, he doesn't slip off with the first guy he meets out of the asylum. I like the way you say we can both come out of this OK. I'd like to know what you have that even comes close to my sick and sorry story."

Karin looked him dead in the eye. "Try my whole family crushed by the train when their car stalled on the tracks. Try being a fifteen-year-old who just told her parents to go fuck themselves and jumped out of the car. And that's the only reason I'm alive and completely alone in the world."

For a split second Ethan didn't believe her. But simultaneously he knew he was the only inexcusable liar in the world. He grasped for her hands.

"Oh my God. It was your family that the train—. Oh, Karin, I'm so sorry, but you never said it was. . . . oh shit, that's why you've been so good to me. You know what it's like. In a way nobody else can."

He hugged Karin who could only leave her arms limp by her sides. Now that she had broached the subject that had made her both a martyr and a pariah in Charlestown, she'd better give him all the details. Maybe only that would inspire him to do the same.

"It had just turned dark, early November, the worst time of year. The trees all sparse after being so pretty. That lonely chill and the first smell of smoke in the air. I'm always in a terrible mood then and top that with being fifteen, maybe you'll understand what I did."

"What you did? How could anyone possibly blame you for—"

"Pop stalled out on the tracks. Mom was on the side facing the train. And my little brother—right between then. I was in the back. We'd been fighting over—get this—the way I didn't react to my brother pulling my hair. It really hurt, but I figured the best thing was to ignore it so he wouldn't think it was so much fun. But Mom goes, "You should scream bloody murder when he does that. Otherwise, he'll never learn. He'll go around doing it to all the girls." And then my father—"I've heard you can lose all your hair that way. Is that what you want, Karin? To be bald?" And Richie was snickering. I couldn't get over that they were blaming me for him pulling my hair."

She started to cry. When he caught a tear with his finger she moved away, refusing his comfort. "I let loose with some insult back, like, better bald than empty-headed like the two of you. And they tore into me. Lack of respect, is this your reaction to us trying to help you? All the while, Pop kept trying to start the engine. After it didn't kick over a few times, I guess he thought it needed a rest, so he joined in. "I work my butt off for you, girl!" We weren't that far from home, so I figured, what do I have to put up with this shit for? And I got out. The last thing I yelled to my parents and little brother was "Why do you all hate me? Like you're so fucking perfect!" And then the train seemed to come out of nowhere. I watched the car get slammed into the gully. Rolled and rolled. Blew right up."

"But that horn. How could they not have heard it coming?"

"The train didn't normally use the horn so much way back then. Now there's a law cause of what happened."

"Way back when? How long ago was it?"

"Exactly eight years ago tonight."

Ethan was speechless. That she would be marking an anniversary like that by mucking in the woods looking for his crashed Jaguar. He wanted to hold her for the rest of the night, but she was still feigning tough aloofness. He was so upset with her for hating herself over what happened, he got the sick desire to pull her hair. Just as suddenly, she leaned against him and kissed his chest.

"Mom, Pop, and Richie—they're all buried in the Hillside Cemetery. The night's not a total loss. I paid my respects." Ethan searched for the right words, but she expected nothing and pressed on. "Esther and Eddie were so nice. She was the one who helped me get started in nursing school. And he was such a charmer, back when he could talk. I went from house to house, learning skills, losing one old person after another. Esther and Eddie were always there for me, but kind of in the background. Then in the fall of '69, after Eddie had his stroke, I was able to start repaying the favor. Their daughter Sandra, normal as pie, was long gone. Dorian's sex life was the talk of the town, Esther had hit the bottle and the house was falling apart. To say they'd changed is putting it mildly. Still, they were all I had."

Ethan felt her warmth but all his eyes could see was the cold shadowy pit of the forest where his car had crashed. "It all happens so fast. Your life is changed. And soon—it's all over."

"Don't say our lives are over."

I didn't mean it like that. Not personally. But maybe she's right to take it that way.

"We'll get through this." Ethan had also started to cry. "Let's get away from this awful place."

"Not just yet. You have to face it. We both do." Seeing his tears, Karin had one of her rapid moodswings.

"Face what?" said Ethan, not wanting to know.

"The pain. Look it right in the eye. And get tougher and tougher till nothing bothers you."

"No, that's not it. That doesn't work."

"Then what does? Everything's so horribly unfair."

"But it happens to everybody. Look at the world-"

"What world? I've never been anywhere. I'm following in Esther's footsteps."

"You will get out. And then you'll see. We're the lucky ones. The top, I don't know, one percent of humanity. We're bound to lose it all. Most other people don't have much to lose in the first place."

"Now that's cause for celebration." Another mood flip-flop and, "Yippee! It's raining hundred dollar bills! Look out, world, I'm gonna hit the next one out of the ballpark!" Karin was dancing around the truck. Ethan hadn't intended to boost her spirits quite that much.

"Don't flip out on me. I need you to—to—"

"And here I thought I needed you."

"You do. Don't you?"

He caught up with her on the other side of the truck, tried to hold her in one spot, and silently demanded a clear connection with her. *This is too crazy. I'm the one with everything to lose now. Next she'll have us dancing nude in the moonlight.*

Indeed, the idea had crossed Karin's mind. Better that than to dwell on what she'd lost, that she missed the musty old Osborne house already, and that Ethan was just one more person she'd inevitably lose.

CHAPTER 22

Dorian led the way through a cornfield whose stalks were low enough for Jeff to see rats, snakes and other creatures which only he could name crawling and skittering at their feet. It was incentive to keep moving even though he was tired and wished they'd stayed at the house. That fight would have blown over like all the others. He fantasized such a battle breaking out if they ever got to his own house. *Dad tossing the Ming vase, the Chippendale table collapsing, Mom rising up out of bed to clobber him with state-of-the-art hot water bag. No such luck. They'll stare at me with those huge hollow eyes, Mom all gaunt and wailing, "something terrible has happened, I can feel it," Dad wisely not overreacting, trying one of his home remedies on me until it's time to cart me off again.*

"Ow!" They passed from the cornfield and went down a pine-treed hillside where a prickly thing had stuck to his arm. Jeff howled in frustration till Dorian removed the burr.

"We're almost there."

Out of the pine woods and through a cow pasture that was familiar to Jeff. After their swim, this was the place they'd come so Dorian could tempt the cows with hay and pat their enormous heads. He was clearly more at ease with animals than other people, enjoying the curious stares and mooing reactions like they had a subtlety human interaction lacked. He knew each cow and greeted it like a friend, but now, even though the creatures were up with insomnia, Dorian walked right by without so much as a glance. "Don't step in their shit," he said.

The town Jeff had come to adore by day was wearing him down in the dark. *How many more hills? We've been down this road. He's as bad as Ethan, running around for the hell of it. I miss my wall.*

Everything in the world was inside my wall. And when I got tired I was already in bed so I just rolled over and blanked it all out. I have to show Dorian my wall, he'll enjoy that...

Jeff only made it to the top of the current hill because Dorian promised it was the last. From there, they looked down at a few scattered houses in a relatively sparse part of town. Set off by itself was a small municipal-looking building with a flag on it.

"That's the park ranger's station. I figured the lights would be on. Now you wait here and I'll come back with some bus money."

"I want to come with you."

"No, that won't work out."

"How come?"

"We can't be together every single minute. It's not healthy."

"You still have other boyfriends. After this, you'll round up the soccer team."

"That's a fall sport, dummy. Trust me, this has nothing to do with you-know-what."

He kissed Jeff and trudged down the hill. The kiss did the trick, making Jeff so happy he kept re-living it for a full minute. By that time Dorian was on the other side of the building. *He'll be back soon. And then I'll get a kiss hello. That's worth waiting for.*

Fred Simms opened the door after some persistent pounding by Dorian.

"Isn't this a nice surprise in the middle of the night?"

"Hi, Fred. Remember that money you owe me? I could use it now."

Fred was accustomed to Dorian's bluntness. Tonight it rubbed him the wrong way. "Money—not just the root of evil, but the bud, the stalk, the whole damn plant."

"It was fifty bucks." If Dorian could endure Bartlett's quotations, Fred might pay up.

"Must've been some night."

Dorian tried to project urgency through his expression, hoping to quickly cut through the ironic double entendres that formed the bulk of his relationship with the ranger. It seemed to work.

"Come on in, Dorian. I'll get it for you."

After the opening foyer, the station consisted mainly of one large room filled with the implements of a park ranger's trade. There was a rollaway bed if he needed to sleep there, but normally there was no cause to keep the station open so late. A poker game was tonight's emergency. Dorian knew the other two guys; they'd just graduated with him, one barely. It was not good to see them again so soon.

"Look who stopped by." Fred's announcement brought an oversized "heyyyyy" from Keith and a too-enthusiastic "whoa, Dorie, man" from Ron, whose hair was long and the same color as Dorian's. Dorian felt slightly more comfortable with Keith who at least had a flicker of intelligence. Guys like Ron astonished him with the range of their stupidity. Dorian said hello to keep the peace, but kept his focus on Fred, hoping to make it out of there in a minute. "That bus comes through about three a.m., right?"

"If it still runs."

"Hell of a time to catch a bus," said Ron, unusually talkative.

"Why don't you join the game, Dorian?" said Keith, "Here's twenty to start."

"I hate cards." Dorian immediately knew he should have ignored the invitation instead of putting it down so fast.

Ron feigned being insulted. "You haven't been by the store in awhile."

"Great prom, huh?" Keith kept the ball rolling while Fred acted like he was looking all over for some money. "Everyone got a kick out of you and Karin playing a couple."

Dorian could take Keith's kidding. At least he didn't get drunk and ask for a blow job, then spread all over school the next day what a fag Dorian was. Like somebody else in the room.

"Off to college now?" said Ron, shuffling the cards with a jerking motion.

"High school was enough abuse, thanks."

"If I had an old man in the Air Force, I'd take advantage of that cheap tuition."

Keith had insight, no question about it.

"If you had an old man like mine, you'd catch the 3 a.m. out of town."

"You've got almost four hours. That's quattuor horas."

"Save it for the tourists, Fred." Keith laughed. Ron didn't get it. "I'll deal you in, Dorie. Jacks are wild."

Dorian regretted not waiting outside. "Could I have my money now, please?"

"We'll help you kill the time." Fred couldn't get over finally having the new hard-to-get Dorian back in his place. "You know, Dorian, it's the simple things in life that form the most lasting pictures—fresh autumn leaves blowing down the lane, postman's mail car coming up the hill, getting buck naked with your old buddies."

"The game's five card stud. Shirts off to ante up." Ron and Keith tossed their tops aside and two bucks apiece into the pot.

"I can open," said Keith while Ron forced Dorian into a vacant chair. Dorian refused to worry yet. He even considered whether he could beat them for a game or two and leave town on a high note. But for once, it wasn't their clothes he wanted to make off with.

"I'm raising you five," said Fred, belatedly stripping out of his official gray shirt.

Dorian calculated whether there was money enough to grab and make for the door. No, not even one fare. And they had put him in the chair least accessible to the exit. Outside that door was the countryside, so perfect apart from f the people that lived in it. Waiting just up the hill was a loopy but handsome guy, to whom he had really not meant to lie. "This has nothing to do with you-know-what." If Dorian was going to walk out that door and return to all the pleasures that were not in this room, you-know-what was going to have everything to do with it.

Jeff was starting to have thoughts that far exceeded the fear of being left alone in the dark. *An open country gate, a warm puppy . . . Dorian, you better be watching out! There are assholes in the hospital* too, but at least they have the excuse of being cooped up with nothing to do. I forgot how terrible it is on the outside. All the strange people who can fake the surface stuff and are raging maniacs inside. It's all too free and loose. Without discipline, attendants, locks and keys, people just wander around waiting for trouble to strike. Jobs, they call it. A sense of accomplishment. Careers, goals, friends in high places, no maps on my taps. I'm the captain of my ship and I'm steering toward my destiny. Yeah, go on fooling yourselves, your boat's full of holes and it's only a matter of time till you sink and drown. I was sailing smoothly through the waves in my wall. Ethan should've never taken me away. He'd be fine and Dorian could play with the soccer boys, the queen of the burgers could have a nice day for the next hundred years. What am I doing here besides spoiling things for everyone? "Aw, don't say you're never going back. Once a psycho always a psycho." Did I say I wasn't going back, Esther? That's all I want to do. I couldn't agree with you more. Freud, Skinner, Jung and Horney have nothing on you. Once a psycho always a psycho. Burn all the textbooks, give everyone work therapy and keep your fingers crossed. "As if you could ever tell the difference between what's real and what's not!" Well, so what, Ethan? Real is your car smashed up in the woods, real is dead cops and dead everyone else, all over Pearl Harbor, in every room of Dad's hospital, hanging over Mom's head in our beautiful mansion. Dorian's paintings are not real—the paint's real, the canvas is real,—see I know the difference, you fucking jerk—but those places don't exist, the colors shine brighter than all the cars you ogle down the highway, even brighter than yours, which is not all that bright anymore. What's real, what's not, who cares? If you do, I don't and my don't cancels out your do, so there goes your proof right down the toilet. "Does craziness run in your family, your family, your family?" Karin's voice appeared most unexpectedly because Jeff had spoken very little with her. *You see for yourself. The answer is yes and no. All in the eye of the beholder. Ethan beheld you and went crazy over you. To me you're just another nurse, one of the attendants instead of one of the patients. Eddie's keeping track of it all. The sick bulletin board. Some people would just call it keeping up with the times. Maybe that's where Dorian gets his artistic talent. Oh my God, so that's why they don't talk to each other—creative jealousy! Stop being so angry, you two. What's the difference when both of you and everyone else are inside my wall? You can fight and hurt each other all you want, but you'll never get outside my wall. Dorian, quit punching the wall. Didn't you hear what I said? You can pound through to the other side and you'll still be in the wall.* Dorian talked as loud as he pounded. *"You don't want to end up like Mom, do you? All those pills, all this screaming and crying just cause you feel crummy. If everything is nothing, how can anyone do anything and ever make it stick? Your whole philosophy comes crashing down the instant you put your arms around me."*

Dorian's harsh words, spoken only hours ago, came back at Jeff like the howling trains that kept attacking Charlestown. Now they echoed and crowded out all his other thoughts. The manic flow reached a logjam, Jeff was thrown out of his head and back down through his entire body. His hands and fingers were cut up, his arms bruised, his legs hurt under his ripped pants, and sticky burrs still clung to his heels.

I'm all scratched and beat up. I can't be inside my wall. I never got hurt in there. Not all over my skin anyhow. Did Dorian really get me out? Or was it Esther? She cured Babyface. Karin keeps losing patients. And there she is, day after day, working with Eddie cause, whatever he is, he's worth saving. Dorian grew up in that house. And he still loves everything he sees. Charlestown can be heaven. Charlestown is heaven. Heaven is real. All this . . . is real.

Helping give credence to Jeff's hard-earned revelation, cries, shouts and curses came from inside the ranger's station. A window was open and the sounds of violence shot up the hillside.

Dorian had seen it coming, but was surprised at how fast.

"This game's too slow," said Keith and off came his pants.

"I'm out." Ron was out of his chair and covering Dorian from the other side.

"One for all and all for one!" yelled the park ranger, completing a three-way crunch.

"Let me out or I'll wake the whole town." Dorian meant to scream, but it was not in his nature. The words came out like a quiet threat. Hardly enough to stop the poker players from lifting him onto the table spread-eagled.

"You'll get your money, Dorian. Just lay back and take it easy." Fred held him down and held himself back. Guests first. Ron and Keith forgot etiquette and both started to mount Dorian at once. The card table came crashing down. Clothes, cards, money, chairs, and three grown men sprawling and groping for Dorian's ass. He fought back, biting the ranger's hand.

"That's the way! Great!" screamed Fred, certain he was about to get his.

"Hey, Dorian, this is for telling Kate I porked you in the woolen mill!" said Ron, by way of foreplay. Keith held Dorian's face to his dick. So much for the flicker of intelligence—he lost all of Dorian's respect in an instant.

The window exploded in a million pieces. A suitcase had smashed out all the glass and a madman followed it into the room. Jeff made the most of Dorian's luggage, bringing it down hard on Keith's head. That freed Dorian to fling his fists at Ron while the park ranger took a moment to wonder about the damage to public property.

"Out of my wall! Out of my wall!" Jeff's monstrous energy, coupled with the element of surprise, enabled him to inflict injury on the strangers who were both bigger than he was. And he needed no impetus to smash Fred Simms. Dorian got off a good kick in Ron's groin, leaving him to squirm on the splintering floorboards. Keith got up and grabbed a lamp. Its cord stuck in the socket and threw him off balance; Jeff got him three times with the suitcase. That was all the punishment the suitcase could take. It flopped open and the contents joined the wreck of the station.

His friends flattened, Fred ran out the door. "Shit! I was someplace else! These guys broke in and wrecked everything!" No wise sayings for this occasion. Just the smarts to realized there was no explaining his involvement in such a thing, plus a skill for lying that had allowed him to function in Charlestown ten years past the time a lesser man would have been tarred, feathered and run out of town. He was already elaborating on the story and his alibi as he zipped up his pants on the fly. He rolled his motorcycle a ways down the road, revved it up and waiting for his hard-on to go down.

Dorian scrambled to pick up as much money as he could. He instinctively realized there was little in the suitcase not easily replaced. Anything of heartfelt value remained back in his room. Even in that last bit of rage at his mother, he knew there was no way he was leaving forever.

Jeff went on yelling something about his wall while using anything at hand, including the ranger's prized walking stick—genuine Juniperus ashei—to make sure Keith and Ron were not faking it. Dorian did not want Jeff to kill them. They were stupid shits, but had meant no real harm, just a little overeager to get their rocks off.

"Jeff, stop! Stop! Out of here quick! Now!"

"It's real! It's real! I'm out of my wall! Out from the wall, Dorian, out from it all!"

"Yeah, yeah, come on!"

They ran back up the hill and down the other side. Through the cow pasture, not avoiding manure this time, and madly through the cornfield. A couple of horses whose fence they crashed into neighed and started to gallop in the dark. The land was erupting around Jeff as the beasts of Charlestown snorted, mooed and barked their sense that Dorian was in trouble. Having made it more than a mile from the luckless poker game, Jeff went down in the mud and Dorian was too exhausted to pull him back up. He collapsed on top of him. They both shivered and hugged and shivered some more. Nothing was going to help now.

"You can see why I'm going to miss this place," said Dorian. The irony was so beyond Jeff he felt an eruption of words coming on. Dorian beat him to the punch, covering his mouth with his own. The kiss quelled everything Jeff had been about to scream.

CHAPTER 23

Almost before he knew it, Karin had Ethan back in the truck and was giving the old vehicle a workout, taking the first possible turn off the Missing Link.

"Where are we going now?" asked Ethan.

"Beats me."

Ethan felt ashamed. It occurred to him he deemed it more awful to be a disgrace in her eyes than to have been involved in the deaths of those police. He was sure that whenever Jeff's pills completely faded from his system he'd feel genuine remorse over what had happened, that it wasn't just a matter of 'us versus them.' He was far too sophisticated to feel superior to anyone else, but his great concern for Jeff had outweighed all other considerations. Only three years separated them and yet his own life had been wonderful, fascinating, never less than perfectly acceptable, while he had watched Jeff's steady decline from the age of twelve. As their contrasting teenaged years flashed before him, Ethan miserably concluded that Jeff's end was in the cards. If it hadn't been the mishap with the medication that launched a high-speed chase, it would have been a hospital overdose because Ethan had decided to not come to New Hampshire. For all one's arduous efforts, there were some outcomes that could not be avoided.

"We'll never find them. Let's head home."

"Are you sure that's OK?" Karin was pleased at his abrupt turnaround. Perhaps being back at the scene of the crash was as effective a catalyst as she'd hoped. Although now she took on some guilt. She would make certain she was not forcing his hand. "I don't want to get halfway there and be told to turn around."

"I'm in no position to help Jeff. He's on his own. Like everybody."

"Don't get morbid on me." Karin shifted into a lower gear.

"Hey, you're the one who was just going 'everyone gets old and dies and—'"

"I don't remember that. Let's just have the directions, please."

Ethan felt her bristle and moved away from her. "It's pretty simple. Head South on 12 to Keene. We'll pick up 2 out of there."

"Tell you what. We'll make one more pass through the town. Just so you'll feel we didn't give up too easily. I can pick up 12 right off Main Street."

"That sounds good." After a silence he added, "Don't give up on me yet."

"I don't know what I expected really."

"I promised to get you out of Charlestown and now we're doing it."

Then again, I made promises to Jeff, to Mom and Dad . . . yep, have to forget about those old expectations. Just take things as they come. Don't look back. There are disasters straight ahead, but also surprises, and sometimes you won't know the difference till long after they've happened.

Staring out at the dark roadside, he got lost in the hypnotic blur. His annoyance with Jeff for ignoring him and gazing off in the same way seemed ages gone by. He didn't even notice the state police pass the other way. But Karin did.

"You know what? You better climb in the back and get under the tarpaulin."

She pulled over and waited for him to obey.

"Don't scare me more than necessary."

"Look, if we're going to be cruising through the center of town, it's better if I'm alone."

Ethan did what she told him to, less because it made sense than that he wanted to please her. Face down in the pickup, with the rough throw-thing doubled over him, he muttered, "I'm getting good at this at least."

Feeling the truck rumble back up to speed, Ethan realized he was putting himself utterly in Karin's hands and that he'd never made himself so vulnerable before. He would very soon appreciate just how vulnerable. For the time being, he relaxed into a semblance of his old self. No matter how often he'd been on the winning side, there was an easygoing quality in Ethan that made even losing look good. Every failure was only temporary, each seeming wrong move was a steppingstone to ultimate triumph. Not panicking, never ruminating on the current less-than-ideal state of affairs—that was the formula for leading a successful life. No matter how low he might fall in Karin's esteem, it was merely a measure of how high he'd one day be, having helped her become a doctor, providing her with a life she'd stopped daring to imagine.

It's not so bad back here, feeling every bump in the road. Tarpaulin stinks, but once we're miles from Charlestown, I'll throw it off and really love the wind on the freeway. I can peek out and watch her without her watching me. Her beautiful hair, that amazing neck, I've already unzipped that dress to slowly reveal her back a dozen times, and I look forward to hundreds, thousands of repeats. If we hadn't met like we did, I might get tired of pulling down that zipper. I certainly have before. "Get in the back of the truck." Fuck, it's the sexiest thing anyone's ever said to me.

A discordant sound censored his thoughts. Bouncing off the walls of the pickup, its repetition chilled Ethan to the bone. A third time reminded him it was the train horn, warning of its entrance to the town. After Karin's story the horn blared hideously, a harbinger of death and destruction that made his own accident a child's game of toy cars. Perhaps he had caused a police car to explode, but he hadn't actually seen it. His only reality had been a jolting few seconds across a field, ending in a virtual embrace by trees. What Karin had witnessed was a blinding obliteration, her whole world blown over, hurtling into a ditch and unleashing her own personal Hiroshima. The increasing pitch of each blast of that horn sent shrieks through his being, the cumulative screams of each family member she'd lost. It was easier to empathize with her pain than come to terms with his own. *That fucking thing goes through town like five times a day, once right in the middle of the night. How can she have just gone on listening to it all these years? I'd have lost my mind. How can she be driving toward it and not be affected?*

Karin was affected, but not in the way Ethan imagined. He'd forgotten that the constantly repeating horn was only the eventual effect of the accident that had killed her family. If anything, the horn was for her what Esther might have called, with perverse humor, a trumpet of salvation. "Think of all the people being saved from now on because they started using that horn in honor of your folks." Denied a normal life, trapped in Charlestown and moving from one strange family to the next and calling it a career, Karin had mostly repressed blaming the train. The horn that everyone in town had to get used to in the middle of the night was for her a kind of revenge against the town's complacency. An unconscious reminder that they would all eventually feel what she did. Death swept through the town in accordance with a precise timetable. If it didn't take anyone in its wake this time, well, just you people wait.

But what about this time? A rare opportunity struck Karin. Every night at this hour she was in bed like most other people. She woke up to the sound of the oncoming train horn, pulled an extra cover or pillow over her head and was soon back to sleep. Whatever emotions fanned through her, in dreams, in half-sleep, they were gone in the morning. Now the years of lonely yearning and silent privation accumulated into a taboo so tantalizing she almost lost control of the wheel.

"I can get across just before the train," went beating through her brain. Back under the tarpaulin to muffle the horn, Ethan sensed something not right. Why was the truck speeding up? Why was the noise getting louder no matter how hard he tried to block it out? He sat up and knocked on the window.

"Slow down!" he yelled, forgetting that he was supposed to be invisible. He could see her eyes in the rearview mirror. Their expression, no doubt exaggerated by the angle and absence of light, looked more warped than anything he'd ever seen in Jeff. He took in the landscape on all sides as the truck barreled forward. Karin was heading straight for the tracks even though the huge freight train was in plain sight. And then he felt her gun the gas.

"Hey!" he pounded on the window. The train bearing down on them was no more terrifying than Karin's psychotic driving, so similar to his own a few days before on the Missing Link. But she wasn't high on anything, there was no excuse! Had she put him in the back for this? She was about to plunge over the tracks and there was nothing he could do about it. The train's headlight bleached him as they shot in front of it. Ethan saw the engine almost on top of him, passing just above his head like a monster jet flying a few feet over the ground. The final blast of that horn, the scream of the engine, the thumping of metal on metal. Nothing else existed for Ethan until fifteen seconds later when he heard Karin's laughter filling the truck's cabin. Her sick ecstasy sent him back under the tarpaulin. Had she been planning this all along? Or did something snap when she heard the train coming? He would find out later that she justified the crazy move in retrospect, saying that most of the patrol cars were on the other side of the tracks. The hundreds of boxcars formed an impregnable wall that allowed her to pass through town and out the other side with a maximum degree of security. Whether it was a valid excuse or not, that glimpse of her wild eyes in the rearview mirror and the mordant peels of laughter accomplished one thing for Ethan. It brought back something he had felt for a few moments before the cop car crashed and he ran off the road. Something equally strange as what he'd just seen erupt in Karin. A strangeness that surpassed even Jeff at his worst.

CHAPTER 24

Esther and Eddie had not moved from where their son had last left them, as if the gunk on the living room floor had stuck to their clothes and they were trapped in a cockroach motel. Eddie lay completely still. Esther was sobering up, but her prayers for his recovery, lacking a response, turned shamelessly to future endeavors.

"Why'd you get in the way anyhow? Like you could defend Dorian. He never took your side. Let's see . . . once I take over your Air Force pension . . . and no more money wasted on that useless girl . . . hell, I may get out of Charlestown yet. Season tickets to the Red Sox. Nice tour of all the palaces and churches of Europe. Can you imagine—that boy Ethan—half my age and he's been everywhere. I'll be happy just to visit my cousin Bonnie in Miami Beach. Now she's always had the right idea about men. Got a new one every two years. Soon as things got monotonous, out they went. None of that 'grow old along with me' bullshit for Bonnie. Boy, am I gonna have fun . . . "

Left alone with that frighteningly familiar but motionless body, not even Esther could keep a fantasy going for long. She switched on the radio and tuned it to her all-religion-all-the-time station. A merciful break in the plea for cash allowed a soprano to put Esther in an ennobled state of mind. She thought of Dorian's paintings, the angels and otherworldly beings, of course, but also that unfinished one that had stunned her when she went rifling through them with Georgie, plotting their dispersal.

"I'd love to know where he found that photo. Pretty strange he paints me from a faded picture thirty years old, instead of having me sit for one in person. 'You never stay still long enough, ' he tells me. Oh yes, I do, there's times when I won't move for hours and he knows it. Course he wanted to do me young, guess he thought that'd be a compliment. Doesn't want to immortalize me with all these lines and bags in my face.

Plus it must've been a surprise, the way it was tucked away. Even so, he should've put you in it too, Eddie, like paint our wedding picture. Am I supposed to be impressed he singles me out? Real touching, don't bother with your Daddy, he'll be gone soon, and if he does hang on, we can always show him the picture and stop his heart on a dime. Aw, what's the point? Like you don't know how he doesn't care about you. You guys . . . no wonder I'm an emotional wreck. I'm the only one around here who lets her feelings out once in awhile. You guys should try it, do you some good."

She slipped back into prayer mode. The urgent thing was to keep preoccupied so she wouldn't have to face the fact that the man on the floor may not answer her ever again.

"I've looked out for you. God knows, He knows you can't make it to church. It's twice as far as the hotel bar. But I put in a good word for you at all five churches and that's fast work on a Sunday morning. Hitting Father Bob's mass at 9:05 so I can whip over to First Congro and catch the tail end of that snooze of a sermon. Then right across to the Episcopal, damn that preacher's good-looking—don't get jealous—and on to the Baptists, grin and bear it, and last the Unitarians which is mostly just some higgly piggly brunch—'we are all one just like this mixed-up omelet'. I'm making waves at the holy gates, bet your ass. So stop worrying about what's to come. Or not. Eddie? Hear me? Eddie! I said wake up and stop worrying!"

She was actually running out of things to say which would have really depressed her, when the screech of a car stopping out front gave her a recharge. A stray mutt's howl as the car door slammed made her put her head on Eddie's chest. Maybe if she pressed down hard she'd go right through him and they'd trade places. Eddie could deal with whatever was about to come through the door and she could curl up and forget about the world and its glut of churches.

It was Tom, the sheriff who'd inspired the barhounds to such mirth at Ethan's expense. He was the one who came by weekly to cart Esther or Eddie off to jail at the request of whichever of them was more sober at the time. Nobody knew if Tom had a hearing problem or if he invented it to remain impartial in all the domestic squabbles he was called upon to break up. Whatever, he talked extremely loud and it hurt Esther's ears. She realized what a blessing it was, most of the time, that Eddie's voice was so soothingly inept.

"Howdy, Esther! Didn't hit him too hard, I hope!"

"Ain't what you think, Tom. I'm scared he finally croaked on me."

Tom took her place and listened to Eddie's chest. "His heart sounds OK. You just couldn't hear it under that damn music!" He swatted the radio several times till it shut up.

"Lucky you showed. I never had time to fix my phone."

"I kind of suspected something was wrong when I didn't get a call."

"Damn, you're clever at police work."

"Let's get him to the medical center."

Esther's genuine condition was evident to Tom; she was trembling so much she couldn't stand up. Tom was patient with her, comforting her until she was able to feign her old take-your-hands-off-me attitude.

"Damn fool brought it on himself," she snorted and got Eddie's feet to help Tom carry him out to the car. Dorian could blithely call her manic-depressive, but that didn't begin to explain to Tom how a sobbing old woman could become a dynamo if you blinked.

"Got calls on my radio about Karin talking to some guys wanted for murder. I couldn't believe my ears!" Tom boomed it out before Esther could protect her own ears.

"Boy, do things get exaggerated in this town. Those guys

couldn't kill a scrawny chicken for dinner if they were starving. Chrissakes, they were the laziest hired hands I ever had."

They had maneuvered Eddie upright in the back seat of Tom's station wagon.

"Wait, wait, Esther. You actually saying you had them here? In the house?"

"In the house, around the house, all I know is I actually saw them only slightly more than I see Dorian and you know that's a snowy day in Hell."

Tom started the engine once Esther was in the back seat propping up her husband. Knowing Esther, Tom hadn't been paying much attention and the whole story still didn't register. He was half-kidding when he said, "Damn! If only I'd looked in on you sooner. Imagine if I'd have caught them!"

"If I catch 'em, I'm putting 'em right back to work. That refrigerator has to go back upstairs. It looks awful laying in the foyer."

"Where was Dorian, by the way?" Tom drove carefully, taking the back way to the edge of town where the small building that passed for a medical center was located.

"I don't want to talk about that moody, selfish kid. He left home and I miss him already. Karin quits, Dorian does what I never though he'd have the guts for. They left me alone with Eddie."

"Aren't you worried about them with a couple of kooks maybe loose in town?"

"They ain't lost! They got Karin and Dorian for personal escorts!"

It finally hit Tom that Esther wasn't bullshitting him. He slammed on the brakes, turned the car around and drove like mad to a part of Main Street where a group of cop cars was gathered. He got out and gave the new information to the trio of officers bunched by one car.

Esther was frazzled by the fuss. What kind of driving was that with Eddie and his heart condition riding in the back seat? But the jolt seemed to be the best treatment. He opened his eyes, saw

Esther absent-mindedly spilling cigarettes on her lap and said, "I want a shmoke."

Esther was unable to hide her joy. "Eddie! Here, have two!"

"Eshter, swee-shweetie, where are, where are, what's this . . . thingthing?"

"We're out on the town." She lit his cigarette.

"Oh, Esther, can't I go to shleep without without being moved here and here and—"

"Hey, don't knock getting chaffeured around. Just watch the scenery go by. A few seconds ago you were travelling one way and that was down."

Eddie saw the cops outside his window. "No, no, no. Why them, not me, it's a mishtake, a mishtake, oh, you know—"

"They're not taking you away. Or me, hate to dash your hopes. Remember those drifters your little nursie dragged in? They're wanted. They're killers. So much for Karin's high ethics. I oughta report her to the nursing board. Then let her demand higher wages for pulling your pants up and down."

"Is she all right? Karin, my Karin, I warned her about them things, them things!"

Tom jumped back in. "Hey, Eddie, glad to see you're still with us! Esther tell you we got some crooks to catch? We'll drop you off at the med center first, don't worry."

"No, no, want Karin, want to, you know, I can, I won't , I—I—"

"What's he saying, Esther?"

"He's OK now, Tom. Hey listen, we ain't accessories, right? We're helping out here."

"I'll say you were both kind of too drunk to notice who was in your house."

"Least that won't be perjury."

"Where would they go, Esther? They're not getting out of town, what with the blockades up and all. And I assume they were on foot, right?"

"Yeah, Dorian hates cars, weird for a kid his age, but he says, I won't get a license unless they torture me. Karin hasn't had a car since, well, you know about that."

"One thing at a time, Esther. Where's a place Dorian goes?"

"He likes skinny-dipping at Devil's Glen."

It wasn't long before Tom was positioned so he could aim his headlights toward the glen, a dammed-up stream formed by water cascading past ancient pines. He got out and looked down. Not that he expected to spot Esther's son and the killer on the lam taking a leisurely moonlit swim, but maybe crisscrossing the town and looking everywhere he might get lucky. He glanced at his pair of dotty passengers before getting back in. All the years of prying them apart, maybe saving their marriage. They could have been murdered in their beds. It was nice to know they were safe and that it was his doing.

"Where else?"

"He loves graveyards. He didn't get that from me." She pinched Eddie who groaned, unable to make even remotely snappy comebacks.

Tom drove through the two smaller cemeteries before tackling the large Hillside that was Dorian's favorite, if not Ethan's. The high beams revealed refuse from the teenage orgy, but everyone was long since gone. Tom gathered such evidence as a crushed beer can, stained underpants and an unopened pack of rubbers. Excited by the leads, he cruised through the entire place with an exactitude that was excruciating for Esther and exhilirating for Eddie. She didn't need to be reminded of how close Eddie had come to being planted here next week, or how long before the entire town and everyone she knew would be six feet under, robbed once and for all of the daily miseries life offered. Eddie felt on top of the situation. Each headstone had its counterpart on his bulletin board collage. Familiar names went by, increasing Eddie's pride in his homemade memorial. The years of war (even though as Esther brayed, "he never got nearer to a battlefield than the base cafeteria.") had resigned him to death being simply a part of life. No reason he should be spared over the millions being slaughtered, starved or neglected into their graves every day. If he keeled over in the next instant, there was nothing wrong with that. And better than to go on living and see Esther or Dorian taken from him.

Tom found nothing else and suspected the beer and rubbers wouldn't make a huge impression on the state police. He probed Esther for more places. Between Devil's Glen and the Hillside Cemetery, they had driven over most of the central part of Charlestown. Even Esther's restless mind was running down.

"Them paintings of his!" She slapped herself as hard as Eddie ever had.

"He's talented, Esther, but right now I think we'd better concentrate on—"

"Listen, listen, Tom. When he's not painting boys in sexy poses, he's jazzing up the local landscape. I ask him where's that pretty field and he tells me you just go up such and such a road. Ha! We've been sticking too close to home. Head over to the road that goes up to Indian Rock. We got him now!"

Tom was refueled by her excitement. Passing other patrol cars whose presence made Charlestown's center resemble a big city precinct, he felt a surge of pride that he and his carload knew the area better than anyone. A competitive thrill convinced him that he was going to be the one to crack this case.

CHAPTER 25

As if searching for a way to top her daredevil stunt with the train, Karin headed high up into the hills over Charlestown instead of going south. Ethan had not recovered enough to wonder why. His renewed banging on the window for her to stop had made no difference. So much for the 'danger' of his being in the front of the truck with her. But at least riding in the back did lead to something he'd given up on and completely forgotten about during her flirtation with doom. Two figures were running in a field to the far left of the road. Ethan would not have seen them if he'd been inside the truck. The panoramic view from the back of the pickup enabled him to spot what he thought was Jeff. He screamed to the sky, no matter now. If Karin was going to act as she pleased anyway, he had to risk everything on the chance that it was his brother running with Dorian. Just put it all out there and hope for the best.

"Jeff! It's me! Hey! Over here!"

Karin slammed on the brakes. The figures went down on their bellies in the field. Karin's voice joining in with Ethan's brought them back to their feet and dashing to the truck. Seeing his brother and Dorian piling into the front, Ethan decided he'd had enough of the dump seat and squeezed in on the end. The dirt-stained, wrecked pair were sandwiched between Karin and Ethan, a tight fit they didn't seem to mind. Dorian, pressed against Karin on his left, rubbed her knee with gleeful excitement.

"So you got away too?"

"Oh yeah. Wait till you hear."

But she didn't know where to begin, so she stepped on the gas and forged into the dark, taking in the blow-by-blow of the brothers' reunion.

"Ethan! You're all right! It's so good to see you!"

"O.K., Jeff, easy there. Well, you're happy. Find some more pills?"

"Pills? Oh those, oh no, no. They're all gone, remember? But I'm fine, I'm great."

"We'll see how many seconds this mood lasts." Having survived Karin's bizarre attempt at a near-death experience, Ethan was in no state to accept anyone's high spirits, least of all his normally miserable brother's. Ethan felt so lousy he pictured Jeff actually rooting on the train engineer as he steamrolled over his head.

"I never felt this good my whole life!"

"No guilt there," said Karin.

Dorian couldn't imagine what she meant. "Did Mom send you looking for us? Cause we're not going back. Where are we headed?"

"We're trying, like I guess you are, to get out of this Godforsaken town. Did he hurt you?" The blood on Dorian had dried, but she could tell he'd been beaten worse than Eddie or Esther had ever tried.

"Oh this? Nah, it was some old friends."

"That jerk who threatened you at the prom?"

"He was one of them. Luckily I had Jeff."

Jeff beamed proudly. Ethan attempted to study the transformation, although they were squashed so close together, objectivity was difficult. "You disappeared for a whole day. You have any idea what I've gone through trying to find you?"

Jeff shook his head—a simple, honest answer. Ethan did not have the energy to tell it all to Jeff right now. It was clear that whatever his younger brother had been doing, it was good for him. *Of course it's only temporary, just one of his sixteen or twenty-nine moods. But what did I do all day? Fuck me if I could unravel it myself, let alone explain it to Jeff.*

Karin found the words for Ethan. "Dorian, did he tell you

what he did? How he caused the crash?"

"Sort of, but I don't believe that. He's been cooped up for months. He has a little trouble with practical things."

"He drugged Ethan's drink! Maybe not intentionally, but still—I hope you didn't eat or drink anything he gave you. The point is there weren't any crazy hitchhikers."

Weren't any crazy hitchhikers, weren't any crazies. . . . she doesn't know about all the people in that hospital, how I got Jeff out of there just in time. Just in time for what? So he could pull me down with him? Karin's so nice to take my side when she wasn't even there and doesn't know the least bit about . . . what Jeff's been going through without me. That's Dorian's problem now. But only because I let Jeff out of my sight. Not just once, not just the one time when he took his pills and put them, put them in my, when he poured them out and poured them into my—she doesn't know anything about that. None of them knows anything about it. Nobody was there except for, except for—

Ethan noticed he was holding the little stuffed pig between his feet. It had fallen to the floor when everyone crowded into the truck and now it was stuck to the mud on the bottom of his shoes. Unable to shake it off, he slammed his feet together, trying to crush the fat roll of cloth. *This pig was there, he was right up there, all the time, dancing and jiggling and making fun of me the whole time. I didn't keep my eye on Jeff, but this little squealer sure kept a watch on me. The faster I drove, the faster he shook his fat little ass, no matter how fast I went, he was right there with me, fucking little fat fucking thing staring back at me from the mirror. Watching me, grinning at me, real impressed with me, like everyone's always been real impressed with me, wherever I've gone, whatever I've done, I can handle this, let me do that, I'll carry that for you, I'm a great guy, just watch and you'll see, watch me go, I'll outrun, out dance, out fuck any guy on the block and no fucking jolly pig's gonna make fun of me—*

Squirming to get the pig detached, Ethan elbowed Jeff who jerked against Dorian. Karin got jostled and drove precariously close to the edge of the road going around a steep drop.

"Keep still! I can barely see!"

She regained control of the wheel. Jeff pulled the pig off Ethan's shoes.

"Can I have this?"

"Yeah, please, take it! I never want to see the damn thing again!"

"Toss it out the window, Dorian."

"No, Jeff likes it."

"You know, we're in a worse mess cause you never reported their car missing, like I told you to."

"You only told me once and I forgot. I was painting. It didn't seem important."

"Not important—the reason I'm practically driving us off a cliff in a stolen truck is cause you ignored me."

Accusing Dorian, justly or not, was a sure way to make him clam up.

"What do you mean stolen? Didn't you ask that person?" said Ethan.

"We can't return it now. With her memory, maybe we've got a few days. We can go pretty far in that time."

"Hm, a few days. And lots of gas? I like this. Kind of a double-date into the unknown." Dorian settled down, having decided to not take Karin's accusation seriously. Jeff held the pig ornament up to the moonlight that came in the truck at the next bend in the road. Once again, Ethan was entranced by it.

"Oh my God, oh, no, no, no—"

"Double-date, why the hell not?" muttered Karin. "It's way too late to tell the truth."

"I told the truth," said Jeff. "I tried to anyway."

I did get mixed up and my pills got into Ethan's coke, but I told him about it as soon as I remembered. It's so hard to remember things, to sort out the past from the future, what you did from what you wished you'd have done and what you're afraid you'll do and, with everybody watching, trying to do what you should do, but then all of them laughing and saying, do whatever you like, don't be so uptight, so you do it and then they come down on you—you did it wrong! But I did tell Ethan I did wrong and he must know how bad I feel about that . . .

Ethan was grumbling and cursing and Jeff got scared he might hit him. But Ethan was only cursing at himself.

"Oh shit, oh shit, yeah, you did, Jeff, you did tell me the truth, but I—fuck, what was I thinking?"

"I didn't know what I was doing. I'm sorry, Ethan. If it's any consolation I don't believe in the insanity defense. Let them throw the book at me. Now . . . remind me. What was it I did?"

Dorian smiled at Karin, "What are we going to do with these guys?"

"I don't know, as long as you don't suggest we swap."

Jeff certainly didn't want to swap partners, but he wasn't positive Dorian wouldn't like a go at Ethan, so he quickly babbled on.

"It's terrible the things I think of doing. And we'll never know if I actually did it."

Ethan grabbed the pig and smacked it against his own forehead. "It doesn't matter whether you did it or not. I never drank that Coke."

"I saw you drink it!"

"Not the same one! When I jumped in the car, you were lying face down and I tried to get you to sit up, but that attendant you'd been looking up and down was getting wise and I was scared he'd come over and tell you to fuck off or worse. I got riled and I—I bumped the Coke off the dashboard."

"I heard a bump. Lots of them. My wall is full of bumps."

"Then you must have been back in your wall the whole time I got out and went to get another Coke."

Karin slowed the truck to a crawl, weaving back and forth across the road. "So, wait—you were drinking a normal Coke?"

"Ethan, if that was a normal Coke, then what went wrong with you?"

"I don't know! I saw those cops behind us and I just flipped! The awful things I saw in the asylum, and you, my brother, a part of all that. I was going to amaze everyone and cure you. But until I walked into that place, saw how you lived, saw the people you were stuck with and worst of all, the people who were supposedly taking care of you, I didn't know what I was up against. Suddenly, nothing was right, nothing could be right if you ended up in a place like that. I watched that fat little dancing pig I had bought for Mom, great gift for her collection, make her happy, give her a split second of happiness in the midst of her horrible pain. The pig danced, just as you liked, so I said, well I can't make anyone else happy, but at least I can make Jeff laugh and I drove faster and faster, making the pig jiggle crazier and crazier . . . The faster I went, the more distance I put between us and that place, that prison, and away from my idiotic life and away away away from everything!"

Karin and Dorian were staring at Ethan with the look that people usually reserved for Jeff. Jeff didn't mind not being the center of attention for a change, but he wasn't at all sure that anyone besides him would understand what Ethan was saying. *Besides me. And besides the pig. Between the pig and me, we know, Ethan. We know that you understand. All these years, you have understood me. You just pretended not to, so they wouldn't put you away too.*

Jeff smiled and patted Ethan on his hands, truly happy finally that Ethan had picked him up from the asylum. Because until this moment he was constantly afraid that they were drifting further and further apart, that the gulf between their minds could only end with them tossed to opposite sides of the universe. And yet, here they were, pressed together like embryos in the same womb. Ethan knew his mind and he knew Ethan's. No way did he want to trade places, definitely not now, but at least by wading into each other's consciousness they knew there was really nothing more to fear.

Jeff's increased confidence did not rub off on Ethan. He trembled to imagine what Karin must be thinking. Even separated from her by two other bodies, Ethan sensed her starting to shake behind the wheel. He had gained a small measure of peace by spewing out the truth, or what he thought was the truth. Now he had to make up something, anything, to help Karin hold a tiny corner of her sanity.

"That's why I wanted to stay here in Charlestown. Because if I couldn't remember what had happened, it might not be a disaster, but an opportunity. My old life was finished. I could disappear and start all over again. Like Jeff. No identity. No expectations."

"You wanted to feel what I did." Jeff took 'no identity' as the highest compliment. "Once you did, only then could you really help me."

"I wish I was that good."

"Better than a few billion, right?"

"What billion?"

"The few billion we're better off than. All over the world. So many less fortunate, so many who never even had minds to lose. Sadness and hardship and hopeless misery in every corner of the globe, but you and me had it made, in our green Jaguar headed for the outer rim of the galaxy."

"I was going to amaze Dad and Mom and everyone else and cure you. Somewhere along the line it dawned on me I should cure myself first."

"If only . . . if only the people in Charlestown understood things the way you do," said Karin. "I might have had some hope."

"What I said, what Jeff is just repeating of my half-baked philosophy—all this gives you hope?"

"Yes. Exactly what you said. It's so true. It's so brilliant."

Ethan tried to comprehend the bizarre look of bliss encompassing Karin. "What is so brilliant about starting out with everything and ending up in a stolen truck bumping through some backwater, wanted for murder?"

"Not everyone can live up to expectations," said Dorian, tickling Jeff and getting Karin to mordantly laugh.

"Dorian, tell Ethan how I got takeout all by myself today."

"Whoa, independence!" Out loud, Ethan mocked Jeff's declaration as sardonically as he felt like mocking himself. But inside, once he considered it, yes, that must have been an amazing feat to see.

"It was worth almost dying to get the truth out of you." Karin reached around Dorian and Jeff and managed to barely touch Ethan on the neck.

"Even if I can't help you anymore, Karin, I'll see to it my parents do. You can become a doctor or whatever you want. Say goodbye to Charlestown forever."

That was not a happy notion from Dorian's viewpoint. "Charlestown gets extra beautiful at this time of year. I've been showing Jeff all my secret places. The Elysian cow pastures, the moon craters behind the town dump. Nobody can find me when I don't want to be."

"That's right," realized Karin. "That is absolutely right! Listen, guys, what about this? You were, you really were beaten up and—and then you wandered around in the woods, completely lost. You got separated. Dorian found Jeff while I found you, and then we borrowed this truck to look for them. Jeff being crazy—sorry, Jeff—and Dorian doing his usual thing of hiding from Esther, it would take us a few days just to find them. Once we do, we drive right to your house. We were lost in the hills and woods of Charlestown, couldn't get to a phone. You never knew what happened to your car or anything."

"Lost in the woods and hills, I'd love that," mused Dorian.

"But can we get away with it?"

"Jeff, we don't have any choice," sighed Ethan.

"But can you forget on purpose the way I forgot because I can't help it?"

"I don't know, but I've learned a few other useful things hanging out with you."

While Ethan and Jeff made up with their eyes, Karin and Dorian looked at each other with conspiratorial glee.

"So let's get started, Dorian."

"I know a great place we can hide first. Take the next right. We'll lose ourselves in the Charlestown nobody knows but me."

Karin followed his directions, driving onto smaller roads and immersing the truck in denser woodland.

Down in the town police cars and vans, unmarked cars and

cruisers had cordoned off all of the main exits from the town. Car radios squawked, information was exchanged, cops got psyched on caffeine at the all-night Jiffy Mart. Search dogs barked and lights were tested, streaking the air like the kleig lights at a movie premiere. A buzz went all through Charlestown, keeping people indoors for fear, while farm and stray animals picked up the tension and bellowed to one another, sensing a coming storm.

But up in the hills where the truck chugged along, it was dark and still. There was a palpable hope apparent in the cooling summer night that two young couples could vanish no matter how far from the town center all that mad activity radiated.

The only imminent threat to such a possibility was a hypersexed park ranger, riding around on his motorcycle with a bee in his ass. He'd lost and found Dorian and Jeff a few times since they cheated him out of a winning strip poker streak. And he'd picked up the scent again, shortly after they managed to hitch a ride in a truck. Now to keep after them till the chance arose to prove once again that Fred Simms always came a winner, no matter what the game.

CHAPTER 26

"Isn't it great? No one will ever find us up here."

Karin did not diminish Dorian's pride one bit when she said, "And we won't ever find our way back out."

"That might be for the best," mumbled Ethan, feeling each lurch and roll of the truck in his stomach. They were moving along a dirt road, so narrow and overgrown no one in their right mind would have attempted it in an army jeep.

"Don't give up, Ethan! I told you I forgive you and I know you forgive me and none of us can help the way we are or what we had to do and all the accumulated little forces that have brought us all together in these rain forests of the Yukon and—and—I forget what I wanted to tell you."

"You told me, Jeff. I think I got it."

Jeff protectively put his arm around Ethan. The gesture actually made them both less comfortable since there was barely room for them to sit up, let alone shift arms and legs. "It's only what happens from now on that matters. It's such a great feeling. This sense of ... no limits. It's just like you said."

"I said lots of things," conceded Ethan. "Which one are you talking about?"

"You can't let the world get you down." Somehow that pathetic cliche coming from Jeff made Dorian and Karin laugh. Ethan didn't find any humor in it, but the giggles were contagious and he was soon laughing out the window at shadows that would like to eat him alive.

Karin kept grinding forward, having suspended all judgement. Until one tree too many scraped the side of the truck. "Dorian, do you have any idea where we're—"

"Yeah, definitely."

Jeff wasn't going to let anything spoil his newfound sense of fun. "If they can't find us for days, they'll call off the hunt and we're home free."

"They'll assume we died from exposure and they'll be right."

"Come on, Ethan, show some stamina!"

Ethan would have traded all the good times of his life for whatever was juicing up his brother.

Karin was still laughing, now thinking about Ethan having used up all his stamina back in her bedroom. Had it been seven or eight times? Damned if she didn't want him again right now, in the back of the truck.

Dorian was excited too, at being the expedition guide. "Wait till you see where this comes out."

A rock jammed the underside of the truck, there was a sound like the transmission falling out, and the vehicle stopped dead.

"Gee, guess we'll never know," said Karin, trying in vain to restart it.

Except for Jeff, who'd been enjoying Dorian up close, the group was happy to disperse from the front seat and get some air. The truck definitely looked like it wasn't going anywhere. It was impressive that it had been gotten as far as it had. Impressively stupid that it had been attempted.

"This way," ordered Dorian, taking them deeper into the woods. The mud deepened, feet sank into puddles, branches snapped and flew into faces.

"We should have taken that kid's flashlight," said Ethan, and the memory of the graveyard made the present surroundings a little less menacing. "I can't see my hand in front of my face."

"I see lots of hands in front of mine!" offered Jeff.

"Well, not completely cured, I guess." Ethan was almost relieved. He loved the old Jeff. If he was changing for the better, all well and good, but there were aspects to his schizo side he would miss, if they ever could be finally cured. *Jeff is cool, no matter what anyone says. What's so great and wonderful about making it in this world?* Before he could leave his question unanswered, Ethan fell into a pit.

"Dorian, wait!" cried Karin. "Something happened to Ethan."

Trying to help him, she fell in too.

Dorian had gotten about twenty feet ahead and Jeff had the most incentive to keep up with the intrepid guide, so Ethan and Karin virtually vanished.

"Karin, where are you?"

"We're in a hole, Dorian! Like, I don't know, some animal trap."

"Keep talking, we'll find you."

But Jeff of-the-many-hands was also hearing many sounds. He found it impossible to focus on Karin's voice what with the crunching of feet, animals scurrying in the underbrush, an overhead plane. Then came a loud rustling noise from the trees.

A trio of grotesquely ugly hunters emerged, their monstrous redneck features magnified by lanterns. Rifles and hunting knives stuck out from their lumpy bodies and two slobbering German shepherds yanked them onwards toward the next victim.

"They got us! They got us!" Jeff went screaming off through the forest. Dorian looked around, trying to imagine who "they" were. If Jeff was helpless before his hallucinations, Dorian was unable to deny the power of his boyfriend's voice begging for help. He followed Jeff yelling "Hold on!" to him , to Karin in the pit, and perhaps to the whole world. He had wrestled his parents apart, barricaded the house from bill collectors, and survived gangs and other cruelties of high school. "Hold on!" had been his motto; it would have to suffice for anyone within earshot.

Jeff's terror kept him charging through impassable foliage, unmindful of cuts and scrapes. He could have fallen face down in the mud and he'd have kept clawing his way down to the center of the earth, but luckily he burst out into a clearing. Groping the air like it was still an obstacle, he went across a large field and down a sloping hillside. Dorian got out of the woods in time to see Jeff's form drop from the top of the hill. He scaled it in seconds and befell the same fate as Jeff, tripping on the steep downgrade, rolling and tumbling treacherously far to a landing cushioned by thick grass and Jeff's battered body. Neither could talk for a long time. They held each other, gasping to make up for lost air. They had gone no more than a thousand yards in the panic, but it could have been another country for the prisoners of the pit.

"What happened to them?" whispered Karin once the yelling and footsteps died away.

"Shh, there's somebody up there." Ethan made her huddle down with him.

"If we've lost Dorian, we're done for."

"Whatever Jeff saw—"

Dirt trickled on top of them and a slight scurrying came and went, leaving Ethan to conclude that Jeff had exaggerated some tiny animal into an enormous threat. Telling Karin that it was probably nothing more than that did not ease her anxiety.

"We'd better stay right here till Dorian comes back or we'll never hook up."

Ethan felt the soft, crumbling sides of the pit and wondered if they had any choice but to wait. His ears became more sensitive to nocturnal things in the woods. He began to doubt that Jeff was overreacting. His mouth found Karin's and they helped each other maintain a cautious and not altogether unpleasant silence.

Jeff and Dorian, their eyes adjusting to intermittent moonlight, discovered they had plunged from one hilltop only to land on another. The truck had done so much climbing before it failed they had achieved a high pinnacle over Charlestown. Even the second perch down offered a vast view of the valley with its deceptively comfortable town wedged between river and hills. More lights were on than usual and once their ears got as accustomed as their eyes the sound of cars, sirens and loudspeakers, though faint and distant, insured Dorian that the town of his dreams had changed far more drastically than a place that had lost trees to Dutch Elm disease.

"Those hunters may have killed them," was the first thing Jeff was able to say.

"I didn't see anyone. Hunters this time of night? It's not even the right time of year."

"Maybe there's a bounty on our heads. They had huge dogs and enough rifles for a commando assault."

"Yeah, there was nothing there, Jeff. I'm afraid you're up to your old tricks."

Jeff looked hurt and Dorian quickly added, "I know you can't help it, but you should always keep in mind that nobody else can see those things and you should just quietly mention it so I can help you make it go away. Your yelling could have gotten us caught, you know."

He's being so reasonable I hate him. It's one thing being inside my wall where you can be quiet and whisper and still reach every corner of the universe. But here we're out of my wall. I know we've been out of my wall ever since the ranger's station . . . ever since Ethan and Karin came in the truck . . . ever since I got takeout. . . . I'm not sure when I left the wall, I knew the exact moment it happened, but now I forget and it's like I've never been in the wall. I don't want to lose that feeling, it's everything that makes me be me, but if I have to lose it, at least let me remember before and after and the moment that made the difference. If I can't remember when I changed, it's like all those years were a waste, I lost most of my life . . .

Closing out Dorian for a few moments enabled Jeff to rev up his malfunctioning mind. The landscape took on the colors he imagined it to have in daylight. Shapes in the sky overhead and on the horizon started to whip and whirl. Land merged into water and clouds swallowed the earth. The ground seemed to drop away and Jeff was suspended in pulsating colors. In another instant he could fall into the radiant swirl or be drawn up into the air to become one with the spirals. Only Dorian's hand on his neck, massaging firmly, kept him rooted to anything remotely resembling a place and time.

"Remember all those dreams we had the first night you stayed over? Well, you're just having another, except you're wide awake. I can do that too, but it's better if it happens when I'm painting. Then I can capture it all and don't have to worry about drifting off and never finding my way home. Because I love Charlestown and I love my house and, believe it or not, I love Mom and maybe even Dad, and I'd rather not have to leave. I know every inch, every speck of my town, even when I'm flying high overhead. Just like in my dreams. Soaring way up over the treetops. Going through a thick mist. I break out into the sunlight! My body's lit up like a sparkling gem. I can take in Charlestown in a single glance. Every part I love is outlined in white light and that makes for a lot of white light. My house, my school, the library, all the churches, they're all breathing like they're alive. Because they are! And the river, look over there, and the fields and woods, yeah, they're glowing in bright vivid colors like paintings by the Old Masters. Animals lit up amidst encroaching darkness like something out of Rembrandt. Townspeople ascending in circles to Heaven by Raphael. Every perfect detail mirrored in Velasquez. And all of it stretched out so far, just like El Greco would make it, you can grasp the longing in your hands, swirl them around in the thick oils and swab your hand across the giant canvas, making it up all over again. Charlestown from a thousand perspectives, the Louvre come to life in my hometown and I'm flying! I'm flying above it all, creating it all, releasing it all, coming back for a perfect landing right in the midst of it all."

Whether it was his touch or his words or both, Dorian also brought Jeff in for a landing. The sky and the hills and the town stopped pulsating and whirling. The brilliance which was almost unbearable a moment before was somewhere inside him, or inside Dorian, and got transmitted through his hand on his shoulder. The night from the hilltop was simply dark and unknowable. It was only as remarkable as he made it and finally it was only remarkable because he was standing completely still with Dorian watching it, absolutely alive in it.

But even once Jeff knew that, he couldn't bring himself to say it. "If only that were true," he said, as if dismissing Dorian's dream.

"Who says it's not?"

"Everyone," shrugged Jeff, for an instant more down to earth than the most levelheaded resident of Charlestown.

"Forget everyone," reassured Dorian. "Just love what you see."

Just love what you see, just love what I see, I can calm down, I can live, I don't have to die . . . I love what I see . . .

* * *

What worked for Jeff stopped working for Ethan once he stopped kissing Karin. His eyes were registering in the consuming darkness of the pit and he saw little to love or long for except the faint light way over his head.

It must have been fifteen minutes before he and Karin were able to persuade each other it was safe to climb out. He was her ladder; as she worked her way up his hands and shoulders, his face was pushed into the sodden wall of the pit. Once she was out she dropped down a thick vine for him to ascend. As he emerged, she couldn't help but laugh. "You look like the swamp monster!"

"I know. You're looking pretty stunning yourself." As the dirty lovers went searching around for a path, Ethan discovered he'd sprained his ankle in the fall. Karin helped him limp along.

"I won't be able to figure out where we are till morning."

"If they did get caught, they must not have told about us."

"He freaked out for no reason and Dorian went to catch him."

"Jeff was really trying to make up with me."

Karin was so angry she stopped walking. "Why are you still rationalizing everything he does? Your brother is psychotic, Ethan. If I was cooped up in a car with him, I might have snapped too."

"The thing is—if it was his fault, they'll stick him back in that horrible place forever."

"So you're just covering up for him. You did drink the doped Coke."

"If I can't say that for sure, you can't, and nobody can."

"You were clearly on something that first day. You were acting weird every time I turned around."

"I thought that was what you liked about me."

Karin took a few steps away from him, half-wishing the woods could swallow her up. Ethan was confident about what he sensed in her, if nothing else. *She's forcing all her doubts onto Jeff. Like hating him will make everything between us O.K. But she doesn't hate him, she enjoys him, thinks he's funny. She's just scared what's going to happen to us. And so she dumps on Jeff.*

"He's had such a shitty life, Karin. It's not fair."

"Nothing in the world is fair. The train company paid a few thousand bucks for what they did to my folks."

Ethan's arms fell to his sides, almost paralyzed. As much as he could feel for her, help her, be with her, he could never make up for her brutal loss. And then the death of the police officers hit him with renewed force. *No matter whose fault, accident or whatever, they had families too, and two reckless guys fucked things up. I have to turn myself in.* "I should give myself up."

"No! I got you this far, didn't I?"

"The more I run, the worse it looks." He dropped to the ground, more from despair than exhaustion. "I could still tell the truth."

"And what's that? You said you really aren't sure which Coke you drank. You don't know the difference between what's real and what's not." The echo of his words of less than forty-eight hours ago to Jeff made Ethan laugh in a silly, high-pitched tone. Night creatures responded from the woods. The notion that she and Ethan were just two more animals in the woods made Karin laugh. In a few moments, they were laughing and crying all over each other. Although neither could have articulated it, both had become suddenly struck with their unreal expectations of each other. But in the silence that followed, they were overwhelmed by the fact of their mutual attraction. Each had, in the past, ample opportunity to love someone like them; it was the very extremity of their personalities and everything that had shaped them that was such a turn-on. The absolute unshakability of such feelings would inevitably defeat their quarreling and frustration.

"You really love your brother. I'm not trying to take anything away from that. But Ethan, we've got to say he did it. Don't you see, that makes you not responsible? And Jeff gets off on the insanity plea."

"He doesn't believe in that."

"So what? Just let him talk for five minutes on the witness stand and you're both home free."

"What's home? What's free?" Ethan just threw out the words, then he realized he was after accurate answers. Karin was not about to fall into that trap. A burst of enthusiasm seemed far more logical.

"We are going to be so happy in Boston. Taking our dog for walks on Beacon Hill. Sailing down the Charles. Your life can become the fulfillment of everything it was supposed to be and mine will change into something I'd almost stopped dreaming about. I will be a doctor and my patients will live for hundreds of years. If that doesn't pay your debt to society, well, society can go fuck itself."

"I used to think it was that easy."

"Yeah? And now you've convinced me. Say it! We're going to win."

"We're . . . going to win."

"Come on! We are! Going to win."

"We're going to win. We're going to win!" Win what? "Honey, I have to take a leak." To close out their positive thinking session he went to urinate into the pit. Karin listened to the long stream and determined that nothing was going to stop their escape, not even him. She checked her shoulder bag, brushing off the dirt and weeds.

Ethan could not believe how long he was peeing, but he was going to enjoy every moment. After taking careful aim down the hole, he let it swing free and stretched his arms back, letting the sense of liberation spread through his entire body.

Both arms were grabbed and pinned to his back. "That's a hundred dollar fine!"

Ethan gasped. He froze as the abbreviated spray dribbled down his pants.

"Do you have any idea what urinary excretions do to foliage?"

"I'm sorry. No, I don't know. If you tell me, I'll hold the rest of it in."

Fred Simms leaned over his shoulder and looked down. "Don't hold it in. Let's see what you've got there. Hm, nice big one. Did you really think you could get away from me, nature boy? I can waive the fine if you'll submit to some community service."

"What do you want?"

"What's best for the people of Charlestown. Why violate their sons and daughters when I can fertilize the tourists?"

Perhaps if he'd known that Fred was really a town official, Ethan would have laid back and enjoyed it, but for all he knew this was the kind of backwoods psychopath he'd feared in the cemetery. He said O.K. in a sultry voice, and when the man loosened his grip so Ethan could face him, he punched him hard in the gut. Simms reacted quick, his hands going for Ethan's groin. A clumsy struggle ensued and Ethan fell into the pit.

"So you want privacy, huh? I can respect that." Simms could tell that Ethan was winded by the fall. Easy pickings were waiting. He took off his hat and shirt and leaned over the pit, licking his lips before jumping in. The needle prick in his arm was a shock, but did not incapacitate him for thirty seconds. He whirled around, throwing Karin off her feet. The hypodermic flew out of her hand, leaving her defenseless as he got his hands around her neck.

"Don't you ever stab me with anything!" He was mortified that he was strangling a woman and he certainly had no intention of killing whoever she was, but his training insured he always followed through in an emergency. Karin poked his eyes out. They flailed at each other in the dark. She took another bad hit across the face before the injection started to take effect. Simms lost control of his arms and legs. Within moments he was roiling in the mud like a wounded animal. He felt a wave of pain that paid him back for what he'd inflicted on Karin, then lost consciousness. Karin hesitated before daring to look at his face. Ruefully she recognized the park ranger. Of course it would be another Charlestown native interfering with her escape.

"Ethan, I got him! Are you all right?"

No response from the pit. Karin leaned down in and tried to make out Ethan's condition. "Did you hit your head? Ethan! Hey!"

She tossed in some dirt to make him stir, though the sense of a final handful of earth thrown into a grave did not escape her. The continuing silence snuffed out the high spirits she'd displayed so boldly only moments ago. That sick overgrown boy scout shot full of sodium pentathol gave her the creeps even if he slept all night. Ethan had to be alive, but she had no idea to what degree he was hurt. Dorian was off on a fruitless quest to reign in the schizo brother. Karin had all the reasons to feel defeated, but something in her hung on. What did it was her romanticized memory of countless evenings with the Osbornes, smiling as Esther finally nodded off and Eddie was left in peace with his cutouts. The house was heaped with junk but she sat in a clean-swept corner, having brought peace and health to a couple that no one else had any use for. What rot! Their lives were over and whether it was her or any other glorified babysitter, the outcome would be the same. Karin gained resolve by debunking each warm false memory. Alone in the woods, surrounded by wild creatures and flawed men in varying degrees of consciousness, at least she was progressing away from those lying recollections. She reluctantly accepted that most likely she'd survive, if no one else did. After all, she lived a 'charmed' existence. The fifteen-year-old who'd lost her family had pitied herself and nobody blamed her; the subsequent eight years had changed her into someone cruelly at ease with life and death. Wherever she found herself was as good as anywhere else and she might as well get on with it. Such was her state of mind when a helicopter soared overhead and a magnified voice announced,

"There are over a hundred officers advancing on your position. Give yourselves up! You are completely surrounded."

The entire area suddenly lit up. Spotlights mowed down the woods. If it seemed a shock that such a desolate area could be so transformed in an instant, Karin was not the person to show it. It was virtually the pattern of her life. Not just the strokes, train wrecks and more recent crashes. Esther's kind offer, Dorian's ability to make her laugh, Eddie's flashes of recovery, Ethan's arrival—they had also come without warning and had ultimately offered some hope. This wave of attack troops would wash right over her. There was no way of knowing if she was headed to prison or the White House. Swirling blue lights, relentlessly blaring sirens, snarling bloodhounds, running feet and crisscrossing searchlights. Karin made a little noise like "hm," and acknowledged that another short-term change was coming.

But she doubly surprised herself. Immediately after settling on that sublimely blase stance, she made a spontaneously bold gesture proving that her survival had not been passively achieved. She kicked the ranger's hat and shirt into the pit and stripped him of his wallet and anything else that marked his identity. It all went into the pit on top of Ethan. She dragged the body as far from the pit as she could before the first group of cops emerged to surround her. At that moment she threw herself protectively over the body of Fred Simms and let out a lifetime of losing in a single shriek.

"It's all over, Miss."

"Get away from him! It was his brother!"

"We'll find out soon enough."

Karin's sobbing broke the heart of each new officer arriving on the scene. They eventually had to separate her from her apparently fallen lover. Her tearful histrionics were a strain, but no one blamed her. She was just a small town girl who'd gotten mixed up with some no-good passing through. Happens all the time. But the needle jabbed in the no-good's arm gave witness that she had wised up. For once, the victim had been able to come out on top.

CHAPTER 27

It was Esther's use of Dorian's painting locales that put her in the forefront of drunken, elderly, manic-depressive detectives. Some luck was involved, but she really knew her son's work quite well. It didn't always show, but she paid attention when he talked about his inspiration and his love for the town where she'd raised him while his father was off not fighting in wars. And when Dorian was out and her legs allowed, she went into his room and stared at the rich colors and idealized landscapes until she either cried or needed a drink. She knew he was talented and didn't need Karin or anyone else in town to confirm it. But when Ethan had taken time between chores to praise a kid he barely knew, that sparked her ambition. The world should know what her son was capable of when he's not trying to get in the pants of some Charlestown boy. And there had been a world of improvement since the last time she tried it. No one would dare shit on these paintings now.

It really didn't occur to her that she was doing anything more than help Tom track down her wayward genius. She wanted to thank him for the surprise portrait before he left town. When Tom radioed the other patrol cars to the vicinity she convinced herself that even cops had a frustrated love of art. "Maybe when they're all having coffee and donuts in the diner after the capture, Dorian can make like it's his gala opening."

Then came the report over Tom's radio—that two boys had been found badly beaten and unconscious in the ranger's station and the scattered contents of Dorian's suitcase indicated that he was one of them. Esther went from her most glorious high to a shattering depression.

"He wanted to go as soon as school ended. I made him feel

guilty, forced him to stay. Now he's hurt, maybe serious. Damn, wish he'd been a little quicker, gotten out of Charlestown before all those bastards got their hands on him."

"What's that, Esther?" said Tom, driving hastily to the ranger's station.

"Nothing. Nothing."

"Don't know if you heard all they said over my radio. They need you to I.D. them, let them know if it's Dorian and his friend. Then they'll take 'em to the hospital."

Tom was being as obnoxiously loud as if this were any old night. It made Esther curse herself for helping him. At the ranger's station a cop came to Tom's window and was clobbered by Tom's booming declaration, "These are the parents in back here! They're ready to help!"

Esther corrected him. "Eddie has to stay here with you, Tom. His heart can't take this and you know it."

"Oh yeah, right you are, Esther. I'll take care of Eddie, but you sure you can handle this alone?"

"I been handling everything alone most of my life." She patted Eddie getting out of the car, hoping he somehow understood that she'd only said that for Tom's benefit.

Escorted into the ranger's station by two state cops, unpleasant memories of her uncle and his lewd behavior flooded over her. But she smiled up at both tall men; damned if she'd act afraid of them.

She felt a short stab of horror as she crossed the threshhold and caught a glimpse of Dorian's suitcase and bloodstains on the floor. In the next instant, though, she knew it wasn't him and had to hide the glee that passed over her face.

"So this is your son, Mrs. Osborne?"

"Huh?"

"I know it's difficult, Ma'am, but which is which? Which is your son and which is the brother he hung out with?"

"I don't know if I'd call it hanging out. They'd only just come to town, you know."

"But there was an immediate connection, so we've heard."

"Immediate connection, yeah, you could say that."

She pointed with her toe at Ron who was lying face up in nothing but his underpants. There was a big welt on his forehead. "This here is Jeff, that guy's psycho brother. And that . . . . that's Dorian." She pretended she couldn't look at Keith who was face down and somewhat more dressed, what with the few clothes spilled from the suitcase partly covering his bare butt.

"Kind of weird they're all alone in the ranger's station. You know the park ranger well, ma'am?"

"Well enough. Fred Simms. I always appreciated there was somebody upstanding in the community to take a strong interest in Dorian."

"Hate to think what happened to him," said one of the cops. Ron started to groan. "If that's the mental case, we won't get a straight answer out of him."

Another cop—Esther had already counted fifteen and was anxious to be rid of them—voiced his appreciation. "You've been a big help, Mrs. Osborne. Your son will be O.K., but we'll have to hold him for questioning."

Esther nodded. As long as Dorian was someplace else, maybe actually getting out of town, she'd agree to whatever these prying sons of bitches wanted. "He's honest, I raised him right, I don't care what anybody says. And wait till you see his paintings. You need something colorful for your living room, sarge?"

She was about to go into a more extensive sales pitch when Karin was hastened in the doorway by two other officers.

"Karin! You all right?"

"This is what happens when you fire someone without references," said the bedraggled nurse, dirt clinging to or dripping from every part of her.

"Where's that guy of yours?"

"He flipped out on me and I had to inject him."

"Hear that?" Esther announced to the cops. "A good nurse

always knows what to do." She was going to enjoy her status as star witness to the hilt.

"So this is your friend's brother, lady?" said a cop, nudging Ron's body.

Karin took in the battered bodies on the floor. She was so accustomed to mayhem and collapsed people, she'd barely bothered to look at first. "Oh these two. They kill each other? Just desserts. That one was especially mean to Dorian."

"Mean?" The cop turned back to Esther. "You said immediate connection."

"Karin, how can you make like you know anything, you out of the house leaving me alone with these two loonies?"

In an instant Karin recalled the constant vertigo of working for Esther. Yet the pleading look in the spent woman's face conveyed that for once there was rationality behind the bizarre demands. Karin knew it was best to shut up.

"Yeah," she mumbled, trying to seem humiliated by all the staring cops.

"No use lying about it, Miss," said a kinder cop. "Your ex-boss told us everything. And we found this on him." He held up a prescription bottle labeled with Jeff's name. Karin figured that if all those kids in the cemetery were strung out on the stuff, it made as much sense that the bottle would turn up on some other local asshole. Thinking of how she was going to get back to Ethan in the pit, Karin was too drained to figure out whatever complications had befallen Dorian and Jeff.

"Then you don't need me anymore."

The cops who had found her after injecting Fred Simms (a.k.a. Ethan Leblanc for the time being) came into the room. Karin had acted the hysterical victim believably enough. Now she could elevate herself to the role of heroine. "I mean, I did do my part to subdue him. In the end I wasn't fooled."

"That's true, Bill," one of the entering cops agreed, taking Karin's arm just to affirm he was on her side.

"Well, we might need you for questioning later on, maybe to be there when he wakes up—"

"Which shouldn't be till well into tomorrow if I gave him as much as I think."

"Yeah, so we'll release you into Mrs. Osborne's custody, as long as she'll vouch for you, and you won't leave town."

"We'll take her back," nodded Esther. "Eddie would like nothing better."

Karin took Esther's hand and went out to Tom's car. Even just seeing Eddie sitting up in the back seat and making his familiar noises with gusto brought a smile to her lips. She was so pleased, in fact, that as Esther kept the conversation going, Karin didn't consider that the savvy woman already suspected the truth.

"Was it hard turning in Ethan?"

"I did what I had to. You know, Esther, there's a limit to what I'm going to let any guy get away with."

"Good girl! There's gonna be other boys. Get somebody stable," Esther declared earnestly.

"I should follow in your footsteps."

"You could do worse." They both stuck their heads through the car window. "Look who's back, Eddie."

"Karin! Oh, Karin, I thought, I thought, you you you, oh well I—I—I—"

"Eddie, it's great to see you out and about."

"Yeah, our first night out together in years. Ain't it been fun, Eddie?" She pulled on the handle and tickled Karin to hurry into the car.

While Eddie was straining either to correct Esther or praise Karin, Tom got back in and released the clutch. "Nobody wants to sit up front with me, huh? O.K. guess you three have lots to talk about." He drove them home.

"K-Kar—she she was always my fav-my favor—oh you know, best best of the bunch." Eddie put his arm around Karin to show off for Tom what a pretty girl he had in the back seat and Esther let him enjoy it.

"And so were you, Eddie. My favorite patient out of all seven or—well, however many I've had and no matter how many more to come."

Tom dropped them off and watched them head up to the porch. He was so pleased with his role in the evening's successful outcome, as well as the picture of unusual familial closeness about to go in the door, he took off. The state cops had told him to make sure Karin remained in the house if they needed her for more questioning the following day. With his limited imagination, Tom would never have thought Karin would go in the front door and out the back. Except for the injuries to Dorian, this was the happy conclusion he'd always wanted to see for the Osbornes. He was not going to stick around to have his hopes dashed to bits.

Karin and Esther put Eddie in his bed and both kissed him good night while he tried to tell them it was practically good morning, but couldn't get past the 'm'. Karin let Esther finish tucking him in and waited for her in the living room. She drank in the last look of the place she hadn't allowed herself when she'd left with Ethan. Esther did not seem all that surprised at her first words when they were alone.

"You two are fine now and I have to go somewhere. That's all right, isn't it?"

"Sure, Karin, you deserve a little time off. Course them cops said to watch you, but they can't expect me to stay up with you every second."

"Thanks, Esther. It's really great what you've done for me. And for Dorian."

"He'll come back when he's ready. He always does. Better off wherever he's at than hanging around with those bullies at Fred's."

"As soon as I can, I'll be back to look in on you and Eddie."

"Hey, I'm a good nurse, too, remember? I'll see to him—oh, he's still awake, for Chrissakes. I'll say goodnight now, Karin. If you disappear between here and your room, that's none of my business."

"Give Eddie another kiss for me."

A few seconds of silence passed between them like nothing else in all the time they'd known each other. The magic of pre-dawn had dissolved a complex rivalry, leaving in memory a poignant fondness that had never existed on a daily basis.

Karin didn't bother to clean or change. It was back to the woods and she was perfectly camouflaged for that. As she made for the hills, Eddie was calling her name. Esther's hand on his brow could not quiet him.

"Eshter, want K-Karin."

"She had to get her rest, Eddie. She's helped a lot of people in this town and it's time for a vacation."

"Vacation?" The way he got the whole word out made Esther realize it had been a poor choice.

"She's a damn good nurse. Can't expect her to just be yours forever."

"She was the best, always the best, want her, want her back."

"You can want her, I can want Dorian, there's some things we both have to get along with less of."

"Dorian, my-my-my shon, is he all right?"

"Yeah, you can bet on it. By the time those dumb cops put it all together, he'll be long gone." She crossed her fingers, then uncrossed them to hold Eddie's hands.

"Is he—is he—off to make a name for himself?"

"Yeah, that might be it."

"Like I did in the war."

"I hope to hell he does better than that." She poked him in the ribs. "Dorie, Dorie, Dorie, my shun and proud of it. Whatever he—whatever—yeah."

"Maybe he'll paint that boy's hallucinations. There were some doozies. Kind of a stretch even for our strange kid. Never know though, I hear there's a big market for crazy art in the city these days."

Eddie gave her his best anemic bear hug. The war, their crumbling house, their kids missing in action, and a world he sensed nobody understood any better than he, even if they could express it better—all of it passed between them in that moment. Their lives could go up in the smoke of a forbidden cigarette, but goddamn, they'd had some fun.

Certainly more than Jeff could contemplate, trying to sit upright in the luggage compartment of a Greyhound bus as it pulled away from the diner. Dorian had unfurled the little flag that indicated a pickup. When the driver pulled over and nobody was there, he got out to peer in the window of the diner. It had stayed open especially late because of the activity in town, but at that time everyone was at the ranger's station or up in the woods. While the driver went in for a quick cup to go, Dorian got the side compartment open (something handy he'd learned from Fred Simms) and closed it after he and Jeff hid among the suitcases. The night waitress apologized for the stop-flag being out, but the driver was grateful for the coffee. He took off down the road with his half-load of night passengers, never to know about his new non-paying ones, who would slip out while the equally distractable man at the Boston bus station slowly pulled out the luggage. Until then, the boys had a bumpy few hours in the dark.

"Yeah, these aren't the most comfortable seats," trying to minimize the chances of another freakout by Jeff. "But at least we saved all my money for when we get to Boston. Let's think of something nice for your parents."

"They have everything. Ow!"

"They don't have a painting by me. I'll do a huge canvas. Any scene they like."

"It won't work. They'll just send me to a different hospital."

"They'll be real happy to see you. Gonna have their hands full with Ethan."

"I miss him. If he hadn't picked me up, he'd still be OK."

"Yeah, he did what he could for you. And he got you to my house. I hope things work out for him and Karin. He's such a weird guy. I hope he doesn't let her down."

Jeff cuddled with Dorian, delighted at the implication that Ethan was as strange as he was. The bus lurched , gears grinded right through him, and he became self-absorbed again. "It figures we couldn't get real seats. I feel like I've been riding this way all my life."

"It's a ride. Just think about this—in your next life you'll have paid your dues and you'll be riding first class all the way."

"I don't mind the dark so much as the smell. At least it's warm. And I kind of like the feeling that we're going home, but I don't have to see it coming. I'll open my eyes and there it will be. Like coming out of a long long tunnel."

"You have those visions. And I make paintings. And in between is everything that's real. Beautiful and real."

CHAPTER 28

Just getting out of the hole took Ethan a long time. Going anywhere after that, doing anything besides laying in the dirt with Karin and sleeping for a thousand years, was but the faintest of possibilities.

"How long was I down there?"

"Long enough for me to save your skin."

"Really? Now can I do something for your skin?"

Karin not only excused the bad joke, but let Ethan, dirty as he was, reach under her clothes and relive the joy of those many times in her airless room. At least now there was a fresh breeze coming through the forest. Above them the trees swayed with approval. Karin wondered how Ethan could take what she'd said at face value and presume that the danger had passed. Again she concluded he had to have taken Jeff's medication by mistake and be experiencing residual effects. Yet it was so novel to be with someone who could actually outdo her, defying the expectations that made day-to-day life such a predictable trial. Surprise was definitely the key element. Was he guilty or not? Did he share a genetic bond with his brother that would ultimately doom him as well? Who were his miraculous parents that could survive the upbringing of two such different but equally traumatizing sons and still be waiting at home with stalwart support, emotional and financial? She had known him all of two days, but even if his ability to surprise her was cut in half each subsequent day, there would be enough to keep her on her toes for the rest of their lives together. He stopped in the middle of a luscious kiss to say, "Who was that creep?"

"Charlestown's eager beaver park ranger. Lucky for you I always carry first aid. I gave him ten times Eddie's dose. Unfortunately Smokey the Bear might live."

"I hope so. I don't want to be responsible for any more deaths."

"If you knew how he treated Dorian, you might not mind in this case."

"And they think he's me?"

"Well, no ID's and I did quite a performance. Still, somebody's going to recognize him sooner or later. Sooner or later, who am I kidding, I'm sure they're all yelling bloody murder right now."

Ethan felt a chill, recognizing that Karin was now truly his accomplice. He thanked her with kisses until 'bloody murder' took on too many meanings for him to ignore.

"So now what?"

"Now we really have to disappear, and without Dorian's help."

"I didn't notice he was that big a help." He stood up on his own.

"I'm happy Jeff found somebody, there is that. So where to now?"

Realizing she would have to take over Dorian's task of trailblazing, Karin mentally retraced her steps in and out of the forest. She didn't say a word for an entire minute and Ethan added, "We're in the wild, just like you wanted."

"Just like I wanted?"

"Wild and free, remember? The only way to live?"

"Oh. Yeah." She had said many dumb things to him, but that remark stood out. She was slightly mortified until Ethan said, "And you were completely right."

"We have maybe an hour till sunup. We'd better make the most of it."

"Right again. I'm going to climb this tree."

He was a few feet off the ground before she could fathom he was serious.

Surprised her again.

"You won't mind if I wait down here."

"That's fine. I just want to get some perspective here." He

made a steady ascent, troubled only by two tricky spots. He dangled from a branch that gave a cracking sound and made the leap to something sturdier. It crossed Karin's mind that he was going to reach the top and jump off. The tree was tall enough for him to die from a fall.

But she should have known better than to project her own fears onto him. He simply wanted a good view.

'I can practically see the whole town," he called down.

"Is Main Street still all lit up?"

"Like Christmas!"

"That's for us."

"Wow! So this is what it's like to make a mark in the world."

"It's only Charlestown, honey."

"Pretty impressive anyhow. I never saw so many churches in a row."

"Esther will be praying for us in every one of them."

"And for Dorian? And Jeff?"

"Of course. But they don't need it at the moment. I forgot to tell you—they got away."

Ethan nearly fell out of the tree. "Yeah? You sure?"

"Esther misidentified two townies. Gave them more time than we have."

She hit the tree with a stick to get him to come down.

"Oh, God, I hope they made it out of town. That would be fantastic. My little brother's on his way! Mom and Dad'll be so pleased when they hear how I've cured him."

"Cured, oh yeah."

"I can see lights across the river from here. That's the Missing Link, right?"

"Now that you have the lay of the land, you want to come back down so we can get going?"

"In a minute, in a minute. What's your hurry?"

Karin slumped down and leaned back against the tree. One surprise too many. She could lie her way out of almost anything. She could always claim temporary insanity if she ended up on trial with Ethan. She'd studied Jeff enough to know the symptoms. And Esther. And Eddie. And Dorian. And a few dozen other citizens of Charlestown.

Or maybe she should join Ethan up in the tree. They could take a flying leap together.

Let somebody else be a great doctor and save the world.

EPILOGUE

Ethan was wishing Karin would come up too, but for a different reason.

This is amazing, what I can see from this one spot. A whole town lit up for us! The river—go south and you're practically at Yale with connections to the brightest and best across the whole world. Go north and you can lose yourself in the mountains, tiny towns where few people ever leave, spots so isolated you might as well be on the moon. And all from this perch of mine. Never knew it. Jeff told me, but all I could think was, that's crazy. Course, he was talking about a wall—"I don't really need to go anywhere. It's all right here inside my wall."—while I have a fucking awesome vantage point on—on what? Why is it different from his wall? I can't go anywhere. I can look at it, I can imagine all the places it touches, but even if I got there, I'd still be here. Cause I'm stuck like everyone else, inside the wall of my brain. You idiot, you never let that bother you before. You're stuck cause you broke the law and now five thousand cops are lowering a giant night stick on your brain. So what the fuck? I can dream, can't I? That's what brains are for, whether they're in fine working order or crumpled up and damaged . . .

His brother, damaged brain and all, was taking Dorian on a tour of Boston's most historic neighborhood. If home happened to be at the center of it, well, every tour should have a convenient rest stop. It helped Jeff enormously to think of his house as a stop along the way; otherwise, walking in the door could seem like the most threatening event of the past week.

"Robert Frost used to live in that building. And Paul Revere had to ride up and down this street to visit his black mistress. Louisa May Alcott kept a pet cow on Boston Common and some really famous historian, I can't remember his name, entertained all the biggies of his day up in that window. "

"And here's number 16 Louisberg Square, where Jeff Leblanc keeps a home when he's not vacationing in various resorts along the grand Connecticut River. You better lead the way, they don't really know me."

Jeff bounded up the steps to stop Dorian who was jokingly holding the door knocker as if ready to bang up a storm. "I have no idea what they're going to say."

"That's the fun of it. But I bet they're going to start with hello. Go on. Ring, Jeff.

Or knock this thing. I guess you don't have a key anymore."

Emboldened by Dorian's enthusiasm, Jeff gave the knocker several sharp raps. There was a long wait. It was early in the morning and they may still be asleep. Certainly his mother, who was in bed half the day. Depending on what day it was, and he had no idea, his father had already left for the hospital or had not come home yet. He kept odder hours than Jeff.

Dorian insisted, so he rang the doorbell a few times. Still no door swinging wide, welcoming or not.

Maybe Dorian thinks I picked any old house and we don't really live here.

But he'll find out eventually. I don't even have to go inside. I remember every inch of it and I doubt they've rearranged the furniture in the last year.

Having easily persuaded himself of the lack of necessity to see his house, Jeff turned and shrugged to Dorian. Nobody home, what now? Dorian's innocent smile seemed to say just keep ringing and knocking, eventually somebody will be home and we'll get in.

But that's silly. We could be here for hours and he might decide I did make it all up. I'll prove it to him! We'll go to Dad's hospital. I'm more at home there anyway. And Dorian will be impressed how the whole place from emergency room to cardiac arrest just makes way when I walk in. "Dr. Leblanc's son is here!

The strange one, the you know—him! Get the doc quickly!" Oh, no, maybe Mom had a bad attack when they got the news about Ethan and me, and she had to be rushed in for vital signs!

He thought of the inside of his house, entirely empty, as devoid of life as Dorian's had been overabundant with it. No, no, much better to start with the hospital, where he could blend in with the other accident and trauma victims, where life passed into death as easily as night into morning, and none of it was his fault. There was a cab dropping somebody off just across the Square. Jeff hollered for it with the kind of confidence Dorian had instilled by making him get takeout on his own. He hustled Dorian into the cab and told the driver "Mass. General please!" The cabbie started to say it was just around the corner, an easy walk for two young guys, but then he saw how disheveled and spent they both looked and figured it was an emergency. As he sped the short distance to the hospital, Jeff held Dorian's hand, looked out the window at the fancy shops and boutiques along Charles Street and laughed at the notion of rich people buying up everything in sight and still not being satisfied.

It was too early for most of the stores to be open, but Jeff had no problem peopling the street and creating chaos at the foot of Beacon Hill. Besides the well-off but perpetually grasping ones, he saw tourists from many countries come to see where freedom once rang, and there were students and loafers, old ladies and cute young guys walking dogs, people looking wasted on steps, loners side-by-side with socialites, ambitious working class stiffs tossing pizza, exhausted no-care types trying to bolster themselves with double espressos. Kids on bikes, roller skates and other wheeled things, heading for the river, looking for good spots to picnic on the grass before an evening concert by Fiedler and the Pops. So many wheels. So much movement, crisscrossing, just missing each other, flying this way and that. By the time the cab turned off, Jeff had remembered Dorian's command, "Just love what you see." and he was laughing at the impossible task of trying to love the excessive varieties of humanity gumming up the antique bricks and cobbled streets of his neighborhood.

Devoid of people it would be nicer. But there's nothing wrong with having them here. They've all got to go somewhere. They'll come and go, just like Dorian and me. It's only their physical bodies, after all. Their souls and spirits and minds are elsewhere, just like mine. And if two souls happen to collide, they melt into one another, just like us. Not like bodies which can get smashed and ruined, blown up or born in pieces. We're outside my wall, moving toward infinity, which is not scary at all. It's my turn to show Dorian the Boston nobody knows but me. My crowded, dirty, ridiculous city and we're flying, flying above it all!

Ethan, perched in his treetop, could not have felt happier at the moment either, even though he had some more awareness why he shouldn't. He pictured himself and Karin escaping from Charlestown in a boat, heading straight up that river and getting lost in the fog. The thick mist of dawn was clinging to the water and nobody on either shore would be able to see what passed down the river's center.

I did some bad things, but I did some good things too. Whatever my failings, they can be rectified. I'm not the only one for whom terrible things have happened behind the wheel of a car. But now I'm standing perfectly still. I can take it all in and know that we're going to be all right. Jeff has known at least a breath of freedom. And he probably will, yeah, I can see it from here—he'll have the best summer of his life.